THE AFTERMATH OF MURDER

Yanking my paralyzed hands away from the metal railing, I went over to the hole and stood staring down into it for what seemed the longest time. The summer evening light was fading fast now, but there was enough of it for me to see what was in there. Even so, I fumbled around until I found my flashlight and turned it on, just to be sure the shadows weren't deceiving me.

They weren't.

I wanted to run, maybe for help, maybe just away. As I hinted earlier, I'm a dedicated coward. But I couldn't get my feet to move. My brain wasn't functioning properly either. All it wanted to record were the unimportant details, that the flowers on either side of the opening were leaning drunkenly, that a lot of beauty bark had spilled over onto the pavers, that the topsoil was really a lovely rich brown color . . .

The fissure was about two feet long, eight inches wide, three feet deep. Sticking out of the far end was the object that gleamed whitely.

It was the skeleton of a foot.

Praise for DYING TO SING:

"Welcome red-haired divorcee Charlie Plato to the ranks of the amateur sleuth! Don't miss this grand new series!"
—*Meritorious Mysteries*

"DYING TO SING is a delightful series debut."
—*Mostly Murder*

MARGARET CHITTENDEN

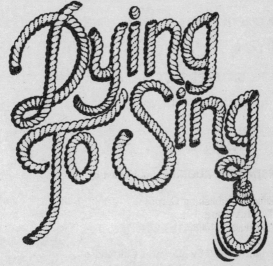

*For Kay
with best wishes
Margaret Chittenden*

KENSINGTON BOOKS
Kensington Publishing Corp.
http://www.kensingtonbooks.com

KENSINGTON BOOKS are published by

Kensington Publishing Corp.
850 Third Avenue
New York, NY 10022

Kensington and the K logo Reg. U.S. Pat. & TM Off.

First Kensington Hardcover Printing: July, 1996
First Kensington Paperback Printing: July, 1997

Printed in the United States of America
10 9 8 7 6 5 4 3 2 1

This novel is dedicated to the following people:

My good friend, Darryll Dewan, who gave me the idea, my lovely daughter, Sharon Chittenden Lundahl, who gave me much of Charlie and all of Benny, and Jennifer Sawyer, my brilliant editor, who saw the wood clearly while I was ricocheting around in the trees.

CHAPTER 1

It was August 23rd. It had been the kind of unusually warm, humid, hazy-sky day Bay area old-timers call earthquake weather.

A shrewd bunch, those old-timers.

Even before the tectonic plates miles below the earth's surface jostled each other, CHAPS was jumping, its large, open interior crowded with cowboy and cowgirl wannabes. On the bigger of the two dance floors, which Zack Hunter had cutely named the main corral, Angel Cervantes and I were demonstrating "The Sweetheart Cha-Cha." Savanna Seabrook was doing the same in the little corral, on the other side of the deejay's booth.

The new line dance was going over big. The guys stomped their boots, grapevined and kicked with vigor. Some of the women, like me, twitched their skinny hips in jeans; others wore shorts and T-shirts or long full skirts. P.J., one of our regulars, whipped her tow-colored ponytail every time she did a quarter turn.

I was envious; my hair doesn't whip. It's long enough, but too frizzy to do more than flop. It's also orange. Not strawberry blonde or red or titian. Orange. As in carrot. Or pumpkin. I'm Charlie Plato, by the way, a thirty-year-old divorcée with an attitude. In other words, depending on your point of view, a nineties woman or a walking cliché.

Any lone stranger peering in at all the cowboy hats might have thought he'd wandered into Texas. But this wasn't Texas. It was a typical Wednesday night at CHAPS, a country-and-western tavern situated in Bellamy Park, which is on the San Francisco Peninsula about midway between the San Andreas and Hayward faults.

At 7:57 p.m. the earthquake thundered along the peninsula like an express train, opening up fissures in the hills, rocking bridges and cracking highways and blasting randomly chosen buildings into heaps of rubble.

Afterward, people said this quake wasn't nearly as bad as the famous temblor, *Loma Prieta*, but at the time we had no way of knowing that.

Remember *Loma Prieta*? "The Earthquake Of The Dark Hill" made its televised debut at Candlestick Park on Tuesday, October 17, 1989, pre-empting game 3 of the World Series.

At any rate, back at the ranch, Sundancer Brown—our fabulous, admittedly eccentric deejay—had just yelled into his microphone, "Put your hands together and give yourselves a round of applause," when I heard the quake coming. Angel heard it, too. Shushing everyone to silence, we both stood as still as the statues of the pioneer couple outside Bellamy Park Library.

At first it sounded like thunder rolling, or a jet going over, or a huge semi rumbling through CHAPS's parking lot. Then the wagon wheel light fixtures jittered and clinked and the electricity fizzled, plunging the windowless room into a darkness as black as the inside of a bad guy's cowboy hat. A split second later the wooden dance floor began heaving and swaying.

People screamed. I screamed. Angel clutched my right hand in his left while he said something prayerful in Spanish. I imagined he was probably crossing himself—he often did so under stress.

It was like standing on a skateboard balanced on a basketball. Everybody in the place shuffled, pivoted and skidded across the floor and fell in a heap. Wine glasses and beer bottles hurtled off tables. From the two bars, the clatter of breaking glass was accompanied by what sounded like every rack and shelf hitting the ground. The smell of alcohol was lethal.

A few more thuds and crashes and screams later, the roller-coaster stopped dead as suddenly as it had started. For what felt like a full minute but was probably ten to fifteen seconds, there was a complete and eerie silence.

Then Angel, who was underneath me, said, "Are you okay, Charlie?"

"Heck no," I said, and people laughed nervously and started untangling themselves.

"Everybody outside," Angel yelled, taking charge, which was unusual for him. I've noticed that people often acquire different personalities in emergencies. Usually Angel is the strong, silent type. Of average height and sinewy, he has a face that's all planes and angles—as if it was cut from mahogany with a chainsaw. A Pancho Villa mustache and black hair drawn back in a ponytail with a leather thong complete the picture of the definitive tough guy, until you look in his eyes or notice his clothing. Angel's eyes are brown and mild, and he's one of the cleanest, tidiest people I've ever known. His white Western shirts and light-blue jeans always look as if they just emerged from the laundry. His cowboy hat is of the finest straw, also impeccable.

Angel is the closest thing CHAPS has to a real cowboy.

When he was in his early twenties he worked on a ranch in Texas and competed in rodeos. That's all he's ever told me about his past. He was born again on the day he entered our partnership, he says.

"This way please," Savanna said politely from somewhere on my left. Savanna is always polite. At 36 she's also seriously gorgeous—a shy African-American version of Dolly Parton with a killer smile, big hair, big bosoms, a big heart.

Savanna and Angel and I each own one-sixth of CHAPS. The other half belongs to Zack Hunter—yes, *the* Zack Hunter. Zack wasn't there. He rarely showed up on a Wednesday, his poker night. Besides which, on Wednesdays most of the patrons were local folks. Zack preferred to save himself for weekends when we featured live music and the place was packed with kids from the university, lawyers and doctors from San Francisco and technoids from Silicon Valley. All categories fairly equally divided between male and female. With that crowd, Zack could be assured of plenty of adulation.

The emergency lights had come on at the exits, and everyone obediently trooped toward them, all talking at once. The guys were being protective of the gals, telling them not to worry. One of the things I love about country-western stuff is that if you put a cowboy hat on a guy, he immediately starts saying 'ma'am' and 'little lady' and walking with a macho swagger.

I was pretty shaken up. I had been living in Seattle in 1989, and I'd watched the reports about *Loma Prieta* on television. There was a major difference between watching and being on the spot—up close and personal, as they say on TV sports programs.

"Charlie?" Savanna said close to me, sounding worried.

I might not be a mother, might even have stopped listening to the ticking of my biological clock, but I did know that in any emergency a mother's first thought was for her child. Savanna was a single mother. She and her two-year-old daughter Jacqueline lived in a tiny apartment in Palo Alto. Savanna had been married ten years before she got pregnant, so Jacqueline was doubly precious to her.

"Go home, Savanna," I told her. "Angel and I can handle things here."

Between the four of us—Sundancer was small but he had a big voice—we managed to herd everyone out onto the plaza. It was a shock—and a relief—to discover it was still daylight. Savanna flashed me a grateful look and took off at a fast clip toward the parking lot.

The air smelled dusty. The California live oaks in the plaza had dropped a lot of branches. Birds were twittering and tweeting and squawking their little feathered heads off. They probably figured dawn had broken, and broken good.

Our *faux* cowboys and cowgirls were twittering just as agitatedly. So were the people pouring out of the Mexican restaurant and the Granada Apartments. Every dog in the neighborhood was barking. Somewhere nearby sirens wailed like banshees, those Gaelic spirits who screech a warning when somebody's going to die.

Angel and Sundancer and I made the rounds. Sundancer still had his headset on, its cord dangling. Amazingly, the only injuries were bruises and a few small cuts from flying glass. People were helping one another mop up. Disasters always seem to bring out the best in everyone. If we had a constant stream of disasters, we wouldn't have any wars. Something to think about.

"I'm going up to check on Benny," I muttered to Angel once we were sure nobody needed emergency aid.

Angel shook his head, his ponytail waggling. His liquid brown eyes looked worried, which was their usual condition. "It's safer outdoors, Charlie. There might be structural damage, and we have to beware of aftershocks."

"It'll only take a minute." I jogged off, detouring around the building to the parking lot to make sure my beloved Jeep Wrangler was undamaged. The whole parking area appeared to be unscathed.

The dim entrance lobby of CHAPS was an obstacle course. The display window on the inside wall of Buttons and Bows—the concession store, which featured Western paraphernalia—had shattered into a million shards. The windows of Dorscheimer's Restaurant—also a concession—were intact. Several branding irons and a couple of saddles had fallen off the lobby walls. As far as I could tell, the wagon wheel chandeliers were okay—because of their weight they'd probably been anchored very securely.

My private staircase seemed to be solid, but I went up it cautiously, feeling ahead in the near-dark. As part of my deal with Zack Hunter, I occupied the upper part of the building—a fairly large loft-like space with minimal furnishings—situated above the main dance floor and bar. It was a pretty good deal. I had successfully argued with Zack that if he let me live there, rent-free of course, I could keep a watchful eye on CHAPS and protect the place from burglars and vandals. I'd neglected to mention that if a burglar or vandal were to show up, I fully intended pulling my bedcovers over my head and pretending I wasn't there.

Inside the loft, I flipped the light switch before I remembered the electricity was off, then fumbled my way around all the windows, cranking open the blinds, a couple of which were lopsided.

"Yo, Benny," I called out as I headed for the hot water heater in the bathroom. I'd read somewhere that in the event of an earthquake or other disaster you should turn off the inflow valve so the water in the tank would stay potable.

Benny wasn't anywhere in sight, though as usual I had left him happily hopping around when I went to work. Benny was my Netherland dwarf rabbit. He was mostly house-trained, and when he fell from grace it was easy enough to scoop up the little black pellets he deposited here and there. At least he didn't chew carpet now the way he did at first—an occasional sock and the upper edge of the baseboard were about it.

The loft was one large room, apart from the bathroom. The whole place looked as if it had been vandalized. Books had plummeted from their shelves; pictures had leaped down from their hooks on the walls. In the kitchen area the upper cabinets had flung open their doors and disgorged their contents, which included teabags, boxes of cereal, bags of dried beans, peas, rice, and bulgur. The bags had burst open, of course.

Luckily the lower cabinets had held firm. My thrift store china and glassware had survived. Setting my cowboy hat onto the handiest chair, I negotiated a path through the debris to my sleeping area, still calling Benny's name, trying to decide where I'd hide in an earthquake if I were a frightened rabbit.

Under the bed.

Grabbing the pocket-size flashlight I kept beside the VCR to read channel numbers by, I fell to my knees and stuck my head under the dust ruffle. No rabbit eyes gleamed back at me.

After searching under, in, and around everything else in the place, I thought to check the closet. I usually left the bi-fold doors open a crack because of a tendency to dampness.

In the bright pencil beam of the flashlight, I could see that most of my clothes had fallen from their hangers onto the floor. Frantically fumbling under the clothing my fingers encountered something fuzzy. "Benny?" I asked, my voice quavering. He didn't feel right. He didn't feel right at all.

Heart in my throat, I set the flashlight down and hastily flung jeans, skirts, shirts and my few dresses over my head to the floor behind me. Benny was under there all right, but his furry brown body was stretched out flat, like a cartoon rabbit that had been run over by a steamroller. It was pretty obvious that he had been, literally, scared to death.

Gently, I balanced his rigid body in both hands, lifted him and laid him carefully on the bed. A huge lump had formed in my throat, and I couldn't seem to swallow past it. Tears spurted hotly out of my eyes and made tracks down my cheeks as I stroked him. That rabbit had hip-hopped his way into my affections. I'd never had a pet before. I was allergic to cats, and I'd been nervous around dogs ever since a neighbor's terrier had sunk its teeth into my ankle and refused to let go as I pedaled my tricycle along a Sacramento sidewalk.

I'd bought Benny three months ago from a kid who was standing outside the local Safeway with a basket crammed with Benny lookalikes. Benny had peered over the side and twitched his whiskers at me as if to say, "Yo, sister, get me *outta* here."

Now his eyes were glossy and lifeless, his long ears motionless. After patting him a couple of times and rubbing between his ears the way he really liked, I covered his body with a towel and stood looking down at him, still crying.

"I have to go help Angel and Sundancer," I told him miserably. In the bathroom, I wiped my face with a washcloth, blew my nose hard on a handful of tissues and promised Benny I'd grieve properly later when there was more time. Then I picked up my flashlight and went back down the stairs, heading for the front door.

Adobe Plaza had pretty well emptied out. Only a few people were still hanging around, excitedly talking and gesturing. Evidently the rest had decided there weren't going to be any aftershocks and had gone to check on possible damage to their homes.

All in all, the tree-shaded plaza didn't look too bad. A few dozen tiles had fallen off various roofs, including CHAPS's, and there were shards of glass everywhere, glittering like cubic zirconias on the historic pavers and on the broad, beauty-bark topped flower-beds that fronted the various businesses.

In a perverse way, the disarray pleased me. Bellamy Park is aggressively upscale, and almost all of the town, including Adobe Plaza, is manicured to a fare-thee-well by Hoshizaki, a huge gardening syndicate that practices sanitized perfection. I often felt an urge to wander the streets blowing fluff from dandelion seed heads in all directions.

Adobe Plaza was originally part of an old Spanish rancho. It is close to the border between Bellamy Park and shabbier, more boisterous Condor.

Next door to CHAPS is the Plaza Bank. Going counterclockwise around the plaza there's a Mexican restaurant named Casa Blanca, an arts and crafts shop, a mini-mart convenience store, a small physical therapy clinic and a huge old apartment building that had recently been renovated and renamed The Granada. The same guy who had put the smart green and gold canopy over CHAPS's street side door had added a fancy new *porte-cochère* to The Granada's side entrance.

With the emergence of CHAPS, the hiring of an outstanding chef at Casa Blanca, and the building of a strip of factory outlet stores a block away, the whole area had recently experienced a renaissance.

We were lucky; CHAPS had lost only one window. Plaza Bank was missing three. I hoped the bank's money—some of which was mine—was safely locked away. The bank's semicircular brick steps had collapsed like dominoes onto the plaza. Outside The Granada, a couple of round picnic tables had turned over on their backs like dead turtles. The accompanying chairs had apparently collapsed.

At first glance, the Mexican restaurant seemed to be leaning slightly, but I quickly realized it was an optical illusion caused by the way the gutters were hanging down.

As I stood there, looking around, feeling numb, still sniffling over Benny, not sure I wanted to go back into CHAPS and face the cleanup, I heard a familiar gurgle of laughter and realized that the two shadows at the side of the bank were my friend Taj Krivenko and her significant other, Joshua Gibson. They were both regulars at CHAPS and had been taking part in the line-dance lesson when the earth began moving. When I'd made my rounds they'd been patting each other down, checking for injuries.

I admired Taj. She was one of those people who never stop giving. Besides working at Plaza Bank as loan manager, she helped out with several charities. One of her projects was supervising the clearing of an acre of land for a kid's playground in Condor. She was a wizard with a roto-tiller, she'd told me. She'd tried to recruit me several times to do something for the community, especially for the children. I couldn't imagine where she found all her energy—or time. But she never made me feel guilty when I said I was too busy at CHAPS.

She was flexing her right leg, I noticed. She had been lame in that leg since she fell off a ladder while putting up Christmas decorations at the Plaza Bank. It had been pretty badly damaged, I'd heard. She'd had to wear a brace on it for a long time. But she'd really worked at therapy, and now she had only a slight limp that certainly didn't stop her from dancing.

Taj had received a settlement from the bank for her injury. She hadn't said how much she'd settled for. Which immediately made me want to know. I'm a nosy person. I read *People* magazine regularly for that very reason. Okay, okay, *National Enquirer*, too.

Taj had a loud voice and the warmest, most infectious laugh I've ever heard. She was good-natured and kind, fortyish, a large, loosely-made and pretty woman who had learned how to turn her size to dramatic advantage. Taj's approach was to smudge charcoal liner around her dark eyes, coat every eyelash thickly with mascara, pin her mass of chestnut-brown hair up in an artistic topknot and jam large-stoned rings on her beautiful, perfectly-manicured fingers. Working at the bank, she wore beautifully tailored suits and silk blouses. When she danced at CHAPS, she wore a full denim skirt, boots, and an oversize Western shirt dripping with fringe. I thought she looked great, a distinct improvement over other large women I had known who wore clinging blouses and outgrown jeans and showed more rolls than the Michelin Man.

I asked Taj once how come she had a Russian name when she was as American as "My Country 'Tis of Thee." She looked so sad, I didn't think she was going to answer me. I was almost ready to apologize for my nosiness. Then she said she and her father and her father's father were all native Californians, but her great-grandparents, Pavel and Irina Krivenko, had escaped Russia at the time of the revolution. They'd had a terrible time getting out, and Pavel Krivenko had suffered from the aftereffects the rest of his life. He'd been a concert pianist, well-born, and a fairly vocal intellectual, so he'd been targeted by the revolutionaries. After he arrived in the U.S., the only work he could find was as a janitor. He hadn't had the heart to play the piano ever again. He and Irina had died before they were sixty.

Such a sad story. I'd heard balalaikas playing in the background, like in *Dr. Zhivago*. I loved that movie. Taj had a balalaika that had been passed down through the generations from her great-grandmother. She'd learned to play it, too.

Involved in thinking about Taj and her ancestry, probably still traumatized by the earthquake, I'd blanked out on Adobe Square. Taj's voice brought me back to full consciousness. "My stars, Charlie, is that you? Are you all right?" she asked, coming toward me. Josh came with her, holding her hand. Josh worked at a swank automobile dealership in Menlo Park. He was thirty-seven—tall, muscular, blond as a Scandinavian athlete, gray-eyed, given to navy double-breasted blazers, white on white shirts, striped ties, and pants with knife creases. Even when he brought Taj to dance at CHAPS, he could have modeled for *GQ*. He was one of the handsomest men I've ever known. And I have known some. I even married one once. Unfortunately, Josh was also weird, which I'll get into later.

I tried to rustle up a smile, but the effort made my face crumple, and I suddenly started sobbing instead. The sobs felt as though they were coming from a deep, mortally wounded place. Some small part of my brain was astonished. I never cried in public. In bed with my head under a quilt, yes, but not where anyone could see.

What can I say? I had loved Benny. He might not bark like a dog or meow like a cat, but he was somebody to come home to, somebody to cuddle. The only family I had.

"I'm fine," I said through the sobs. "How about you?"

Taj hugged me to her large soft breasts, which felt very comforting. People who live alone never get enough hugs. "My leg's a little painful where I fell on it," she said in an apologetic way. "I think somebody else fell on it too, but I can't quite remember, it all happened so fast. Was there much damage to CHAPS? Did you see the bank's steps? What a mess! What do you think, magnitude six and a half maybe? Seven?"

I wasn't exactly experienced at gauging earthquakes, and I had no idea yet how much damage CHAPS had sustained, but I couldn't talk while I was sobbing anyway. "I guess she must be in shock," Taj said over my shoulder to Josh.

"My rabbit died," I managed to blurt out.

"You're pregnant?" Taj exclaimed.

How could I not laugh? Taj set me away from her and stared. After a few seconds, she lifted her right hand tentatively. If I hadn't managed to stop laughing, she would probably have slapped the hysterics out of me. With the

knuckleduster rings she wore, that could have been hazardous to my health.

"Benny," I explained hastily. "My pet rabbit."

Taj's face cleared. "My stars, Charlie," she exclaimed
again. It was her favorite expression. "You had me scared
for a minute. I know young women don't worry about single
parenthood nowadays, but all the same. . . ."

"Honeypot, I really think we should get you to a hospital and have your leg looked at," Josh interrupted.

Taj's round face softened with love as she looked at him.
I wished for the umpteenth time that I could like Josh more
than I did. If a man is loved by a generous-hearted woman
like Taj, there has to be something lovable about him.
Wouldn't you think?

"I'm afraid Taj may have re-injured her leg," Josh said
to me.

Taj patted his face gently, and he put his arms around
her and palpated her big body here and there with his strong
hands while they did kissy-face and baby-talk. Josh is the
only adult male I ever heard actually use the term "love-
muffin."

When the smooching frenzy was over, Josh told me
someone across the plaza had heard on his Sony Walkman
that the quake had barely affected San Francisco. Bellamy
Park wasn't too bad off either. Dennison and Condor had
suffered the most damage.

"That figures," I said. Neither of the neighboring towns
were as upscale as Bellamy Park. "Even God favors the
well-off."

"Charlie," Taj chided. "Maybe most people in Bellamy
Park have money, but almost everyone goes to work."

Taj finds something kind to say in any situation. Smiling

serenely she shook her head at me, then she and Josh went back to discussing the earthquake. I didn't want to talk about the earthquake anymore, so I wandered over to the steps in front of CHAPS, sat down and stared at the scuffed toes of my Code West boots, concentrating on sending a telepathic message to Josh and Taj to go away so I could have a few minutes to mourn Benny before going inside.

Why didn't I like Josh? Maybe because he was always so perfectly dressed. Maybe it was the way his perfectly straight nose twitched whenever Taj mentioned her "settlement," which she did frequently. It gave me the idea he was interested in her money. As I mentioned earlier, I also thought he was a little on the weird side. But then again, I seem to think that about more and more people, so I've begun to wonder if maybe they're normal and I'm the weird one.

On the other hand, there was definitely something weird about Josh. For one thing, he talked with the sepulchral tones of a funeral director. Whether he expressed sympathy or amusement, it sounded phony. Also, his smile was seriously strange. In repose, his handsome, unlined, smooth-skinned face showed little expression at all, but then quite suddenly his eyes would pop and shine, and he'd show all his teeth as though some invisible cameraman had just yelled, "Here we go, Josh, say cheese!"

All of a sudden, he was standing over me. "Would you like me to take care of Benny?" he asked lugubriously when I jumped. "I could drive him to the Humane Society. They have . . . facilities. You can't possibly bury him here. Hygienically speaking it's not . . ."

"I'll take care of Benny myself," I interrupted, my voice flat.

"She's still in shock," Taj said tenderly, excusing my rudeness, which I didn't want excused.

"I am not in shock," I insisted loudly, and after exchanging a glance full of pity for the bereaved, testy carrot-top, they decided to check on their townhouse and maybe try to get Taj's leg x-rayed.

As they ambled around the side of the building, hand in hand, Taj limping, the last rays of sunlight glinted on something, and I noticed that a man was standing under one of the nearby live oaks in the plaza, staring over his metal-rimmed spectacles at CHAPS. He was an older man, in his seventies maybe. Tall and stout, he wore a flat British tweed cap and a sport coat. Very natty. I remembered seeing him hanging around the area a couple of times before.

"Hey!" I called out. "Are you okay?"

He stared at me over his glasses for a while, just long enough for me to feel squirmy. Then he walked toward me and said, very politely, with a phony-sounding British accent, "Have you got a leak in your water pipes, madam?"

Alarmed, I stood up and looked around but saw nothing unusual. "Not as far as I know," I said. "Did you see water running?"

Without replying, he switched his gaze back to CHAPS. Then he muttered something to himself, shook his head and marched off across the plaza. Literally marched. Smartly. His back was as ramrod straight as an old soldier's.

The old guy was probably a couple of slices short of a cut loaf, I thought. Or else suffering from post-quake shock. Whichever, he seemed to be functioning fairly well physically. I put him out of my mind and started back up the steps.

I was almost at the top when the aftershock hit. It

wasn't a big one as aftershocks go, but the ground was already weakened and it shook like a bowl of Jello.

I dropped the flashlight, grabbed hold of the ornamental black stair rail with both hands and hung on for the ride, noting that the shrubs in the flower border were vibrating. The delphiniums were thrashing around like primitive dancers spaced out on firewater. As I stared, the beauty bark that topped the border suddenly exploded upward like popcorn.

When the shaking stopped, I saw that a fissure had ripped apart the flower border as neatly as if it had been zipped open from below. Something white shone inside the gap.

Yanking my paralyzed hands away from the metal railing, I went over to the hole and stood staring down into it for what seemed the longest time. The summer evening light was fading fast now, but there was enough of it for me to see what was in there. Even so, I fumbled around until I found my flashlight and turned it on, just to be sure the shadows weren't deceiving me.

They weren't.

I wanted to run, maybe for help, maybe just away. As I hinted earlier, I'm a dedicated coward. But I couldn't get my feet to move. My brain wasn't functioning properly either. All it wanted to record were the unimportant details, that the flowers on either side of the opening were leaning drunkenly, that a lot of beauty bark had spilled over onto the pavers, that the topsoil was really a lovely rich brown color . . .

The fissure was about two feet long, eight inches wide, three feet deep. Sticking out of the far end was the object that gleamed whitely.

After some time, I allowed myself to admit that the object was a human foot. But even while the horror of it was shuddering through me, I still didn't want to acknowledge the fact that the foot wasn't a whole, healthy-looking foot with flesh and toes and toenails.

It was the *skeleton* of a foot.

CHAPTER 2

In order to protect itself the human mind plays peculiar games. Mine produced a memory of one of my college professors intoning: "Albert Einstein's theories of relativity forced people to think of a space-time combination in which strange things that contradicted common sense could happen."

Right on, Professor Kuznetsky.

I don't know how long I stood staring at that damn foot. The human mind also seems to compress or expand time depending upon circumstances. I felt completely alone, lost in a wilderness in which a cold wind was blowing.

When I came back to myself, I was gulping air and my body was still requesting immediate flight. As I gazed blankly around, it dawned on me that there was a lot of activity going on at the corner of The Granada. Focusing on the group that was milling around, I recognized that they were all male.

I'm ashamed to confess that I thought, *aha, yes, men would know what to do with a dead foot.* The fact that a nineties woman allowed herself to think this shows how much effect the trauma of my discovery was having on my thinking processes.

All the same, my body obeyed the only instructions it was getting and chugged toward my neighbors. The crisis apparently centered around a damaged water main that was spewing water in all directions. I wondered if this was the leak the big old guy in the tweed cap had been confused about.

I danced around the edges of the group for a minute or so, but the men were all busy shouting instructions at each other. The only instruction that made sense to me came from a stocky dark-haired man who yelled that someone should call 911. I immediately trotted away to call in a report on the foot.

Crunching glass underfoot, I raced into CHAPS's office, waving my flashlight, grabbed the nearest phone and dialed 911. Which, judging by the rapid sound of the busy signal, was what a million other people on the San Francisco Peninsula were doing. Right about the time I was going to hang up and redial, the phone went dead.

Still requiring action, my body charged into the main corral, following the flashlight's wildly lurching gleam. Spotting light and movement around the back bar, I veered in that direction, skidding to a stop when I saw Angel and Sundancer shoveling debris into a large garbage container and our senior partner Zack Hunter kicking broken beer bottles toward them.

The bar counter was an inch deep in shattered glass. In the middle of the mess a Coleman lantern roared a welcome, radiating a large circle of light. I had a sudden understanding of how comforting it must have been for nomads of long ago to come upon fellow travelers gathered around a campfire.

"Yo, Charlie!" Zack exclaimed cheerfully. He was wearing full Western gear even though he'd been off duty all day. He usually wore it, saying it was good advertising. It was my opinion he knew very well how sexy he looked with his lower parts packed just right into his black jeans. The rest of his clothing was black too—tapered Western shirt, cowboy hat, Tony Lama boots. He'd adopted a sort of Western-movie cowboy drawl to go along with this Johnny Cash man-in-black image. He was actually born and raised in Beverly Hills.

Angel wiggled expressive brows and gave me his rare smile. "Benny okay?" he asked.

I shook my head, my eyes immediately puddling up again.

Angel grimaced in sympathy, then went back to shoveling, his muscles bunching under his Western shirt. Angel had trouble expressing emotion, but I knew he'd liked Benny.

Sundancer shook his head. "Earthquakes," he muttered, which I took as an expression of sorrow. Zack had hired Sundancer because he looks like a clone of Larry King, even to the trademark suspenders. That's Zack for you—he's most comfortable with things and people who can be connected in some way to television or the movies.

Sundancer is strange and brilliant—two traits that often go together. He studied sound wave theory at MIT before becoming a deejay. I suspected he didn't even care about the lyrics, but just chose songs whose sounds formed patterns that suited him. Luckily, his preferred patterns suited everyone else, too.

Zack handed me a mop.

I looked at the mop, then at him, and opened my mouth to tell him about the foot.

Nothing came out. Deep in my throat I could feel the pressure of the sobs that were waiting to explode the minute I tried to speak.

Mute, I looked around, trying to distract my brain with observations so that the pressure on my larynx would ease. The damage in here seemed limited to stock. Zack's prized wine captain, a huge cooling cabinet that kept wine chilled to perfection—60° for red, 50–55° for white, sparkling at 45°—was intact, but racks of wineglasses had dropped onto the bar and scores of beer bottles had fallen out of the wide-open refrigerator unit. You could get drunk on the smell.

Zack had turned away and put on a pair of thick work gloves so he could safely sweep glass fragments off the long bar into a plastic bucket. "When the quake hit, I was eatin' dinner at the British Bankers Club—that classy eatery in Menlo Park," he said. "You know the one? Stained glass windows? Tiffany lamps?"

He'd probably been entertaining one of his usual Barbie clones, some still functioning part of my brain suggested.

"I hit the road fast I could," he went on. "Couldn't finish eatin' for worryin' 'bout my investment. Melissa said . . ." He broke off without revealing what pearls of wisdom his latest dolly had imparted. "Claims adjuster's already been and gone," he added casually. "I called him from Menlo Park—he was here soon as I was."

The power of a celebrity name never fails to astound me.

I was still clutching the mop as if it were a lifeline. Eventually Zack noticed I wasn't responding with my usual repartee. He turned his head, his straight black eyebrows slanting inquiringly above his nose in the puckish way that always makes my insides clench in a sort of sex-deprived Gordian knot. It had been a while since my divorce became final, a while before that since I'd seen any action.

Though I pride myself on my intelligence, it is flawed where men are concerned. And while I have absolutely no intention of killing off my self-esteem by getting involved with Zack Hunter, I can't persuade my hormones to stop standing up and shouting for attention whenever Zack is on scene.

Trying to trick my voice into operating, I thought up an innocuous question. "Did you dash up to my apartment the minute you arrived? To see if I was still alive?"

Judging by the flash of Angel's dark eyes and whiter than white teeth, the question wasn't all that innocuous.

Zack looked blank, which wasn't unusual for him. The first time he met me he asked where I got a name like Charlie Plato. I explained that the Charlie was an improvement on Charlotte and the Plato was from my Greek grandfather who always said he was descended from the same family as the philosopher.

"Which philosopher would that be?" Zack had asked.

Zack Hunter, as you know if you haven't lived in a cave for the last few years, is 6'2" tall, 35 years old, tough-looking in a rangy, breath-stopping, sexy sort of way. He has thick black hair that always looks boyishly tousled, a lined forehead, a slightly crooked, once-broken never-quite-fixed nose and hard green eyes that are permanently narrowed as if he's squinting into a dust storm. He also has a jagged scar on his left cheek, which according to Zack was bestowed upon him by a bull's horn.

Sure it was.

For non-TV watchers, if there are any such, I'll explain that for seven years Zack Hunter played Sheriff Lazarro on the wildly popular, totally improbable hit series, *Prescott's Landing*. Before that Zack had played in several less than successful movies, but *Prescott's Landing* had catapulted him to the status of a cult icon. Exactly two years ago, for some unknown reason, his character had been killed off. Sixteen and a half months after that, he'd acquired this building and turned it into CHAPS. Lately he'd been showing up in a Hawaiian Sunshine Soap commercial, vigorously scrubbing his tanned, washboard-stomached body under a waterfall, looking at the camera from under half-closed eyelids in a way that made my inner parts go *whomp*!

Now that my voice had been restored, I wanted to tell Zack about the foot, but I was suddenly afraid I'd hallucinated the whole thing. Maybe the earthquake combined with grief over my poor little rabbit had caused pressure to build up in my brain.

Not wanting to make a fool of myself, I decided to be discreet. "I want you to come and look at something," I said, glancing over my shoulder. Wielding flashlights, Angel and Sundancer were rolling the garbage container toward the lobby, evidently intending to empty it into the dumpster out back.

"What?" Zack asked.

"I'm not sure," I said evasively. "That's why I want you to look at it."

He frowned.

"Just come with me, okay?" I snapped. Leaning the mop against the bar, I headed toward the plaza door, counting on Zack being curious enough to follow.

It would have been dark by now, except that a full moon had shot up from nowhere—maybe the earthquake had dislodged it from its resting place. It was remarkable how much brighter the moon shone in the absence of electricity.

The foot skeleton had not been a hallucination.

Zack gazed down into the fissure even longer than I had. Then he said, "It's a foot, darlin'."

"I can see that," I said with astonishing patience.

"You said you didn't know what it was."

"I didn't want to shock you."

"Oh." He looked back at the foot. "I thought the idea of you stayin' in the loft for free was to prevent this kind of thing."

"That foot's obviously been in residence longer than I have."

"You may be right." He slanted a glance at me. "He doesn't look like one of our regular customers."

I closed my eyes in sufferance over this remark, then pondered the pronoun. "What makes you think it's a he?"

"Kind of a big foot for a woman." This was a highly perceptive remark for Zack, and it stunned me to silence.

"Maybe we could just cover it up again," Zack said with a crafty smile. "It would save a whole heap of trouble. Shoot, nobody would even know."

"Is that what Lazarro would have done?" I asked. "I thought he was supposed to be a good cop. Surely he'd know you can't go around covering up murder."

Zack looked at me suspiciously, evidently suspecting I was making fun of Lazarro. Which I did from time to time. Who could resist? "How can you be sure this foot was murdered?" he asked.

"Not too many people bury their own foot," I pointed out. "And I doubt Bellamy Park was ever a burial ground for spare parts. It's also entirely possible this foot is attached to a whole skeleton. And if someone buried a whole person in this flower border rather than in the local cemetery, it stands to reason that someone most probably killed . . . him. In any case, we need to report our find to the police."

He gazed at me solemnly, his brow creased in thought.

"On *Prescott's Landin'*, people were always thinkin' if they were first to report a crime, Lazarro would commend them for their honesty and integrity. Instead, old Lazarro used to check that person out big time. He always suspected that the dude who supposedly found the corpse was the murderer. You might want to think on that."

"That was fiction, Zack," I said wearily. I was forever saying things wearily to Zack Hunter.

He looked indignant. "We had advisers from the local police force." Squatting, he gingerly scooped a little dirt out from around the foot with an index finger.

"I don't think you should touch anything," I said.

He stood up, wrinkling his nose, looking a little pale around the eyes. Wiping his hand on the seat of his jeans, he nodded briskly. "Maybe you'd better call 911."

He was evidently going to regard it as "my" foot. Loping off into the plaza, he picked up a fallen live oak branch, trotted back and draped it over the hole. "I tried 911," I said patiently. "I got the fast buzz that means all circuits are busy, then the line went dead. We'll have to drive to the police station."

He looked at his wristwatch. "It's gettin' late, Charlie."

"The police station is probably open, Zack. We just had an earthquake."

"Yeah, right." He carefully adjusted his cowboy hat to its proper angle and patted my shoulder. "You go ahead and do whatever you think is right, darlin'," he said kindly. "I'll get on with the chores."

"Zack!" Sometimes his name came out sounding like a cuss word. It felt that way in my mouth, too. "Half of CHAPS is yours. I only own a sixth. That makes your responsibility for this foot much greater than mine."

I thought he'd probably frown over that for some time,

but he just shrugged and gave in. "Okay, but we'll take my pickup. I'm not riskin' my neck in that jeep of yours."

"I'll get my purse," I said before he could change his mind about going with me. "The police might want to see some identification."

In my living room area, I avoided looking toward the towel draped on my bed as I studied myself in the wall mirror. My face was so pasty my freckles stood out like polka dots. For all of five seconds, I thought about putting on makeup and spritzing my hair with water, which sometimes calmed it down. My hair has a mind of its own. My dad used to say it always looked as if a mischievous kitten had played in it for a week or two.

I suddenly missed my dad and mom so much my throat ached. This happened a lot, especially at times like this when life seemed incredibly tough. I was still mad at my parents for getting themselves killed when their stupid little Cessna went down in bad weather on a trip to Tahoe. I was eighteen at the time. I kept wishing they'd been content to fly Alaska Air or United like everyone else.

I reached for my cowboy hat, which was black like Zack's. One big benefit to Western gear, if you're having a bad hair day—which for me means most days—you can just jam on your hat and cover most of it up.

I was doing just that when I heard the sound.

A scratching sound.

A familiar sound.

Holding my breath, I peered around the door to the bathroom.

Benny was squatting in his litter box, doing his twosies like a good little bunny, ears and nose twitching, eyes gleaming.

My heart swelled, and tears started flowing freely once

again. As soon as I was sure he'd finished, I swooped down
and grabbed him out of there. As I burbled all kinds of joy-
ous mother noises at him, he nuzzled my nose, nibbled on
my ear, then thrust his head under my hand so I'd pet him.
He was vibrating gently, happily. If he'd been a cat he
would have purred. It was a miracle.

After several minutes, I remembered Zack was waiting. I
reluctantly placed Benny in his cage, patted him one more
time, checked his food and water containers, then carefully
closed the gate. As I trotted down the stairs, I wished with
all my cowardly heart and soul that the same miracle that
had restored Benny to me would work its magic on the foot
in the flower border and make it come back to life, too.

Somehow that didn't seem too likely.

CHAPTER 3

In the absence of functioning traffic signals, Bellamy Park residents were directing traffic at downtown intersections. Drivers scrupulously took turns, waving each other forward. Drivers are always polite in Bellamy Park. When they get down the road into shabby old Condor, though, it's every jerk for him or her self. Who says environment doesn't affect behavior?

As far as I could see in the moonlight and the lights from passing cars, downtown damage consisted mainly of fallen moldings, acres of broken glass and an occasional downed tree. There were several spirals of smoke in the night sky, but no obvious fires. The rosy brick facade of an office building next to the police department had slid off its front wall and spread out to the middle of the road, like a sheet of wallpaper someone had forgotten to apply paste to.

The population of Bellamy Park is around 28,000, give or take several million tourists who drive through on their way to or from San Francisco and occasionally stop off to eat or drink or shop. The city has a fair-sized police department, but tonight the lobby was deserted apart from an attractive but tired-looking brunette dressed in a crisp white blouse and dark skirt. She was stationed behind a long wraparound counter, alternately talking into two telephones. Her vocal cords sounded as stressed-out as she looked.

An extremely tall thirty-something black man came in through the front door just as the woman hung up the phones. "Hey, Sheila, when did you get here?" he asked. He turned in a circle, massaging the back of his neck. "Where did everybody go?"

"I came in as soon as the ground stopped shaking," she told him. "Took me a while to get here, but I figured I might be needed. Midnight watch came in early, went out again, doing building checks, looking for victims. We've been lending officers out like we're a cop library." The phones on her desk were jangling, and she put a hand on each but went on talking. "There's some trouble over in Condor—a gang of youths roaming around looting stores, beating up local residents who try to intervene. Dennison's acting up too—dispatch got a report about a couple of shootings going down."

With a tired shrug, she lifted both phones, said "Hold on," into one then spoke into the other.

The man was a detective sergeant named Taylor Bristow. As Zack was uncharacteristically keeping his lips zipped, it was left to me to explain about the hole that had opened up in the flower border outside CHAPS. "A fissure, I guess you'd call it."

The tall sergeant had a great smile and no hair. "Yes, ma'am. The department you want is . . ."

"I'm not concerned about the fissure. I'm concerned about the foot that's in it."

"Ma'am?"

"Do you suppose you could possibly stop calling me ma'am?" I asked. "My name is Plato. Charlie Plato."

His eyebrows climbed. "Like the philosopher?"

I shot a triumphant glance at Zack Hunter, then started in again on Bristow, only to discover he wasn't listening. He was staring at Zack instead. "You're Sheriff Lazarro!" he exclaimed, just as I was about to explain that the foot was missing its pound of flesh.

Zack's mouth drew back into the thin-lipped bad-boy smile he was famous for. One hand went up automatically to remove his cowboy hat so the other could rake boyishly through his thick dark hair. "Used to be," he said modestly, replacing the hat at a sexy tipped-forward angle.

"Well, give it to me with both barrels!" Bristow said, quoting a nauseatingly over-used Lazarro expression. Then he hummed a few bars of *Prescott's Landing*'s theme song, which had plagiarized several of the more flamboyant chords from the old *Bonanza* introduction.

Next thing I knew he was shaking Zack's hand as if he were a long-lost brother returned to the fold. "Do a little acting myself," he said. "Shakespeare in the park? I used to watch *Prescott's Landing* all the time. Catch the old reruns when I have a chance. Way more excitement in that town than in Bellamy Park."

I liked Shakespeare in the park myself, and Bristow certainly had the voice for it, deep and vibrant. I could easily imagine him declaiming, "If it were done when 'tis done, then 'twere well it were done quickly." Which words I wished he'd live by before my patience wore any thinner. "I'm trying to *tell* you about some local excitement," I said wearily.

The men exchanged a glance fraught with male forbearance. "There's a skeleton of a human foot in the flower border outside CHAPS," I stated, cutting straight to the point this time. "The earthquake opened up a hole in the ground and out popped the foot. It looks as if it's attached to a leg, maybe a whole body."

Bristow's eyebrows climbed again. "That right?" he asked Zack, thus innocently risking my undying hostility.

"It's a foot," Zack agreed. "Guess it must have been there for quite a spell. No flesh on it that we could see."

"I'll be damned," Bristow said. "CHAPS, huh? Heard you were the man behind that. Country music? Adobe Plaza? Keep meaning to get out there, heard it was a happening place." Glancing at my face, which may have shown some increasing impatience, he added hastily, "Hold on, I'll get a dispatch card."

After disappearing into the nether regions, he returned with a card and took down a brief statement. Then he went behind the desk and typed up a few more details, managing to talk to Zack at the same time.

Bristow's mother, it transpired, was wild for Sheriff Lazarro. Well, sure, no problem, Zack would be happy to give Ma an autograph. Yeah, it was no lie that police work wasn't as exciting in real life as it was on the boob tube, but hey, who'd watch a show where a bunch of macho guys sat around doing tedious grunt-work, writing reports, hanging around courtrooms?

"Since Zack got fired from *Prescott's Landing*, he's been doing the Hawaiian Sunshine Soap commercial," I cut in sweetly. "Maybe you've seen him cavorting under a waterfall in a plastic lei."

"I do not cavort, darlin'," Zack protested. "I bathe. Sensuously. And that lei is made of real orchids."

Sheila hung up her phones once more, then leaned forward over her desk, gazing at Zack with hot hazel eyes.

"You were a terrific sheriff," she said with great sincerity, then hesitated. "I never did understand why they gave a Midwestern sheriff an Italian name though."

"It's all about bein' politically correct these days, darlin'," Zack drawled. "First off the writers had an Irish cop in mind, mostly because they thought I looked Irish. Then they decided an Irish cop was a cliché. So they made him Italian to please the Italian-Americans—they get ticked always bein' the bad guys."

Sheila obviously found all this insider stuff fascinating. "I missed the last episode you were in," she said. "Why'd they take you off the show?"

"Yeah," Bristow asked, apparently as entranced as Sheila. "How come you quit?"

Zack removed his hat again and frowned down at the sweatband. He seemed at a loss for something to say, and I suddenly remembered a story in *People*—a couple of years ago maybe, when I was living in Seattle, still married. After allegedly getting in a fight—a real knock-down-drag-out-fisticuffs-fight—with the director of *Prescott's Landing*, Zack Hunter had walked off the set. *People* magazine had "revealed the shocking story" of Zack's past violence and heavy drinking, which had apparently stopped just short of alcoholism. According to the *People* reporter, Zack had been well-known around the studio for his hair-trigger temper and explosive reactions.

I'd forgotten all about that story. If I'd remembered it, I might have thought twice about going into partnership with Zack.

Sometime after that Zack had been written out of the series, without explanation. And he had disappeared. Nobody seemed to know where he had gone. I'd never heard any explanation for his disappearing act or the preceding violence.

An image of the skeletonized foot in the flower border poked up in my mind with a question mark attached to Zack's name.

Nah, I thought. Nowadays, Zack rarely drank more than a beer, and he was terminally good-natured. I certainly hadn't noticed any violent behavior since I'd been working with him. In fact, I'd never heard him so much as raise his voice to anyone.

All the same, I found I was staring at him speculatively, and quickly lowered my gaze to the counter.

"Hey, listen, I didn't mean to pry," Sheila murmured into the taut silence.

Zack zinged one of his sexy under-the-eyelids glances her way, and she drew in a shaky breath and put her hand to her bosom.

"It's a natural enough question," Zack said. "I just get to feelin' bad when I think about the writers killin' Lazarro off. Hard for me to talk about, darlin'. They didn't even write Lazarro a glorious exit. They sent him off in the woods on a manhunt and had him come down with Lyme disease, caught from a tick, which gave him some weird kind of arthritis."

Sighing, he tipped his cowboy hat at an even more fetching angle. "Supposedly, Lazarro couldn't walk very well after that, so then he got run over by a bus."

"Yeah," Bristow said. "I do recall that now you mention it. Ma was upset for a week."

"Lotta women mourned," Zack said, shrugging bravely. "Lazarro always did receive more mail than the other lead characters. Made for some jealousy, you know?"

I thought it was interesting that Zack always referred to

Lazarro in the third person—as if he were a whole separate person. Maybe that was the way all actors thought of their characters.

"So now you're sticking to commercials?" Sheila asked.

"Just restin' on my residuals, darlin'," Zack said, green eyes glinting. "Runnin' CHAPS until my agent comes up with a series I can live with—and I do mean *live* with."

This very minor witticism was greeted with great amusement on all sides. It was truly amazing to me to see how enthralled these two intelligent people were by Zack's presence. A commentary on the influence of television.

By the time Sergeant Bristow got through with our statements and came back around the counter, he and Zack had made a date for a beer on the following Wednesday night. Sheila would join them if she could get a babysitter for her nine-year-old son Harry. She was a single mother, she let Zack know.

Leaning my head back I made eye contact with Sergeant Bristow. It was unusual for me to have to strain to look up at a guy—I'm 5'10" myself. Bristow had nice eyes, I noticed—golden brown, almost amber, sincere. My former hostility faded. "So what are you going to do about the foot?" I asked.

He sighed. "We'll try to get someone out there ASAP, Ms. Plato, but I have to tell you we've a lot going on. I'm sure you understand. A floor fell through in Cassie's Cashmere Clothing. Couple customers trapped. Fire department's got a crew down there, but I want to go back and see how they're getting on. We've had several people hurt here and there, flying bricks, trees coming down. Gotta couple buildings in danger of collapsing. Besides providing mutual aid to Condor and Dennison."

He paused, then added, "I'll try to get a patrolman out

to CHAPS to take a look tonight. Might get a crew on the job sometime tomorrow. Medical examiner and coroner's investigator will want to take a look first—the examiner will be the one to direct the excavation and take the remains to the hospital for autopsy."

My face must have shown the attack of nausea brought on by the words 'remains' and 'autopsy'. Sergeant Bristow gave me a sympathetic smile. "I understand how upset you are, Ms. Plato, and it's for sure you've got a unique problem there, but it's not exactly a life-threatening situation and we do have a lot going on right now."

I hate it when men say I'm upset, but I could see he had a point. "What do you suggest we do with the foot in the meantime?" I asked with commendable patience.

"Keep people away from it," he said promptly. "Don't tell anybody about it. And don't disturb it. Cover it up maybe."

"I already put a tree branch over it," Zack announced.

"Good thinking." The sergeant rewarded Zack's brilliant foresight with a proud smile. "Best to leave it as undisturbed as possible. Don't mess with anything in the hole—might be a clue or two around."

He shook Zack's hand again, then picked up the paperwork and disappeared into a back room.

I had a feeling of anti-climax as I hoisted myself into Zack's pickup. My body was still geared for action, and no one was acting. "Damn it all, anyway," I muttered.

Zack gave me a startled glance. "You still upset? What with? I thought you said your rabbit was okay? You steamed at Bristow? Seemed like a pretty cool dude to me. Looks like Michael Jordan, don't you think?"

I gave him a look, then reminded myself I was in partnership with this man, and life was much simpler when all parties to an agreement could live in harmony.

The thought crossed my mind that if I'd stayed in Washington State, I wouldn't have had to deal with somebody's buried foot. Maybe it would have been better if I hadn't answered that ad in the *Seattle Weekly* four months ago—Wanted: Investors with capital, a sense of adventure, and a love of country music.

Buying a sixth share in a country-and-western tavern might have seemed an impulsive act to some. My ex certainly thought so—though it was none of his business, considering that our divorce had been final for several weeks. It had been a very simple divorce. Rob gave me nothing, and I did likewise, though he'd had the nerve to suggest he was entitled to some of the money I'd inherited from my parents. To recompense him for loss of a wife, he said. As if I were some kind of stolen property.

Anyway, the ad had appealed to me immediately. I'd been hard-core country long before the music went mainstream. The timing was good, too: I had the aforementioned inheritance, I was desperately anxious to remodel my postdivorce life from attic to cellar, and after twelve years of self-imposed exile I was ready to return to California.

I grew up in Sacramento. My folks used to take me to San Francisco or Half Moon Bay whenever they wanted to escape the summer heat of the San Joaquin Valley. The whole peninsula evoked some of the happiest memories of my life.

In fact, I had to admit that until this evening, I'd been having a blast at CHAPS. How could I let one bony old foot spoil things for me?

To my surprise, a patrol officer arrived at CHAPS about

the same time we did. He shone his flashlight into the hole, agreed with Zack that there was a foot in there, took a few notes and measurements and covered up the hole again.

The camp lantern was still hissing merrily, and Angel was still cleaning up when Zack and I walked into the main corral. Sundancer was nowhere in sight. The whole place reeked of beer.

"Lookin' good," Zack said.

Angel's face didn't register any pleasure over the compliment. "I was worried," he said, looking it. "Where did you two disappear to? I thought maybe you dropped into a hole."

Zack and I exchanged a glance. Perhaps Angel was psychic. Zack didn't say anything. I gathered he had taken Bristow's injunction against talking to heart.

"It's about time you showed up, girlfriend," Savanna said lightly from behind me. "Sundancer took off the minute I arrived. Said he had to go see his psychiatrist." Her smile turned naughty. "I guess the earthquake shook up his id."

She was wielding the mop Zack had wished on me earlier. She had yanked her fabulous black curls back off her face into an elasticized scrunchy, managing to look as breathtakingly beautiful as always. It hardly seemed fair.

Setting the mop aside, she gave me a hug. "Angel told me about Benny. I'm sorry," she murmured.

I'd been so caught up in worrying about the foot I hadn't even reported back. "Benny wasn't dead after all," I told her and Angel. "He was just temporarily paralyzed with fright. Last time I looked he was all bright-eyed and bushytailed."

Angel's rare smile flashed.

"I wasn't expecting you to come in again," I said to Savanna.

She had gone back to work with the mop. "Jacqueline slept through the whole earthquake, according to the sitter. The apartment complex barely shook—no damage except for a couple pieces of fence that were falling down anyway. Figured I might as well be useful here."

I was relieved to know Jacqueline was all right. I thought of her and Savanna as family. Jacqueline was a good little kid, and she and her mom seemed to feel I was family too, though unlike me Savanna did have one of her own. It was large, but none of them had had anything to do with Savanna since she married Teddy Seabrook, a white man.

Teddy and Savanna had separated just before she bought her share of CHAPS, so I hadn't met him. Which was no great loss to me, Savanna insisted, though she looked sad when she said it. So far she hadn't told me what had led to the breakup, though I had certainly asked. As usual, my enquiring mind churned constantly with the need to know.

Savanna had not yet told her family about the separation because they were all waiting to jump up in the air and clap hands and yell, "We told you so," and she was way too proud to give them the satisfaction.

Angel said he thought we should make a plan, so we held an impromptu board meeting then and there and decided we'd have to close up for cleaning and repair and an inspection for possible structural damage. This would probably mean missing a couple of profitable weekends, but most people would be doing their own cleanup anyway.

"Well, as long as everything's under control, maybe I'll run along and see what happened to Melissa," Zack said when we were done. "I'll check again with the insurance company when mornin' comes. We're pretty well covered, accordin' to the guy who was out here earlier."

"Oh no, you don't," I snapped before he could make his getaway. "There's a little matter of that bony extremity in the flower-bed. Angel and Savanna have a right to know about it."

"A bony extremity?" Angel echoed wonderingly, squinting at me.

"A foot," I explained.

"Bristow said not to tell anyone," Zack reminded me.

"Angel and Savanna aren't just anyone. They're our partners." I glared at him. "Speaking of which, you're as able-bodied as the rest of us. We can't let beer and wine swill around the dance floors all night. It'll destroy the finish. And the lobby's still littered with glass. You're strong enough to handle a mop or a broom. There's nothing in our contracts says you're the sleeping partner."

Tugging at one end of his drooping mustache, Angel looked from Zack to me and back again.

Savanna appeared as bewildered as he did. "What was that about a foot?" she asked.

Instead of answering, I gestured with my head for her and Angel to follow me. Zack came along, too. After he removed the oak tree branch all four of us stood looking down at the foot.

Angel crossed himself.

"How did it get there?" Savanna whispered, clutching my arm for balance.

"We reported it to the police," Zack said importantly. "That's where we were just now—at the police station. We don't know how the foot got there. We think he was murdered. Stands to reason. Why else would he be buried here?"

I decided to let him take the credit for this piece of deduction.

"Could this be an old Indian burial ground?" Savanna asked. "Federal law requires protection of Indian burial sites. They'll kick us out of CHAPS."

"You think it looks like an old Indian foot?" Zack asked.

There are times when I'm tempted to kick Zack's shins hard enough to make his eyes water.

"You have any ideas, Angel?" he asked.

Angel made a sort of grunting sound. As I said earlier, Angel is the strong silent type. Though this grunt didn't sound like anything I'd heard come out of him before.

We all looked at him.

His skin, which was normally a healthy bronze color, had turned a sort of fireplace-ashes gray. His skin was drawn tight over his high cheekbones. His body was swaying. Before we could reach for him, he fell straight across the fissure, face down in a dead faint.

He regained consciousness within seconds, but seemed disoriented as we helped him to his feet.

Almost immediately, his wooziness passed, and he shook us off gently but firmly and started brushing loose soil from his white shirt. We all stood there like village idiots, gaping at him.

"What was that all about?" Zack finally asked.

"Maybe Angel's not used to looking at a dead person's foot," Savanna said chidingly. "It's not exactly on my usual agenda either." She touched Angel's arm lightly. "Don't you fret none, honey. Doctor I knew used to say big tough loggers were the first to faint at the sight of blood. This isn't exactly blood, but it's still a shock to anyone's system."

"Are you okay now?" I asked, touching his other arm. "I guess maybe I should have explained about the foot before showing it to you. I almost passed out myself when I first saw it. I didn't even want to believe it was real."

Angel still didn't say anything, but he did look at me. It was as if he had suddenly gone far away, and there was nobody there to respond to me. Gazing into his eyes, I felt enveloped in a sadness so deep it was like grief.

I'd seen Angel get mildly upset once—when he had to bounce a patron who was actively harassing me and Savanna, but there was no comparison between his unhappiness then and whatever was affecting him now.

"What is it?" I asked. "What's wrong?"

This time, my voice seemed to bring him abruptly out of the gloom that had surrounded him. He attempted a grin that didn't quite come off and left him looking sicker than ever. "What's wrong?" he echoed. "What d'you think's wrong, Charlie? What d'you expect? You tell me to follow you, I follow you. So what d'you do then? You show me a dead person's foot. A *skeleton*. No warning. Not even a hint. Just bam—this big shock. Then you wonder why I fainted."

He looked down at himself. A few particles of soil still clung to his blue jeans, and he swiped at them, then looked at his hand. "I need a shower," he said, turned on a boot heel and jogged off toward the parking lot.

"I swear," Zack said into the silence that followed, "I never would have put Angel down as the type of dude would go around faintin'."

"He hasn't exactly made a habit of it," I pointed out. "People have different ways of reacting to death. It doesn't mean Angel's a weak person."

Savanna pulled the scrunchy off her hair and twisted it

around her fingers. "Angel looked so sad," she said wonderingly. "Not shocked. Sad."

"Methinks he protested a little too much," I murmured.

"What kind of fool talk is that?" Zack asked.

"Shakespeare, dear heart," I told him wearily. "I must
have caught it from Sergeant Bristow. Loosely translated, it
means I think there was more to Angel's reaction than
meets the eye."

CHAPTER 4

It was almost two a.m. before Zack and Savanna and I had CHAPS looking and smelling wholesome. We stopped and stared at one another several times as gradually weakening tremors shook the chandeliers. Occasionally, one of us would comment on Angel's behavior, which still puzzled us.

But by the time I staggered up the stairs to my loft, I was much too exhausted to stay awake worrying about anyone's reaction to anything, or to contemplate cleaning up my own debris. I carried a pot of camomile tea to bed, but I didn't get halfway through it before I dropped into a fitful sleep.

When you experience an earthquake of some magnitude, you lose your basic if undeclared trust that "God's in his heaven, all's right with the world." Subconsciously, you are waiting, anticipating, even *expecting* the earth's bosom to heave again. When you've suffered the additional shock of discovering a skeleton of a foot within tossing distance of your bedroom window, you find yourself dreaming, in vivid color, what might be attached to that foot.

The morning after the earthquake I woke feeling weary and anxious. I put out my mental antennae to test the sounds and scents of the day before opening my gritty-feeling eyes. My plaza-side window was open, and I could hear voices—several voices—one or two of them mechanically amplified and accompanied by static. There were also some light thudding sounds that I couldn't identify.

Raising my head off the pillow, I risked cracking my eyelids. Daylight was streaming around the lopsided edges of the blinds. No good little elves had sneaked in during the night to shovel up the mingled beans and grains and teabags from my floor. My books and the framed woodblock prints of the "Sixty-nine stations on the Kisokaido" series, left by the previous tenants, still lay in tumbled heaps.

I glanced at the clock radio on my nightstand. 7:57. The exact time the earthquake had struck. The power was still off. My wrist watch told me it was actually seven-thirty a.m. I groaned. I am not, at the best of times, a morning person.

Naked, I shuffled through the debris, pushed my hair off my face and peered through the miniblind slats. The scene below looked more like an action movie set than the usually tranquil oak tree-studded Adobe Plaza. A couple of police cars were parked on the ancient pavers. The historical society would have a conniption. One car's front window was open. The police radio was the source of the metallic-sounding voices. Men wearing jumpsuits and particle masks were digging up the wide and formerly flourishing flower-bed, some with spades, a couple with their gloved hands. They seemed to be running the soil through some kind of sieve. I couldn't actually see the foot or whatever else might have been revealed—a trio of uniformed officers were bending or crouching over this side of the hole, one taking photographs.

A good-looking middle-aged man in a suit stood on the far side of the flower-bed, observing. Det. Sgt. Taylor Bristow loomed next to him, his naked but shapely brown head glistening in the early sunlight.

A short distance away, lingering among what seemed to be a knot of idle onlookers, was the natty elderly man in the British tweed cap who had asked me about a leak in the water system. Next to him, dwarfed by his size, Bernie and Frannie Lightfoot, the owners of the mini-mart, were craning their necks to see around the sturdy figure of Leah Stoneham, the physical therapist from across the plaza. They were all watching a petite blonde woman in a dressed-for-success blue suit talking with Zack Hunter.

Our man in black had adopted his thumbs-in-waistband, cowboy-hat-tilted-over-eyebrows-in-an-aggressively-sexy-manner pose. Never in my memory had Zack appeared among those present before four o'clock in the afternoon.

Cussing under my breath, I pulled on jeans, shirt and boots, checked Benny's food and water supply, rubbed the spot at the base of his ears that always made his whiskers vibrate, rammed my cowboy hat on my sleep-tangled hair and scrambled down the stairs.

Yellow crime scene tape had been strung around a fairly large area, keeping the bystanders and TV crew at a distance. The wide strip of soil in front of CHAPS looked more like an archeological dig than a flower-bed.

The blonde in the blue suit was gazing up at Zack like a flower searching for sunlight. "Couldn't get through on 911. Stands to reason with the earthquake and all," I heard Zack say as I drew near. "Lines might even have been down. So the minute I realized it was a human foot, I hightailed it to the Bellamy Park police station and reported in to Detective Sergeant Bristow. He's the tall black dude over yonder."

My role in last night's drama had evidently been erased from Zack's memory banks. He went on to modestly disclaim the petite woman's praise for his timely action. Any minute he'd be doing his John Wayne impression: *A man's gotta do what a man's gotta do.*

"Why in blue blazes didn't you call me?" I demanded. "You could use a telephone if the stairs are too much for you. Or just holler up to me. Throw rocks at my window. Shoot some flares. Didn't it occur to you that I might be interested in what was going on down here?"

"Reckoned you needed your beauty sleep, darlin'," he drawled, with an amused eye for my sleep-rumpled appearance. Raising a wry eyebrow at the blonde, he added, "This here's one of my partners, ma'am. Charlotte Plato. Lives on the upper level over yonder at CHAPS. Unofficial security guard. She went with me to the police department."

The blonde became animated. "Could you share with us your feelings about this body, Ms. Plato?"

"Us?" I echoed. My major feeling at that second was fury with Zack for calling me Charlotte, which he knew I hated.

Us? Peering around—I wasn't yet operating on all frequencies—I noticed that the man in jeans and Stanford sweatshirt standing nearby was pointing a sound boom in my direction, and a similarly dressed guy had a humongous videocamera on his shoulder. Belatedly, I recognized the woman in the blue suit as a terminally perky reporter from one of the San Francisco television stations.

"Who in blue blazes called the media?" I demanded. And knew the answer even as Zack favored me with his bad-boy smile. "The only bad publicity is no publicity," I'd heard him say on more than one occasion.

"Charlotte's inclined to be cranky first thing," Zack explained to the camera.

"My feelings are that everyone should stay away and let the police get on with their job," I said to the blonde with my sweetest smile.

About then, Taylor Bristow caught sight of me and waved me over. He introduced me to the suit, who turned out to be the county coroner slash medical examiner, Dr. Martin Trenckmann. "What have you found out?" I asked Bristow once the preliminary politenesses were over and Trenckmann had turned away.

Bristow cocked an eyebrow. "Early days yet, Ms. Plato, ma'am. This isn't *Prescott's Landing*. We don't solve a crime an episode the way your boss used to do."

"Zack Hunter is not my boss," I said indignantly, but Bristow was already turning away in response to a gesture from one of the diggers. He and Trenckmann squatted down next to the now-sizeable trench in the flower-bed. After one glimpse, I decided I could get by nicely without seeing any more of what the two men were studying. Even so, the grisly image of a dirt-encrusted skull topping an entire dead and naked person who was part skeleton, part flesh, had burned itself into my brain. So had the words Trenckmann muttered to Bristow. Something about the unusual amount of rain in recent weeks and it being tricky to move the cadaver because the flesh was sliding off the bones. I could have lived my whole life without hearing that. I didn't even want to think about the word "cadaver." I decided that from now on I would refer to my discovery as Mr. X, which was anonymous enough not to paint lurid images in my mind, yet conferred some human dignity on the corpse.

The members of the work crew stood back, resting from

their labors. One of them went to stand under a tree and lit up. I hadn't smoked since an aborted attempt in my teens, but I found myself following the man and seriously considering bumming a cigarette, if only to take the taste of the eye-watering smell from the grave out of my mouth. Luckily, good sense prevailed before I caught up with him, and I mingled with the crowd and began easing my way toward the man in the tweed cap. Bernie and Frannie Lightfoot said hi to me, and I paused alongside them, keeping an eye on my quarry.

"Isn't this something, Charlie?" chubby Bernie said. "Big city news comes to Adobe Plaza. Have you any idea who the body is?"

As I shook my head, Frannie frowned at him, evidently disapproving of the note of excitement in his voice. A fussy little brown wren of a woman, she always looked disapproving. I imagined she nagged Bernie constantly. And he probably deserved it.

The crime scene tape snapped a little in a suddenly brisk breeze. In response, the watchers became festive. A man wearing a bicycle safety helmet and aviator sunglasses told the old joke about what happens if you play country music backwards. "You get your wife back, your money back, your job back. Maybe CHAPS should try it, see if the body would come back to life."

Bernie Lightfoot laughed his high-pitched laugh, guaranteed to set any listener's teeth on edge.

"I don't care much for country music," a young pear-shaped woman in spandex shorts said solemnly. "Give me R & B, give me traditional jazz, give me the Digables."

Bernie screeched again. "Hey, they'd be pretty apt in this situation. The Digables, get it?"

See what I mean about more and more weird people showing up nowadays?

The blonde reporter was gazing toward the trench now, chatting away while the cameraman panned the scene. The breeze was wafting the odor of death toward us, and her complexion acquired a green tint like the tinge on a cauliflower.

Stepping back to get around the Lightfoots, I noticed that the big man in the flat tweed cap was no longer with us. He was marching away across the plaza, heading toward The Granada, shoulders back, head high, a furled umbrella tucked like a swagger stick under his left arm. I elbowed my way through the crowd and jogged after him.

"Excuse me, sir," I said when I caught up with him. "Do you live around here?"

His gold-rimmed glasses were riding low on his straight nose. They glittered in the sunlight as he looked down at me over the top of them. "You may call me Prinny," he said. "It may seem a rather familiar form of address, but I was never one to stand on ceremony."

"Prinny?"

"Exactly. It's easier for colonials than 'Your Royal Highness,' don't you think?"

I realized my mouth was hanging open and snapped it shut. Either the man was joshing me, or I'd been right earlier when I suspected he didn't have both oars in the water. I tried again. "What do you think about all this, Prinny?" I asked, gesturing behind me.

He cupped his right hand alongside his nose and mouth, and confided something about somebody doing something to someone named Frenchy.

A jagged bolt of excitement sizzled through me. "You know who he is? The body? You *know* him?"

A pained expression flickered across his somewhat weathered face. "Frenchy was my archenemy," he said. "The trouble between our peoples has . . ." He stopped, then examined me carefully as if he were seeing me for the first time. "Do I know you, madam?" he asked.

"Charlie Plato," I said hastily. I was beginning to get another crick in my neck. He was almost as tall as Taylor Bristow. Much much bulkier though. "You were talking about some kind of trouble?"

He shook his head. "We are dealing here with state secrets, madam." With that, he shouldered his umbrella, did a smart about-turn and marched away. Stupefied, I watched him until he turned in under The Granada's porte-cochère.

Okay, so probably he was just a harmless nut, but how much of a line was there between nut and maniac? And hadn't I read somewhere that a murderer often returned to the scene of the crime? Was that fact or fiction?

Angel showed up around ten a.m. and went right to work in the bar. When Zack let me know he'd arrived, I found him taking inventory by lamplight—the main corral didn't have any windows. Standing behind the counter, making lists of supplies that needed replacing, he looked much as usual, which is to say quiet and industrious and efficient. But when he finally glanced up and saw me, a shadow appeared in his normally clear gaze, along with a certain evasiveness in his manner.

Hoisting my rear onto one of the bar's high stools, I brought him up-to-date on police doings, managing not to mention that it seemed distinctly weird that he hadn't asked.

He nodded once in a while, but didn't comment. I studied him for a couple of minutes when I was through. He looked as healthily bronze as ever. A faint pink flush painted itself on his high cheekbones as I continued to squint at him.

"You feeling okay this morning?" I asked him when it became clear he wasn't going to make any overtures.

Zack and Savanna, who were checking the stability of nearby chairs and tables, lifted their heads alertly.

Angel tugged at one end of his mustache. "Fine and dandy," he answered flatly, without looking up from his list.

From the corner of my eye I saw Zack and Savanna move on to the next table. "You're sure?" I persisted. "You went down pretty hard."

"I'm sure."

Zack and Savanna drifted farther away, evidently satisfied I wasn't going to pry anything more from our tight-lipped friend and partner. You'd think I'd have had enough sense to give it up too, wouldn't you? Fat chance!

"That was some weird reaction you had to seeing that foot," I ventured as Angel started counting beer bottles.

He shrugged.

"I'm sorry I gave you such a fright," I offered.

He finally straightened and looked at me. Very directly. The skin at the back of my neck tightened, and I caught my breath, almost expecting the sadness to envelop me again.

Angel's brown eyes maintained their usual mild appearance. He did inhale deeply through his moustache and teeth before speaking, but all he said was, "It's okay, Charlie." Then he turned his back on me. "If you'll excuse me, Charlie, I'm trying to count stock here," he said politely.

I was seething with frustration, but Angel's shoulders had acquired an obstinate set.

This time I did give up.

Zack's interview appeared on the noon news, a few minutes after our power came back on. I watched while I swept beans and bulgur into a dustpan. He looked sexy as all get out, as always, and sounded intelligent to boot. I showed up looking as if I'd slept in my clothes at a public shelter. Actually, I struck an unintended humorous note—the sound man had obliterated my voice, so all the viewer got was a minute or so of my mouth moving as if it were motorized, while Miss Perky did a voiceover explaining who I was. According to her I'd had nothing to add.

Within an hour we had an even larger mob hanging out in the plaza. The power of the box. A few people brought along sack lunches. I remembered reading about sightseers filling the San Francisco marina area after *Loma Prieta*, getting in the way of rescue attempts and firefighters, gawking at people who were trying to dig out possessions from the rubble. Supposedly, during the French revolution, women brought their knitting along to watch people get their heads relocated by the guillotine. I've never understood what attracts bystanders to disasters. Are they thinking, "There but for the grace of God go I?" Preening over their own good sense in avoiding death and destruction? What?

Our skeleton rated a couple of soundbites on the six o'clock *CNN Headline News*. More was said about Zack/Sheriff Lazarro than about poor Mr. X.

That newscast brought a few more tourists and a phone call from my ex in Seattle—the well-known, one might even say famous, Rob Whittaker, plastic surgeon to the stars. Yes, in Seattle. His patients came all the way up from Hollywood, mostly to avoid publicity.

"You had to wait for something sensational before calling?" I grouched. "You didn't think to check if I were still alive when the earthquake was first reported?"

"I tried to call last night," he said in the same bewildered, what-on-earth-have-I-done-to-deserve-this tone he'd adopted when I told him I was leaving him. He hadn't been able to imagine why I wanted out of our marriage. He'd always known he was flawed, you see. I hadn't. I'd fallen in love, as most people do, with the person I believed him to be. At the time he had almost literally saved my life, *and* given me a job, so I had been justifiably blinded by gratitude.

"I couldn't get through," he explained. "I guess a lot of people have loved ones in the Bay area."

Loved ones.

My bones melted. Quite suddenly Rob was walking around in my mind, tall, slender, with thinning fair hair and a forehead lined by his intense compassion for all living things, wearing his white doctor coat, looking at me with that absent-minded but loving gaze of his, his eyes brimming blue.

There was nothing false about the loving gaze, by the way; Rob genuinely loved me. But then, he'd never met a woman he *couldn't* love. Age was no barrier—twenties, forties, fifties. Race didn't matter either—he was an equal opportunity adulterer.

"I thought for a while that Benny was dead," I said, sniveling partly over that and partly over the memory of how completely I had adored this man before I discovered his fatal flaw.

"Benny? The guy you work for?"

Rob had never been good at remembering minor details—such as the fact that his office manager was also his wife.

"My rabbit," I said crossly. "Benny's my rabbit. After the earthquake, I found him in the bottom of my clothes closet, stiff as a board. But he came to after a while. He's hopping around just fine even as we speak."

I paused to check on Benny's whereabouts. He was underneath the coffee table, his little round eyes gleaming as he looked up at me through its glass top. I drummed my fingernails lightly on the glass, and he leaped two inches into the air then shot under the nearest armchair. This was one of his favorite games. He'd taught me how to play it the first week he had me.

"I *told* you I'd bought a rabbit," I complained to Rob.

"Of course you did," he said in his soothing doctor voice.

"You might also try to remember that I don't work *for* anyone," I went on. "I'm a *partner* in CHAPS. Angel and Savanna and I own half of it, Zack Hunter owns the other half."

"I'll try to remember, Charlie. I'm truly sorry." How could anyone stay miffed with a man who responded to criticism with abject penitence?

I could. Nothing to it.

"They showed him on CNN," he went on. "Zack Hunter. Cocky sort. Some kind of has-been TV actor?"

"He's hardly a has-been," I protested. "He's just on a hiatus right now." Why on earth was I defending Zack? Probably because since I left him, Rob tended to very gently put down any aspect of my new life that came up in conversation. He didn't mean to be critical—it was just that he was still hurt because I'd *deserted* him. His words, not mine.

"I hardly recognized you when you showed up at the end of the interview," Rob went on. "You looked tired, Charlie. You ought really to think about getting your eyes done. I'd be happy to . . ."

"My eyes are fine—I was short on sleep is all. I'd gone through an earthquake and found a dead person."

During our marriage Rob had kept finding parts of me that could do with a makeover. My own fault—he'd started out that way when we first met, and in the beginning I hadn't objected.

We met at a party. I'm skinny now, but then I was thin to the point of emaciation. I'd somehow stopped eating when my parents died four years earlier and hadn't got back in the habit again.

Rob took me off in a corner, asked me a few very personal questions, then told me I was anorexic and if I didn't get help I would die. Soon. Discovering I'd just graduated from the U-Dub and didn't have a job yet, he'd given me one, then made me eat five times a day. He'd also made me consult a shrink.

All of which was good. But when he wanted to snip the frown line above my nose, I told him if I felt like frowning, I wanted everyone to know it. And when he thought my breasts would look better bigger, I pointed out that was his fantasy, not mine. And no, thank you, I didn't want my freckles dermabraded with a wire brush.

"So who's the corpse, then?" he asked. "How did he get there?"

"We don't know yet. The detective said he'd be in touch later. I call him Mr. X."

"The detective?"

"The body."

"Why?"

"To personalize him. I guess I feel a certain responsibility for him because I found him."

"They said on TV that your boss found him."

I gritted my teeth. "Zack is not my boss—" I broke off. Complaining that Rob never really listened to me hadn't done any good when we lived together. Why should anything be different now?

"I didn't sleep all night for worrying about you, Charlie," he said. His voice throbbed with sincerity.

I softened again, even though I doubted he was telling the truth. The man was an Olympic-class sleeper. Fatigue went with doctor territory, he used to say.

I have to admit he was a *busy* doctor. I'd worked for five years as his office manager as well as his wife, so I could attest to the long hours he put in. His devotion to his patients went way beyond the call of duty. His female patients, that is. His examinations were thorough. Until the end I hadn't known *how* thorough.

But once he was through with his evening "consultations," zap went his head on his pillow. In our early days, when his chronic sleepiness seemed cute to me, before I learned that it was his *extra*-medical activity that had worn him out, I'd joked that in five years I'd be older than he was. I was right. At least I *felt* older.

"I'm fine," I said. "My loft didn't sustain any damage—a few things fell out of the kitchen cabinets is all. CHAPS had a lot of breakage, but only lost one window. If it wasn't for Mr. X, we'd be in fairly good shape."

I went on to explain how my discovery had come about, adding that Dr. Trenckmann had carted the remains off in a body bag along with a goodly amount of the soil Mr. X had been buried in. As far as I'd been able to determine, Mr. X hadn't been accompanied by any clothes. Perhaps they had disintegrated during his sojourn in CHAPS's flower-bed.

"I'll be back," Detective Sergeant Bristow had said to

Zack and me just before he hoisted his long legs into his car. A threat or a promise, I'd wondered. Earlier, Bristow had talked to us both at some length and had promised to let us know whatever the coroner found out. Neither Zack nor I had mentioned Angel's fainting fit to Bristow.

I suddenly realized Rob was still waiting patiently on the telephone. Rob was always patient. Visibly so. Irritatingly so. "Sorry," I murmured. "I guess I drifted off."

"No problem, Charlie," Rob said. We talked for a few more minutes. "I still miss you," he said just before he hung up.

I felt the pull of old affection and was teary-eyed as I continued cleaning up earthquake litter from my loft. I'd had a good life with Rob. I had loved him. I'd also loved the beautiful Tudor house on Puget Sound that we had diligently restored, the accessories and furnishings we had selected together. We'd still be married if I hadn't walked in on him in examining room #2 to report an emergency that required his immediate attention.

He was examining Trudi at the time. Yes, *the* Trudi— the world-famous model. He'd just recently done some liposuction under her chin—she'd begun to develop a double one, poor dear.

Trudi was in for her post-op checkup, so Rob certainly belonged in the room with her. But did he have to be on the examining table with her, his pants around his ankles? Suddenly, the reason for his insistence on an uninterrupted thirty-to-sixty minute consult with certain patients before the nurse came in to assist began to make more sense. So did all the comments about his terrific bedside manner.

Apparently Rob had always thought sharing his sexual largesse with a goodly percentage of his female patients was a necessary part of their post-surgical therapy. Especially those who made the pilgrimage from Hollywood. Maybe he looked upon it as a travel bonus, like frequent flyer miles. Or maybe he had a Pygmalion complex that caused him to fall in love with his own handiwork.

I'd immediately stopped going to bed with him, much to his disappointment; talking about his exploits had turned him on. I found myself having to explain that in the age of AIDS, indiscriminate sexual behavior was not only hazardous to *his* health, but also to mine. Wouldn't you think a doctor would have known that?

Because I loved him and he was so repentant, I'd naively thought that now I'd found him out, he'd mend his ways. We could wait six months, have our blood checked, then go on with our lives, I suggested. Our Lady of Forgiveness.

Ha!

So you'd think once I realized he had no intention of giving up his little hobby, I'd have had the sense to take off. Instead I'd kept putting off a decision, mostly because I was reluctant to give up my very generous salary and medical benefits, not to mention the Tudor house and all it contained.

I might have still been hesitating, but one Thursday morning, lingering over coffee while Rob was supposedly on hospital rounds, I read a quote from Voltaire in the "Horse Sense" section of the *Seattle Post-Intelligencer*. "Man is free as soon as he wants to be."

I automatically pencil in the word "Woman" to all the quotes the ancients left us out of. Reading the improved maxim, I realized I had only myself to blame for the fact that I was wretchedly miserable. I had given material possessions, things, power over me, so that they owned me.

They had turned themselves into a trap that was keeping me in a sham of a marriage.

In the wake of this epiphany, I folded the newspaper neatly and set it aside, stood up and said, aloud, "Let it go. Let it all go."

Then I packed my clothing and drove away in my Jeep Wrangler, reasoning it was okay to hang on to a possession that was mobile. I left behind not only the house but my favorite walnut table, my antique linens, my beautiful little rocking chair and my entire collection of 243 blue willow dishes, which I had amassed piece by piece at antique shows and flea markets.

I vowed as I let myself into the studio apartment I rented in West Seattle that I would never again own a house or a stick of furniture. That way I could be ready to move on at a moment's notice, whenever the fancy struck. A few months later, after the divorce was final, I had done just that, in the wake of Zack's advertisement in the *Seattle Weekly*.

CHAPTER 5

The post-earthquake looting in Condor and a fire in East
Dennison took media attention away from our Mr. X once
his remains had left the premises. The sightseers gradually
stopped coming around to take pictures of the gaping pit
that had once been our flower-bed. The area still looked as if
a brace of giant mutant gophers had gone berserk, the
uprooted shrubs wilting in the heat of the mid-day sun.

"Let it be, just in case," Detective Sergeant Bristow advised us, without additional explanation. He and a patrol
officer had come around to take individual statements the
day after Mr. X was disinterred. Now he'd returned to report on the post-mortem. Zack and Angel and I met with
him in the tavern's office. Savanna was running late—
Jacqueline had a cold.

"So, okay, here it is," Bristow said. He was sitting in a
relaxed position on the sofa we kept for occasional nap-tak-
ing, long legs stretched in front of him. I wondered where
someone that tall found his narrow-legged jeans. With
them, he wore a dark blue short-sleeved shirt, his Bellamy
Park police department ID clipped to the breast pocket. He
didn't look intimidatingly professional by any means, but
the three of us sat tensely on the edges of swivel chairs, our
spines straight, all our attention concentrated on him.

"The autopsy showed the victim was a man in his early to mid-seventies, Caucasian, six feet plus, malnourished," Bristow began.

"He *starved* to death?" Zack exclaimed.

I sighed. "You're not thinking this through, Zack. He'd hardly be likely to bury himself in the flower-bed. You think maybe the birds dug a hole for him and then covered him up? Obviously, someone bumped him off. Starving him would be a very slow way of going about it."

"Violent death isn't something to make jokes about, Charlie," Angel said. There was an unmistakable chiding note in his voice.

Zack and I both looked at him. Angel never criticized any of us. And his nice brown eyes looked sad again. His skin was tight over his cheekbones.

So, okay, none of us was too happy about finding Mr. X in our back yard, but our usually easy-going partner's reactions seemed a teensy bit out of line here.

"Being facetious is my way of handling horror," I explained in lieu of an apology.

Angel's gaze held mine for a long moment, then he shrugged and his mouth twitched at one corner in a way that looked vaguely apologetic. I was about to demand to know what was really eating him here, but then I realized Bristow was looking from one to the other of us with great interest.

"Maybe somebody buried Mr. X *after* he starved to death," Zack said. He always found it difficult to let go of an idea once he had one.

"Why would anyone bury a body that didn't need to be hidden?" I asked.

He chewed on his lower lip for a minute or so. He could

make even pondering look sexy. "I guess you're right, darlin'," he said at last. "He must have been murdered."

We all looked at Sergeant Bristow, who had been waiting patiently. "Your Mr. X *didn't* starve to death, but he
might have had trouble eating," he said. "Poor old guy
didn't have any teeth to call his own."

I blinked. "None at all?"

"Evidently he wore dentures, but we didn't find any
with the remains and we did look. Maybe he'd put 'em down
somewhere and forgotten where they were. Ma does that
with her glasses all the time." His mouth twitched. "Maybe
somewhere his smile is sitting around waiting for him to
come back to it."

He and Zack seemed to think that was pretty funny.
Angel scowled at both of them as they guffawed, but I
figured they needed their ways of handling horror, too.

"Cause of death was a blunt force wound to the head,"
Bristow said when he'd wound down. "Something heavy. A
sledgehammer maybe."

Zack winced. Angel's face went ashy.

Bristow added, "He had grey hair. Hair is composed of
protein. It's not biodegradable."

"I didn't see any hair," I objected.

"No?" He paused. "It had—separated," he said.

Mr. X's grisly remains popped up in my mind like a prop
in a house decked out for Halloween. I had an idea that
nightmare assemblage of soil-encrusted bones and decom-
posed flesh was going to haunt me for the rest of my life. I
cleared my throat. "I noticed Mr. X didn't have any clothes
on. Did *they* . . . decompose?"

"Nope. Evidently he was buried as is. That's the one
thing we can be sure of. Everything else is open to question.

The body had deteriorated considerably, which makes things difficult."

Angel swallowed audibly. Obviously, he still didn't relish anything to do with our dead body. I was fairly repulsed myself, but I'd always been fascinated by the how and why of murder and I still felt a proprietary interest in Mr. X. "Why would a murderer strip his victim?" I wondered aloud.

"The perpetrator might have been injured—if there was a fight, for example," Bristow said. "He might have been afraid he'd splattered his own blood on the victim's clothes. Maybe he thought the clothing might be traced by its labels, or a dry-cleaning tag, or else it was really distinctive—a uniform, perhaps."

He shrugged. "It's also possible the victim was already naked when he was struck."

"I remember once on *Prescott's Landin'*, Molly Carstairs beaned her lover with an iron skillet," Zack said with a nostalgic gleam in his eye. "Afterward, she put a swimsuit on him, hauled him away in her car and dumped him in the river. He was supposed to look as if he'd dived off the high bank onto a rock."

"I remember that episode," Bristow said. "Molly had found out the guy was two-timing her with her long-lost twin sister who had just shown up in town a few weeks before."

Zack nodded. "*He* was in her bedroom naked as a jaybird when she popped him. Trouble was, Molly's Weimaraners started playin' tug of war with the dude's clothes and dragged them out in the street and then after the dude supposedly disappeared, Sheriff Lazarro found the clothes in an alley." He paused for effect. "There was blood on them."

"Did he slap his forehead and say 'Aha!'?" I asked sweetly.

Zack looked at me sorrowfully. "I just thought maybe Mr. X might have been naked because *he* was killed while he was havin' sex with some chick."

"Without his teeth in?" I protested. "Yuk. I'd sooner believe he jumped out of his bathtub like Archimedes and chased through the streets shouting 'Eureka' until some passing citizen struck him down thinking he'd gone bonkers."

Zack's eyes had glazed over. He was probably trying to figure out what movie Archimedes had appeared in. I shot a glance at Bristow. "Was Mr. X killed right there in our flower-bed?"

He shook his head. "He was moved after he died."

"From where?"

"That we don't know. Yet. Though we have our suspicions."

"Well, it can't be from very far away," I said, without really taking in what he'd said. "I mean, who's going to kill some old guy in East Dennison, say, and then suddenly think, 'Hey, I know, I'll take all his clothes off, drive him over to Bellamy Park and plant him in the flower border outside CHAPS.'"

Bristow's smile was appreciative. "I like your reasoning, Ms. Plato. You must have inherited some genes from the philosopher."

His face sobered. "You're right, as it happens. We're pretty sure he was killed very close to where he was buried."

I ran over in my mind what he'd said a moment ago about suspicions. A chill went through me. "You think he was killed here, don't you? Inside CHAPS."

My suggestion earned me a hard-eyed stare from Zack and an approving but slightly suspicious glance from Bristow. "Hey, listen, I've only been in California for four-and-a-half months," I reminded Bristow. I'd told him that when he took Zack's and my original statement, but he might have forgotten. "That poor old man must have been buried longer than that," I added.

He raised an eyebrow. "Did I make any accusations?" He paused. "This may not even have been CHAPS at the time."

"How long ago was he killed?" I asked.

"According to the M.E., probably about seven to nine months."

I'd hoped he was going to say Mr. X had been done away with several years ago, long before any of the people I knew and was fast becoming fond of had appeared on the scene. "That's as close as he can come? Probably?"

Bristow nodded. "When you don't know all the circumstances surrounding a death, and the death took place that long ago, it's pretty difficult to pin a precise date on it. Trenckmann's basing his conclusions on a previous Dennison victim who looked similar after being buried in the same kind of soil under the same kind of climatic conditions. That one had gone missing eight months earlier. This one we haven't managed to date precisely. Dr. Trenckmann's bracketing his educated guess with a month either way."

He sighed. "There's another problem because of the length of time involved. We have a saying in our business that a criminal brings something to the scene of a crime and takes something away with him. In this case, any clues that might have existed don't appear to be around now."

There was a silence. Zack had bought the building seven or eight months ago, I remembered suddenly. I caught myself involuntarily glancing at him.

"Like I said before, this place was empty six weeks before I bought it," Zack said, narrowing his eyes at me.

Bristow sat up straight, brought a pen and a small notebook out of his shirt pocket, flipped through it and nodded. "Let's go over it one more time."

Zack groaned. "Give me a break, man. I've told you everything I know twice already."

"Sometimes it helps to go over stuff," Bristow said easily.

"You want to see if we trip ourselves up and say it differently?" I asked.

He gave me a look, and I apologized. "I'm just interested in how you go about this," I told him with all the innocence I could project.

"You studying to be a junior detective?"

I use a lot of sarcasm myself. I hate it when someone uses it on me. "Maybe," I said, lifting my jaw.

He grinned at me, shook his head, looked at Zack. "You took possession when?"

He hadn't answered my question, I realized. Which probably meant I'd hit it right on the head. He was hoping we'd trip up. Did that mean he suspected one of us of being the murderer? Zack? Angel? Me? I had a sudden premonition that Mr. X was going to cause us a lot more trouble than just some mounds of dirt in the yard.

"The Watanabes' agent handed over the keys on the eighth of January," Zack said. "I started remodelin' right away. Opened CHAPS in March. March fourteenth."

"I arrived in mid-April," I put in.

"I signed on March 1st," Angel said. "Savanna came along the same time."

Bristow looked at him, his eyes showing interest. "Savanna? Yeah—I took a statement from her last time I was here—I was hoping . . . *expecting* to see her today. She's a waitress, right?"

"She should be here soon," I told him. "She does some waitressing, some bartending, yes. But she's a partner, too. We all have various jobs. I keep the books. Angel helps tend bar and occasionally evicts unruly customers."

Bristow looked appraisingly at Angel as though measuring his muscles. "All three of us teach dancing," I said to distract him. "Zack provides the glamour," I added snidely.

Zack looked pleased.

"You don't have to worry about Savanna," I went on. "She's the sweetest woman in the world. Warm-hearted. Shy. Everybody's sweetheart. We all love her."

"That we do," Zack said, green eyes glinting.

I was surprised. I'd never noticed him paying *that* kind of attention to Savanna. Oh, he was always charming to her. But then Zack was like my ex in certain particulars—he apparently felt a need to charm every woman who crossed his path.

Had Mr. X had a daughter? I wondered. Or a young wife? Had he surprised Zack and—no, it was Mr. X who was naked.

"Before you all owned CHAPS . . ." Bristow began.

"This was a Japanese restaurant," Zack said. "Tomodachi. It means 'friend.' It was divided up into little bitty rooms with tatami mats and shoji screens—that kinda thing. People sat on the floor, and the waitress came in and cooked on a little charcoal stove right there in the room.

Owners were Mr. and Mrs. Joe Watanabe. Older couple, I reckon. Never met them. Before they bought the place it was a dance hall—big band stuff in the forties and fifties. Happenin' place, I've been told. The Watanabes came in 'long about the late sixties."

Bristow was making notes. "Where are the Watanabes now?"

Zack shrugged. "The real estate agent told me they sold out for a couple reasons. One—business wasn't too brisk. Two—Mr. Watanabe's folks were ailin', and they wanted their son and daughter-in-law to come back to Japan and take care of them. Seems that's the duty of the eldest son."

"Where in Japan?"

Zack shrugged. "What do I know about anyplace outside the US of A?" He thought for a minute. "Might have been an address in among the paperwork. Maybe Charlie could dig it out of the computer."

Bristow cocked an eyebrow at me. "You want me to look now?" I asked.

"If you don't mind."

I scooted my chair around the desk and booted up the computer.

"Way the agent talked, the Watanabes were decent folks, quiet, hard-workin'," Zack offered. "I wouldn't have thought . . ." He broke off and shrugged again.

I came up with an address in Osaka, and Bristow copied it down. Then he flipped through his notebook some more. "So," he said, after a long pause, "seems the victim could have been buried in the flower-bed while the Watanabes were still here, or while the building was standing empty, or . . ." He glanced without expression at Zack. "Or maybe while you were doing the remodeling."

"I was thinkin'," Zack said, frowning mightily.

Bristow waited.

"That kind of wound you said. Blunt force. Would there be any blood?" Zack said.

We all sat very still, staring at Zack.

Bristow was very good at hiding whatever he was thinking. "It could have produced some blood spatter, yes," he said calmly.

Zack took off his cowboy hat, briefly studied the inside of it, then replaced it just as carefully on his head. "Occurred to me that might explain the stains," he said.

Bristow squinted at him.

"The stage in the main corral," Zack offered. "That was the one place the Watanabes hadn't covered with tatami. The agent told me they used it for Kabuki plays and ceremonial dances. Couple boards had some kind of brownish stains on them. Kinda faint. I thought maybe somebody spilled some liquor, or coffee."

"They *had* stains on them?" Bristow asked. His amber eyes were suddenly very alert.

Zack crossed his right foot over his left knee, gripped it a moment then set it down again. "Hell, how was I to know? I had *all* the floors refinished."

"Sanded?" Bristow queried.

"And varnished," Zack said, looking worried.

Bristow stood up. "Lay on, Macduff." He caught my eye as we all trooped out. "A lot of people think that's 'Lead on, Macduff,' " he said, "but it's not. Macduff and Macbeth are having a sword fight, and Macduff's jeering at Macbeth about what would happen if he gives up, and Macbeth says "Lay on, Macduff." I think about that when I get into tight corners."

I got the idea he was trying to defuse the sudden tension. I decided I liked Taylor Bristow.

In the main corral, Zack indicated an area near the front of the stage. Bristow boosted himself up, got down flat and squinted at the boards from a couple of angles, then sat back on his heels and looked at Zack. He wasn't hostile, but his usual friendliness wasn't in evidence. "When *pre*-cisely did you notice the stains?"

Zack took off his hat again. Maybe that aided his thinking processes. Oxygen to the brain.

"After the agent gave me the keys," he said, squinting into the middle distance. "January eighth. I came in with the contractor—Yaroshek—to look the place over, decide what had to be done where, that kinda thing."

He put his hat back on. "They weren't the only stains, Sergeant. All the floors were worn-lookin', kinda grimy. Dust seeped through the tatami maybe. Floors are very important in a country-and-western bar—people come here to dance, they want a good floor."

Bristow nodded. "Was that the first time you looked at the floorboards?"

"Nope. I checked the place out several times before I made an offer."

"So did you notice any stains on the stage *those* times?"

Zack looked puzzled, as though he wasn't sure what the sergeant was driving at. It was perfectly clear to me. If Bristow could establish the approximate date on which the stains had appeared, that would pretty well date the murder.

Zack chewed on his lower lip for some time, then shook his head. "Can't say I did. Noticed most of the floorboards would need to be refinished, like I said, but that's all. The stains didn't stand out that much, you understand. They were just a little different color from the rest."

"Were you alone when you first looked at the place?"

"Yeah. I didn't bring the contractor in until I'd bought the buildin'." He hesitated. "Well, Darlene let me in, but she pretty well stayed out of my way and let me look around on my own."

"Darlene Standish? The Candlewick Agency?"

Zack nodded.

"I'll talk to her." Bristow stood up, then squinted at the boards again. "Might be something left in the cracks. I'll call in the lab boys to . . ."

Instead of finishing his sentence, he clamped his mouth shut and gazed directly over our heads. We turned. Savanna was standing near the bar regarding us as she removed her shiny white raincoat.

Savanna was wearing her favorite fringed red shirt, tight-fitting blue jeans, black cowboy boots. Remember now, this is the woman with the Dolly Parton breasts and handspan waist. Her dark curls, spangled with raindrops, tumbled riotously around her face and shoulders. Her lipstick was the exact color of her shirt. Her earth mother smile lit the shadows.

"Z'appenin'?" she asked brightly.

Bristow's sigh had a yearning sound to it.

I glanced up at him. He had the silliest expression on his face, more like a smirk than a smile. His eyes looked unfocused. Imagine someone who's just walked into a glass wall and has no idea what hit him.

Savanna often has that effect on men.

It took Bristow only a few seconds to pull himself together. But even after we'd returned to the office his gaze kept straying to Savanna. Either he suspected she was the murderer, or the man was smitten. The fact that his voice faltered every time he glanced her way convinced me it was the latter. Well, that was a good thing, wasn't it? Bristow seemed like a nice guy. Savanna could use one in her life. So could Jacqueline. So maybe he should be encouraged. As long as he wasn't married.

"How does your wife feel about you being a police officer?" I asked him.

He looked startled. Probably because I'd interrupted his discourse on methods that crime labs could use to detect the presence of blood even if an attempt had been made to clean it up.

"I don't have a wife," he said tersely.

I pressed on, wanting to be sure of his status. As I've already said, Savanna is like family. "You've never married?"

He had to be Zack's age. Zack hadn't married yet, but that was because he was in love with himself and was deathly afraid of commitment. He'd told me the second part himself; the first part I'd witnessed personally on a couple of occasions.

"I've been divorced for ten years," Bristow said.

"No children?"

"No children."

He was regarding me with suspicion edged with nervousness. Probably he thought I was after him myself. Ha! I wasn't interested in going after anyone.

"Sorry to interrupt," I said.

"Charlie's a natural-born one hundred percent snoop," Savanna said, giving me a fond smile. "She found out I was separated, she asked me a jillion questions, too. Not that I answered any of them."

"Uh-huh," Bristow said, his gaze fixed on her beautiful

face. Evidently he had caught that she was separated. His amber eyes were glinting.

Savanna was still smiling fondly at me. She was no dummy, but there was an innocence about her. It obviously hadn't occurred to her that I was asking questions for her benefit.

"What happens now?" Angel asked. This was the first question he'd contributed, and we all looked at him. He was very solemn, but he didn't seem upset anymore. "How d'you go about finding out who Mr. X is?" he asked Bristow. "How d'you go about finding the person who did this thing?"

Bristow replaced his notebook in his pocket and leaned back against the sofa cushions. Although he very politely looked at Angel while he answered his question, he kept sneaking little glances at each of us in turn. As if he were watching for behavioral responses. Guilty expressions. Nervous gestures. Hoping we'd make comments that would give ourselves away.

Maybe I'd watched too many *Murder She Wrote* episodes.

"Now that we have a general description of the victim and an approximate time of death," Bristow said, "we're pulling reports of missing persons from the computer for that time frame. Looking for that *type* of person. We also have the computer doing a check of other police agencies."

He spread his hands. "So far we've come up empty. We've questioned your neighbors in the plaza, but hey, who remembers what they were doing last week, never mind last November, December and January?"

"Nobody was reported missing during those months in Bellamy Park?" I asked. "I mean, I would suppose that would be the first place you'd look."

"Not too many people disappear in this town," Bristow said. "It's not that kind of town. We're not accustomed to homicide either. We had one last year, none the year before that."

"What about Condor? There's always something going down in Condor. Is anyone missing there?"

"The building that houses the Condor Police Department sustained heavy damage in the 'quake. Their whole computer system is down. It'll be a while before they can function properly."

He looked at Angel. "To answer your second question, there's not much we can do toward finding the perpetrator until we know who the victim was. Once we have an identity, then we can check out places he went, people he knew."

"On *Prescott's Landin'*," Zack said, "Lazarro found the identity of a murder victim by checkin' dental records." His eyes crinkled at the corners. "Guess you can't do that with our dude. Considerin' he doesn't have teeth."

Savanna gasped. We hadn't filled her in on the details yet.

"You okay?" Bristow asked her in the gentlest voice imaginable.

She nodded, but she looked anemic around the mouth.

"We're circulating x-rays just the same," Bristow said to Zack. "It's possible we might find the dental lab that made dentures for him."

"What about fingerprints?" I asked.

His eyelids hooded slightly. "His hands were—we couldn't—he was in that ground for a long time."

I suddenly felt anemic myself, but I persevered. "If that *was* blood on the front of the stage—couldn't you track him down through his DNA?"

His smile flashed for the first time that day. "Guess everybody's an expert on DNA nowadays." He shook his head. "DNA's great stuff. We don't even need the blood for that. They say your complete DNA 'genome' shows up in a single hair or fingernail clipping. You can extract it from skin, bone, body fluids, tissue, as well as blood. Problem is, if nobody has anything on record to match it with, we won't be any closer to identifying your Mr. X. In any case, it'll probably take months to find out if there is a match on record anywhere. Crime labs are notoriously understaffed and underfunded."

"But you'll keep trying."

"Of course. If we can find bloodstains between the floor-boards and connect it with your Mr. X, it will be a step forward. It will at least locate the crime scene." He glanced at his wrist watch. "I'm going to put in a call for a forensic team. Keep everybody out of the stage area until they're through, okay?"

The four of us groaned in unison. "We were hoping to open tomorrow," I said. "Labor Day's Monday. It's a long weekend."

He looked apologetic. "We'll get out of your hair as quickly as possible. That's the best I can promise." He stood up, glancing again at Savanna.

I came close to saying something about his interest in her as she seemed so oblivious, but I decided I'd better wait and see how she felt about getting anything started. I wouldn't want anyone trying to matchmake for me. For all I knew, she might feel the same way.

I got to my feet. "You'll keep in touch?" I asked.

"For sure." He shook hands all around, lingering predictably over guess whose slender fingers.

"You'll get someone to put the flower-bed back together again?" I persisted.

"For sure," he repeated distractedly. Savanna had just given him the benefit of her killer smile, which was always something to see. He appeared a little woozy. I had the feeling he'd stopped listening to me.

CHAPTER 6

We reopened CHAPS on the Wednesday after Labor Day and drew our biggest crowd ever, many of whom were disappointed when none of us would own up to knowing anything about the skeleton.

By that Saturday night Mr. X was pretty well forgotten. Most people entered CHAPS from the parking lot, so they didn't have to pass the torn up flower-bed.

We were back to business as usual, Sundancer flitting around his booth with his headset, glasses and suspenders, his wispy hair on end, while Angel and I led the line dancing, and Savanna served drinks and spread sunshine. Zack was present, cheerfully helping the bartenders serve up beer and wine and water, adding in buckets of charisma, autographing napkins or denim jackets for newcomers, smiling his bad-boy smile for their cameras.

When the live band arrived and the general dancing got underway, I slid into a booth opposite Taj Krivenko and her Josh. They were working their way through some giant-sized bowls of Dorscheimer's five-alarm chili. It was the first time they'd shown up at CHAPS since the earthquake, and I'd been worried about Taj's leg.

"It's coming along fine," she assured me with her

usual serene smile. "I've been going over to Leah Stoneham's clinic in my lunch hour. First time I ever went to a
masseuse. She's really good. You ought to try her,
Charlie."

Somehow I'd never been able to whip up any excitement
about getting a massage from a woman, especially a woman
I barely knew, especially if I had to pay for it. I nodded
without committing myself.

"I'd have dropped in to check on you, but we had a ton
of cleaning up to do at the bank," Taj went on. "On top of
that, our condominium was damaged." She gestured dra-
matically with her ring-encrusted fingers. "Our bedroom
ceiling came down. So did this huge oil painting we had
hanging over the living room fireplace—a wonderful abstract by a Swiss painter—*The Geneva Yacht Basin*. Josh
paid four hundred dollars for it last spring."

"It had real gilt on the frame," Josh said mournfully.
"Totalled. Positively totalled."

Taj patted his cheek, and he twisted his face to kiss her
plump hand, leaving traces of chili sauce on it. "Imagine if
that picture had been hanging over our bed and we'd been
under it," she said cheerfully after beaming love at him and
wiping her hand delicately on a napkin. "We could have had
our heads cut off."

I shuddered.

"Don't ever hang anything over your bed in earthquake
country, Charlie," she added solemnly.

"I won't," I promised. "I had a couple of shelves come
unstuck myself. In the bathroom."

"Would you like me to fix them for you?" Josh offered.

"For heaven's sake, Josh, this is the nineties. Charlie's
perfectly capable of putting shelves up." There was an edge

to Taj's voice all of a sudden. Surely she didn't think I'd jump Josh's bones if he came up to my loft.

"Well, I'm not too sure about molly bolts," I said, to tease her.

This brought me a lecture from Josh on the subject, including detailed drawings on a napkin.

"Just don't put the shelves over your bed," Taj warned again. She was all smiles now that I hadn't accepted Josh's offer. I hadn't realized she was that insecure in their relationship. But he was surely demonstrative enough. Too much so, in my opinion.

"I've hardly been able to sleep since the earthquake," Taj went on. "I just lie there staring up at the ceiling, trying to keep it up there by sheer will. Poor Josh has to hold me all night, every night."

I didn't want to imagine Taj and Josh in bed together.

That thought made me feel guilty. Savanna had suggested that maybe I disliked Josh because I doubted a man that good-looking could be genuinely devoted to a fat woman, but I'd honestly never felt that way about overweight people. It would be a boring world if everyone were the same size. In any case, even though my weight problems had been a different sort, I could empathize.

Anyway, I was very fond of Taj myself, so why should I find it difficult to believe someone else could love her?

About then Josh's eyes popped the way they did, and he bared his teeth at me in what was supposed to be a smile and I thought, nah—my dislike had nothing to do with Taj's weight. It had to do with Josh's weird personality.

"I'm not sleeping too well, myself," I admitted to make amends for my critical thoughts. "I keep worrying about Mr. X."

Taj blinked.

"The body in the flower-bed," I explained. "I call him Mr. X because I hate to think of him being anonymous."

"The police don't know who he is, do they?" Taj asked. "They haven't released any particulars."

"There's a statement coming out tomorrow, according to Sergeant Bristow," I told her. Considering that, and because Josh and Taj were regulars and she worked next door, I didn't feel I needed to keep my lips zipped in front of them.

"They do know who he is?" Taj gasped, leaning forward.

"Not yet."

She looked disappointed and went back to eating her chili. "Have they at least figured out how he got there?" she asked around a mouthful.

I shook my head. "All we know is that he was a man, probably in his early to mid-seventies, Caucasian, around six feet tall, undernourished."

"Undernourished?" Josh echoed, a spoonful of chili hesitating halfway to his mouth.

"That's what Sergeant Bristow said. Well, perhaps he said malnourished. He also told us the poor old guy didn't have any teeth. He wore dentures, I guess, but he didn't have them in when he was buried."

"No teeth. Malnourished," Josh repeated. He shuddered a little, then looked at the spoonful of chili and set it back down in the bowl. Taj glanced at him as if she were afraid he was going to throw up.

"My stars, Charlie," she said. "I just can't imagine someone being buried right in front of CHAPS and none of us knowing about it. Think how many times we must have passed him. You and I even sat and talked on the steps there a couple of times during the summer."

I had thought about that. I was trying not to anymore. I had also noticed how wonderfully blue the delphiniums were. I didn't want to think about that either.

"Do the police know what he died of?" Taj asked with another concerned glance at silent Josh.

"The medical examiner says somebody hit him on the head," I said. "It must have been something pretty heavy, I guess."

I didn't mention the bloodstains Zack had seen on the stage. They *had* been bloodstains, evidently. Some lab examiners had come in within an hour of Bristow's call and gone over the area with something they jokingly called a blue light special. They'd found traces of blood down the front of the platform. They had also scraped minute amounts out of the cracks between the floorboards.

None of this was to be included in tomorrow's statement. Neither the police nor the four of us wanted that news made public. The police wanted to keep some particulars under wraps, and we didn't feel a need for any more notoriety, whether it was good for business or not.

Since the discovery that the murder had most likely taken place inside CHAPS—what were the odds of some other human's blood being spilled that close to Mr. X's grave, after all—Bristow had once again questioned everyone who worked in the building, including the restaurant and concession store employees, our bartenders and waiters and bouncers. Some of these people were native Californians, some were recent imports from other states and Mexico, one was Canadian, one turned out to be an illegal alien from some country I'd never even heard of. I didn't know if any of them had owned up to being near the area during the three month period in question.

"Did Sergeant Bristow question you?" I asked Taj, remembering she qualified as a work neighbor.

She glanced mischievously at Josh. "Sergeant Bristow's the police officer I told you about." She looked back at me. "Doesn't he have a *great* smile! And such nice manners."

Josh's mouth had turned down at the corners.

"What did Bristow ask you?"

Her wonderful laugh gurgled. "He wanted to know if I'd ever noticed anyone digging in CHAPS's flower-bed. I said sure—Hoshizaki, the gardening syndicate. They dig in the bank's flower-bed too, I told him." Her smile faded. "I'm sorry, I shouldn't make jokes about something so serious. I pointed out that whoever buried the victim would hardly do it during bank hours, and as neither CHAPS nor Casa Blanca was open at that time, I didn't hang around this area outside bank hours."

She shrugged. "I guess he asked me the same questions he asked everyone else at the bank. If I'd seen or heard about anything unusual happening during last November, December and January. If I had known of anyone who had disappeared around that time. If I had any thoughts at all about the body that was found here."

She sighed. "I couldn't help at all." She was silent for a minute, then looked up at me, her usually smooth forehead furrowed. "He also asked me if I knew the Watanabes, which I didn't really, except for eating in the restaurant a couple of times. The food was okay, but I don't much care for sitting on the floor."

I could certainly see why she wouldn't.

"The Watanabes seemed like real nice people. Quiet. Sort of gentle. Do you suppose one of them killed him?" she asked.

"I have no idea. Yet whenever you read about somebody going berserk, everyone always says, 'But he was so nice, so quiet.' So I guess the Watanabes would qualify." I sighed. "It seems so bizarre to bury a naked man in a flower-bed outside a public building. I would think whoever did it had to be crazy, and I haven't run into anyone who seemed . . ."

I broke off. Taj and Josh stopped eating and regarded me expectantly.

"Do you know a big old guy called Prinny?" I asked. "He may live over in The Granada. Wears one of those flat tweed caps. Sport coat. Natty. Sort of military bearing. He's quite a bit taller than me, but much heavier—portly, I guess you could call him."

Josh shook his head, but Taj was frowning, resetting the carved ivory pins that held her topknot in place. "Prinny," she repeated. "That sounds familiar." She leaned her elbows on the table, cupped her chin in her hands and squinched her eyes half-closed.

The lead guitarist-singer was crooning a Mary Chapin Carpenter song—"The Last Word." Both dance floors were full. Angel was slow-dancing with P.J., a regular at CHAPS. When the song ended, he escorted her back to her table and left her. She looked disappointed, and I felt sorry for her. P.J. was no beauty. Her eyes were a little too close together, her mouth was a little too large, her chin receded. None of which was her fault. She was no more responsible for her facial features than I was for my orange hair. There are really very small differences between features that add up to beauty and those that don't, but people do tend to judge by those differences.

So I felt for her, but I was sort of torn about her dancing with Angel all the same. On one hand I was glad to see Angel

dancing outside of lessons. He'd been awfully subdued since
Mr. X showed up in our flower-bed. But I had to admit, to
myself anyway, that I wasn't too happy about his choice of
partner.

This had nothing to do with P.J.'s looks. I'd been a part
of CHAPS for going on five months now, and it hadn't
taken me long to realize P.J. was on a serious manhunt. She
usually sat on a stool at the main bar, and I'd watched her
head swivel every time an unaccompanied man walked in
the door. Her expression was always so eager it bordered on
desperate. When the dance called for partners, she made a
beeline for the nearest unattached male. Not that there was
anything wrong with that, but it all added up to a pattern.
So did her black bodystocking with black tights and the
bright, gauzy mini-skirt that fluttered around her thighs
like butterfly wings, a choice of dress that was hardly appropriate for her age—late-thirties—or for a country-and-western tavern. She had a great body, though it might be a little
too muscular for some tastes—Zack had told me he'd seen
her working out at Dandy Carr's gym.

I'd seen Angel dance with customers before, of course,
and he *always* walked away, just as he had from P.J. As far
as I could tell, Angel didn't have a love life. Nor did I for
that matter. Nor did Savanna. Zack made up for all of us.

P.J. was probably older than Angel by six or seven years.
Not that a difference in age matters. She wore her long,
straight honey-colored hair pulled back from her face and
fastened with a wide black ribbon. I've tried to do my hair
in that style. It looks great with a cowboy hat, but even if I
wet it down and wrestle it into place, it pulls free and frizzes
up again as soon as it dries.

The cheers and whistles greeting the band's rendition of

Tracy Byrd's "Watermelon Crawl," a CHAPS favorite, startled me.

Taj's brow had cleared. "Do you mean Mr. Perry?" she asked when she saw she had my attention.

"I thought he said his name was Prinny." I tried to recall if there were any details I hadn't passed on. "He's probably seventy-five or six."

Taj nodded. "It sure sounds like Mr. Perry. He comes into the bank once in a while and just stands there looking vaguely officious. One of our security officers usually turns him around and points him back toward the apartment building."

She pondered for another few seconds. "Everybody says he's harmless, but he waved his umbrella and shouted at me one time when I was driving away from the bank. And one of the tellers said he threw a humongous rock at her windshield. He missed, luckily."

Her eyes widened. "You don't think Mr. Perry killed that man!"

"I'm just casting around," I said hastily.

Nodding, she went back to spooning chili. "Mr. Perry lives with his daughter at The Granada. You probably know her as well as I do—she comes in here a lot. She's here tonight; I saw her dancing. P.J., they call her."

The skin on the back of my neck crawled. I glanced around but could no longer see P.J. Maybe she'd gone to the rest room.

"I've notarized documents for her," Taj continued. "I can't think of her full name—it's not Perry; she was married and divorced. I could look it up if it's important. She handles all her father's affairs. Some time ago, she obtained a court order appointing her his guardian because of his incompetence. I advised her on it." She frowned again, then shook her head. "I'm hopeless with names. I'm surprised I remembered Perry."

"He has Alzheimer's?"

"Last I heard the doctors weren't sure of the exact nature of his illness. It could be Alzheimer's. He's surely confused."

I shrugged. "It's probably not important. Last time I saw him, he grumbled about some kind of trouble and someone being his archenemy. Frenchy. I wondered if he meant Mr. X. He was hanging around outside right after the earthquake. The guy in the cap, I mean. Prinny, Perry, whatever."

Taj laughed again, nudging Josh. "Well, my stars, Charlie, Josh and I hung around after the earthquake."

I made a face at her. "You and Josh were dancing at CHAPS when the earthquake blasted through. Then you were looking at the damage to the bank. The big guy didn't have any excuse for being where he was. Of course, if he has Alzheimer's . . . like you say, he certainly seemed to be . . ." I hesitated, searching for a tactful way to put it.

"One sandwich short of a picnic," Josh said, popping his eyes and teeth at me.

"One taco short of a combination plate," Taj added.

"Kangaroos in his top paddock," contributed a *faux* cowboy who happened to be passing the table.

The three of them laughed, but I didn't think their little exchange was funny. I might use expressions like that when someone seems a bit weird, but not if I know they really do have mental problems. I excused myself abruptly and left.

I'd noticed that Josh hadn't asked any questions about Mr. X. Wouldn't most people be curious? Of course, Taj always had lots to say, and he was probably used to letting her take the lead.

"Check on P.J.'s name for me, will you?" I asked Taj as she and Josh left the main dance floor after doing a stately waltz.

"Sure, Charlie, anything for you," she said.

I walked over to Zack who was leaning against a post near the bar, arms folded across his chest, cowboy hat tipped forward. He was watching a group of boisterous dancers doing the Texas Ten-Step. It's a funny thing with Zack. The women are all crazy for him, but most don't approach him the way they do Angel. It's as if his stardom or his presence intimidates them. They wait for him to proposition them. Which he does.

"Hey, Charlie," he said with the appraising under-the-eyelashes glance that always activated my red blood cells. I'd never had hot flashes before I met Zack. At first I'd worried about premature aging, but I'd learned to accept and even enjoy the rush. It was probably good for my complexion.

I told Zack about P.J. and her father. He didn't know P.J.'s full name either. "She's always hot to trot," he drawled.

"I've noticed. Did she—did you—?"

He sent me another zinger glance. Back off, Charlie.

"I told Taj and Josh just about everything I knew about Mr. X, apart from the connection to CHAPS," I said. "Josh didn't ask a single question. Doesn't that seem odd?"

Zack looked puzzled. "He's a guy, Charlie. Guys don't bother with stuff like that. Gals are the nosy ones."

I let out the long-suffering sigh that always accompanies any conversation I have with Zack.

"You wanna dance, Charlie?" he asked as if he'd mistaken my sigh for yearning.

So call me stupid. But Zack Hunter is one smooth dancer, and the band was taking a break. Sundancer had just started Travis Tritt's "Can I Trust You With My Heart?" and I'm a sucker for romantic songs.

I'd call Bristow in the morning, I decided as Zack and I two-stepped around the dance floor. I'd meant to tell the detective about my strange conversation with the man in the cap the day Mr. X was dug up, but I hadn't gotten around to it. Now that I knew the old guy's proper name, I'd do it.

In the meantime, I'd concentrate on steppin' and twirlin' in the arms of one of our nation's premier sex-symbols, and enjoy the envious stares of every female on the floor.

CHAPTER 7

"Okay," Bristow said into the telephone.

"That's all you're going to say?" I demanded. It was Monday morning, around eleven a.m. After cleaning Benny's cage and brushing him to get rid of his loose hairs, I'd sat down to pet him and decided it was a good time to reach out and touch a cop.

"What do you want from me, Charlie?" Bristow asked.

Charlie, the man said. We were getting to be friends.

"Don't you think the stuff about Mr. Perry might be important?" I asked. "I mean, he's definitely unbalanced. He just might be crazy enough to kill someone. All that stuff about archenemies. Who talks that way nowadays?"

"We'll see. Was that all you wanted to tell me? I have some people . . ."

"I want to know some stuff, too. What about the Watanabes? Did you track them down?"

"Not yet."

"Are you working on it?"

"You sound like my mother." He sighed. "We're operating on taxpayers' money here, don't forget. We have a few other crimes that require attention. No one fitting the very uncertain description of your Mr. X has shown up on any missing persons reports so far. The case will be held open, okay? We don't give up on murder."

"But this particular murder is not high priority?"

"You can't always hurry things along, Charlie," he said evenly.

"So, after going to all that trouble of digging him up and sifting the soil, you've found out he was an old man, toothless and malnourished, which seems to indicate he wasn't one of Bellamy Park's leading citizens, and all of a sudden there's no hurry?"

Somebody had to stick up for poor old Mr. X. Imagine dying alone and naked, violently, and nobody even noticing you were missing. You might as well not have existed, if nobody cared enough to miss you when you no longer did.

"We're looking into it," he said. "I'll let you know when I have anything."

The phone rang the minute I hung up. I thought it might be Bristow calling back to apologize for not seeming more impressed by my helpful information. Then I heard some seriously heavy breathing, and goosebumps prickled all over my body from scalp to sole.

"Miss Plato?"

The goosebumps became goosemounds. It wasn't that the words were threatening. It was the mechanical nature of the voice. It reminded me of something, but I couldn't place it for the moment. I couldn't even tell if it were a man or a woman. It was very low-pitched, a touch more baritone than contralto, but basically sexless, like a robot. It was probably a recorded advertising message, I thought, and tried to make myself believe it. Something stopped me from hanging up right away.

"Who is this?" I asked.

"I want my money," the robot voice said, enunciating each word.

"Is this some kind of joke?" My stomach had tied itself into a giant pretzel. "If so, it isn't funny. I suggest you get off the line before . . ."

"Five thousand dollars," the voice said.

I gulped. "Excuse me?"

Benny climbed up to my shoulder and began nibbling my hair. He loves my hair. Which is nice, considering nobody else does.

"He stole five thousand dollars from me, Miss Plato."

"Who did?" It had to be an advertising gimmick. Pretty soon someone human would get on the line and tell me . . .

"The skeleton in the flower-bed."

I moved the receiver away from my ear and looked at it. This was major weirdness, almost on a par with Mr. Perry's, but I still couldn't bring myself to hang up. Especially as the robot was calling me by name.

"You found the body," the voice continued. "You have my money. I want it back."

"Are you speaking through a computer?" I asked.

No answer.

"Look, Mr. Robot, whoever you are, you've got a wrong number here in more ways than one. There was no money. The skeleton didn't even have pockets."

"Five thousand dollars," the voice said again. And then added, "I know where you live."

I can't begin to describe how menacing that sounded. It made me lose my voice the way I had when I saw Mr. X's foot. Once again, I opened and closed my mouth a couple of times, and nothing came out. I should hang up right now and call Bristow, I told myself.

Benny had gone to sleep against my free ear. I could feel his warm fuzzy-fur body vibrating. I wondered if I'd gone to sleep too and this was a truly stupid and tasteless dream.

"They showed the tavern on television," the voice continued. "The reporter said you lived upstairs."

Standing, I eased Benny off my shoulder and into his cage, carried the cordless phone to the door and checked that the deadbolt was on. Having my whereabouts made public was not bringing me any pleasure. On the weekend, two of our cowboy wannabes, well-tanked, had suggested accompanying me upstairs for a little private entertainment. Evidently, they had watched the newscast also.

"I came there and looked at the place where you live," the robot said. "I saw you come out of the tavern and get in your Jeep Wrangler and drive away. I recognized you by your hair. You have very distinctive hair."

A thought popped up in my paralyzed brain. My voice came with it. "Who *is* the skeleton? If you know he stole your money, you know who he is."

"His identity is not important." It was creepy, listening to that mechanized voice slowly sounding out each word in such a tinny way. I suddenly realized who it reminded me of—

"You sound like Igor," I blurted out.

"Igor?" the robot sounded irritated.

"He's one of the talking schedulers on Sound Blaster Pro."

Zack had installed the Sound Blaster card and software on the office computer so he and Angel could play computer golf when business was slow. Zack liked the sound effects: birds tweeting, hands clapping, a sympathetic voice saying, "Your ball is in the rough."

Savanna had discovered the talking scheduler and had entered Jacqueline's doctor appointments and her babysitter schedule into it. She'd chosen Igor from three possible reminders, setting his speech low and slow.

"You may call me Igor," the voice said.

"I don't want to call you anything," I said. "I'm hanging up now."

"No," the robot voice said. There was so much menace in that one syllable that I continued to press the receiver against my ear.

"I do not want to have to kill you," Igor said.

"You killed Mr. X?"

There was a silence during which the heavy breathing started up again.

I persevered. "You killed the body in our flower-bed? You buried him?"

"If I had buried him, I would have my money. I will kill you if you talk to the police about this call. I do not want to hurt you, Miss Plato. Give me my money, and I will not hurt you."

"I don't have five thousand dollars," I protested. I did, actually, but I wasn't going to give any part of my inheritance to this creep. "There wasn't *any* money in that hole. Not even a dime. Trust me. The police sifted every inch of that ground looking for clues. They didn't even find the old guy's teeth."

Igor went on inexorably, still enunciating carefully in his robot voice. "I am a patient person. I will wait one month from today for my money. If you go to the police, I will have no choice but to kill you." He paused. "I will be watching you. If I see you with a police officer, or hear that you consulted one, I will visit you personally. I will be waiting for you in the dark, and I will use a very sharp knife to cut your throat. I know how to do it so that it will look like suicide. Suicides make tentative slashes before they get the courage to cut deep enough. I will do this to you. Each slash will go deeper and deeper and deeper until your blood spurts out."

This conversation was definitely going downhill.

"How are you going to get your money if you kill me?" I asked. I had aimed for a brave and casual tone, but my voice came out a high C.

"You need not worry about that. Worry that I mean what I say. I will give you one month to find my five thousand dollars. If you do not give me my money, I will kill you in the way I have described. I will kill you like an animal."

The TV screen that hangs out in my imaginative brain presented an image of a deer my father had killed when I was seven. He and some buddies had gone hunting in Utah. After gutting the deer, they had hung it upside down from a tree branch. They'd taken photographs. *Color* photographs. I had cried for hours after seeing those pictures. I'd had nightmares for a couple of weeks. I'd made my father promise he would never, ever go hunting again.

Igor cut off the connection.

I sat down hard on the sofa as my terrified legs buckled under me. My heart raced. Filled with a sense of doom, I dialed Bristow's number with shaking fingers, but before he could answer, I remembered him saying less than ten minutes ago, "You can't always hurry things along, Charlie."

I hung up. I could imagine Bristow treating my "suicide" the same way. I could imagine him telling everyone in the department that I'd been threatened by someone who talked like an animated computer icon. The other cops would tell their spouses, who would share the story at the office or a club meeting or their friendly get-togethers. Igor would find out.

This might be a good time to pack my clothes and Benny in the Jeep Wrangler and move on, I thought. There was a clause in my contract that said the other partners in CHAPS would buy me out if I decided tavern management wasn't for me. They hadn't wanted to agree, but they'd really needed another partner's cash, and after I'd explained my phobia about getting too attached to a place or to things they'd given in.

So, I could probably make my getaway.

Did I already mention that I'm not one of your brave soldier types? I don't even read horror novels or watch movies about bodysnatchers or chain saw massacres. A few bars of creepy music and the TV is *off*.

I'd actually started planning which suitcase to pack first when it occurred to me that I wouldn't be able to live with myself if I let Igor run me out of town with one phone call. And I certainly wouldn't want to spend the rest of my life looking over my shoulder to see if Igor had caught up with me.

One month.

I got up and went into my kitchen area, noted the date on the wall calendar Lenny's Market had given me and counted down four Mondays to the ninth of October. October's illustration was a cheery pastiche of witches on broomsticks and jack-o-lanterns with jeering grins. It seemed fitting.

After turning back to September's more inspiring autumn leaves, I went back to the sofa, pulled my knees up to my chest and wrapped my arms around them. After a while I realized I had taken up a fetal position, which meant I was probably more scared than I'd ever been in my life. I huddled like that for some time, staring at the telephone as if it were one of those cobras people in India teach to sway to music.

My mind kept replaying that awful robot voice. "Each slash will go deeper and deeper until your blood spurts out." Igor might be a robot, but he certainly had a way with words.

CHAPTER 8

I may have mentioned already that Bellamy Park is an up-scale town. Ritziest of all the residential areas is the Paragon Hills region surrounding the golf course and country club. Picture wide, shady streets, live oaks (of course,) maple, willow, pepperberry, and magnolia trees, which at this time of the year were blooming with plate-size flowers. Whatever the season, there are always masses of flowers in Paragon Hills, and the lawns are always green. For all I know, the sky's always blue. It certainly was when I drove up there a couple of hours after Igor turned me into a quaking blob of jelly.

Paragon Hills, naturally, was where Zack had chosen to live, in a single-story, Spanish-style, red-roofed adobe house built around a central courtyard complete with swimming pool and hot tub.

I wasn't sure Zack was home—all of the houses in Paragon Hills have enclosed garages with space for three or four cars and a boat, and you rarely see a vehicle parked in a driveway. I suppose it would be considered tacky.

I parked my Jeep Wrangler in Zack's driveway and hoped it wouldn't instantly lower property values. Walking up the steps to the veranda, I tried to convince myself that I was doing the right thing, bringing my troubles to Zack. But an incredulous voice in my head kept saying, *"Zack? You're expecting help from Zack? Zack Hunter?"*

I'd been in Zack's house once before, but that had been for my welcome party and a greeter had been stationed at the open door. This time I had to ring the doorbell. I half expected it to play a few chords from the *Prescott's Landing* theme song, but it ding-donged like any other.

It took a few minutes for Zack to show up. I spent the time admiring the planter boxes, which overflowed with cascading nasturtiums. When I was a little kid in Sacramento, Petey Shackleford and I spent hours hunting through nasturtium leaves for caterpillars. Just as I impulsively squatted down to check out this batch, the door opened.

"Yo, Charlie," Zack said cheerfully. "You lookin' for another foot?"

I'd never really appreciated Zack's sense of humor, but that wasn't why I didn't respond with a snappy comeback. In the instant I laid eyes on him, I was robbed of speech. Probably because my brain stopped functioning at the same moment my stomach went whomp!

I seem to remember saying something earlier about how sexy Zack looked in his all-black Western gear? Well, I'm here to tell you he didn't need the black clothing to look great. What nature had endowed him with was sexy all by itself.

No, his sun-bronzed body wasn't completely naked. He had on a pair of cuffed white shorts. Very short shorts. His stomach was totally flat, with grid marks on it like you see on guys in body-building magazines. The rest of his muscles were also well-defined, without being grossly overdeveloped.

I'd never been attracted to hairy men, and you'd sort of expect a man who had a wealth of tousled black hair on his head to be similarly hirsute on his chest and arms and legs and maybe even, (yuk,) his shoulders, but Zack's body was smooth. Hairless. Buffed. I'd seen Zack's body on the Hawaiian Sunshine commercials, of course, but that was on my 19″ television screen and his chest could have been waxed. This was real life, and it hadn't.

I was inside the doorway without any memory of getting there. Still speechless. Gazing at Zack, who was, surprisingly, gazing at me.

"Charlie?" I heard him say, as from some distant galaxy.

Was that electricity arcing between us?

Somewhere in the back of my benumbed brain a synapse perked up and sent me a message that Zack had sounded a little short of breath. A second later—or it might have been five minutes—he cupped my cheek gently in his right hand and touched his thumb to my closed mouth, exerting just enough pressure to cause me to open my mouth a little, so he could bring his face closer and . . .

"Hi!" a female voice said.

Zack dropped his hand, smiled his wry and lazy smile and turned to the woman who had appeared in the vestibule carrying a garment bag and a small suitcase.

Did I say woman? Let me rephrase that. Imagine every dazzling physical attribute a woman could possibly possess and wrap them all up in one willowy body dressed in a navy blazer, white shirt with floppy bow tie, straight beige skirt. Don't forget the ash-blonde—*naturally* ash-blonde—shining hair that hung from a side part in a perfect bob that swayed like a bell when she moved her head. Nor should you leave out the cute *retroussé* nose, the shell-like ears, the violet eyes, the generous mouth whose smile instantly gave tribute to the orthodontist who had used his skill in exchange for a mere four or five thousand dollars some nine or ten years ago.

She couldn't be much more than twenty. Maybe twenty-one.

"Melissa, this is one of my partners, Charlie Plato. Charlie, Melissa Freshan. Melissa's a flight attendant."

Melissa's smile flashed into my eyes like a searchlight beam. "I saw you on television with Zack," she said. "It was too bad the sound went off just as you arrived."

I opened my mouth, but my sound had gone off again. It was becoming a habit.

"Charlie's imitation of a fish," Zack said, sounding fond.

Indignation made my blood circulate again. "I need to talk to you," I managed.

Melissa beamed forth another smile. I wished I'd worn sunglasses. Such radiance was more than I could bear. "I have a flight to catch out of San José," she said. "It was nice meeting you." Turning to Zack, she draped her arms around his neck. "Goodbye, sweetie," she murmured. "As usual, it was wonderful."

He put his hands on either side of her waist and pulled her in against that wonderfully flat abdomen. Then he kissed her. It was like watching television on one of those home theaters where the heads show up larger than life.

Zack had had a lot of practice kissing in public, of course. More than kissing, sometimes. When you're used to doing that sort of thing in front of cameras, directors, makeup people, hairdressers and whoever else gets involved in filming a love scene, who's going to notice an audience of one? I must say, Melissa was as uninhibited as Zack. She kept running her hands over his bare shoulders and upper arms as if she were tracing his muscles into her memory to comfort her during the long, lonely hours in the air.

They took their time about the kiss. I wasn't sure about the etiquette of the situation. Should I gaze at the ceiling and hum as if I'd forgotten they were there? Try to ease around them and make a cup of coffee in the kitchen? Or should I simply back through the still-open front door, skedaddle to my Jeep and drive away?

I was leaning strongly in favor of the latter, when they finally broke the clinch. "Take care, darlin'," Zack muttered huskily, turning Melissa loose with obvious reluctance.

"I will, sweetie, I will. You too, okay?"

"Sure 'nough."

One more searchlight smile flashed in my direction, and she gathered up her bags and headed for a side door, which I supposed led to the garage.

The vestibule seemed dimmer for her passing. "I suppose you've already had lunch?" Zack asked.

I nodded. I religiously eat three healthy meals plus two healthy snacks a day. Hi-carb, low-protein, no added fat. Concentrating on health, not weight. My own personal mantra. I don't let even major traumas like anonymous threats to my life disturb my eating routine. That's the way my ex programmed me to get beyond my anorexia without lining my arteries with lard. The formula worked, and I don't mess with success.

"I'm havin' some cold pizza left over from last night," Zack said, his voice rising a little to make the statement a question, as if the suggestion would tempt me.

I shuddered.

I could see he was curious about my reason for dropping in unannounced, but I was still fumbling for a way to introduce the subject. I couldn't seem to concentrate. "Could you please put a shirt on?" I asked.

He looked startled. He was so comfortable with his body I guess he didn't notice when it was uncovered. That devilish smile of his showed up as soon as he realized his lack of clothing was getting to me. "I was catchin' a few rays," he explained. "Let's go out to the patio. It's too warm a day to waste indoors."

It was a lovely house—airy and cool-looking with vaulted ceilings and a sunken living-room, furnished with light wood and white upholstery. The route to the patio took us past the master-bedroom suite. Zack excused himself to pick up a shirt. My peripheral vision—ever on the alert—noted that the bedroom had a chaotic appearance at odds with the neatness of the living-room. Twisted sheets hung off the bed, a fluffy white blanket had been flung onto a nearby chair, the pillows were on the floor. The clothing that had apparently been hastily dropped was not all Zack's. Unless he had a secret penchant for ecru lace.

"Take a seat," he said from the walk-in closet. I continued out to the patio and sank onto a chaise that was apparently stuffed with down. The sunshine felt wonderful. A thermometer on a nearby post said it was 74°. I wished I'd worn shorts and a tank instead of a frumpy long-sleeved shirt and jeans.

By the time Zack joined me, juggling a plate and a couple of mineral water bottles and wearing a '49ers tee-shirt, I'd given my hormones a stern talking to. This didn't stop me from noticing that the tee was snug enough to show his muscles, without being sleazily tight. Gratefully, I accepted a bottle from him and took a long swig.

"I had this anonymous phone call," I began as he set down his bottle and plate on an elaborately wrought metal table.

He lowered himself to the edge of the chaise next to mine and began chewing happily on a slice of congealed pizza. His eyes brimmed with interest. "An obscene phone call? Heavy breathin'? I'm-standing-here-in-my-birthday-suit kinda phone call?"

"No, Zack, *not* that kind. It was a threatening call." Without trying to be succinct, I spelled it all out for him— the robot voice, the demand for "the money," the threat that the caller would cut my throat if I contacted the police.

"You'd better tell Bristow," Zack said.

I scowled at him. "Weren't you listening, Zack? Igor said he'd kill me if I went to the police. He said he'd make it look like suicide with little tentative slashes at my throat and then deeper and deeper slashes until my blood spurted out."

The image those words conjured up made me shudder. "It sounded to me as if Igor meant it," I added. "I'm not taking any chances it was a hoax."

Zack was frowning. "Who's Igor?" he asked. "I thought this was supposed to be an anonymous phone call."

I explained the origin of the name. Zack was not a computer person, but he caught the drift.

"So if you can't go to the police, what can you do?" he asked.

"I was hoping you'd help me find some answers. You're seeing Bristow socially—you could ask him casually if there *was* any money. You might even pretend there was a similar episode on *Prescott's Landing*, and you wondered if money were involved in this one."

"You know, I do believe there *was* a story that had to do with blackmail. Raymond had some nude photographs of Molly, or somethin'. I'm not sure I recall . . ."

"You don't have to recall," I said. "You just have to ask Bristow."

"Okay, Charlie," he said patiently. "I reckon I can do that."

"Don't tell Bristow about Igor," I warned. "Igor said he'd be watching. He said he knew where I lived. Not that he's the only one, since you revealed the location of my home all over the airwaves."

He looked blank, and I didn't follow through. I was trying to think of a diplomatic way of phrasing what I wanted to say next. "I thought I'd try to persuade you to help me find out some other stuff."

His eyes narrowed. "What kinda stuff?"

I held up two fingers. "Who is Mr. X? Who killed him? Answers to those would get us off to a good start."

Zack selected another slice of pizza. "Do we really care? I mean, it all happened before I opened CHAPS. We don't know who the old guy is and . . ."

"*I* care," I said hotly. "That poor old man doesn't have anyone worrying about him as far as Bristow's been able to tell. Besides which, I have a personal stake in this now. I happen to care about my own neck. Throat. If I can find out who Mr. X is and who killed him, I'll be that much nearer finding out what happened to the money Igor's concerned about."

"You don't think the investigation would be better left up to the police?" Zack asked.

"I think the police have a lot of other stuff to do that they consider more important." Maybe a little flattery would help. "I also think people might talk to us easier than to the police—especially to you. You have a certain kind of . . ."

He stopped eating so he could listen. He was his own favorite subject.

"Charisma," I finished.

He smiled modestly.

Now that I had his undivided attention, I went on. "It seems to me the logical way to get answers is to ask questions of the people most likely to be involved and to watch their behavior, their body language."

"Which people?"

"Well, I don't know yet, but I should think a good place to start would be with the people who work at CHAPS. I'll check the computer records to find anyone who was also around when the Watanabes were there. I thought you might question them because they all idolize the ground beneath your Tony Lamas."

He looked modest again.

"After that, I thought we'd start on the neighbors. It would be easier, I should think, for someone who belonged in the neighborhood to get away with burying a body in the flower-bed. We could begin with the people we know and sort of fan out from there to others who have been in the neighborhood long enough. People such as the old guy I told you about. I thought he called himself Prinny, remember, but Taj Krivenko said his name was Perry. His daughter comes to CHAPS a lot. P.J. I mentioned her . . ."

"Patty Jenkins," Zack said.

I set my empty water bottle on the table and frowned at him. "You told me last night you didn't know her name!"

"I asked around afterwards. I was gonna tell you tonight."

"That's great!" I exclaimed. "We're already ahead. So
then, P.J. and her father. Taj." I hesitated. "I'm not sure
we should include Josh, but . . . yes, we should—he's been
going with Taj a long time, so he might have joined her for
lunch or dinner after work, or picked her up. He might have
seen something and not realized it was important. I think
we have to approach everyone that way, ask them 'Were
you in the area? Did you see anything that struck you as
fishy?' And so on. The sort of questions Bristow asked us."

Zack nodded. "The people at the mini-mart, Frances
and—" He squinted. "I think the pudgy dude's name is Bernie. They opened the store a few years back. How 'bout
Leah Stoneham, at the massage parlor?"

"That is not a massage parlor, Zack. Leah's a physical
therapist."

He grinned, unrepentant. Sometimes I think he says
things he *knows* will get to me. Other times, I think he's not
smart enough to be that subtle.

"Leah came after I did," I pointed out. "I think we
should focus on people who've been in the neighborhood
since the beginning of January or earlier. What about Jorge
and Maria Blanca from the Mexican restaurant? When did
they open Casa Blanca?"

"They didn't buy the building until the end of February." He regarded me from under his eyelashes. "Am I
going to get paid for all this work?"

He was joking, of course. I think.

"Think of it as a civic duty," I suggested. "Sacrifice
yourself. Do it for free."

"Charlie," he chided, "I only do one thing for free."

He was gazing at me again. The sun was behind him, his

face in shadow. But I could see the glint in those green eyes
of his. "And that I do gladly," he added.

Whomp! went my stomach.

I stood up, walked over to the pool, took two deep, calm-
ing breaths and reminded myself that this was the man
whose genes had at some time been marinated in testosterone, the man who had just risen triumphant from a wres-
tling bout with the radiant Melissa, a man who was
probably not given to practicing safe sex.

I walked back and sat on a canvas captain's chair a little
farther away from Zack. "Friendship's harder to come by
than sex. Let's stick to friendship, okay?"

Wry smile in place, he arranged himself at ease on the
chaise—long sun-bronzed legs stretched out, hands clasped
behind his head. "If that's the way you want it," he said.

Which was as good as saying he wanted it the other way.
Don't be ridiculous, I scolded myself. Coming on to a
woman was just a habit with Zack—it had no more meaning
than a handshake to a normal person.

"That's the way it is," I said firmly.

"Okay."

Did he have to give up so easily?

"Maybe after you talk to the staff we should get *all* the
neighbors together," I said, forcing us back to business. The
more I thought about that idea, the better it seemed. "Everyone who works or lives on Adobe Plaza. If we get them all
in one room, we might be able to figure out who's *not* liable
to be guilty of the murder. At the very least, maybe somebody will say something that'll give us a lead to something
else. Hercule Poirot used to do that sort of thing all the
time."

"Hercule Poirot? Didn't he have his own TV series?"

"Sure, Zack," I said wearily.

He pondered some more. "One time Sheriff Lazarro had people sign a guest book when they came to somebody's weddin'. He had 'em put in where they were from, like what state, so he could track down if they had records. Maybe we could have a guest book out when the people come to CHAPS."

I wasn't sure this was a workable idea where Mr. X's murder was concerned. For one thing, there were laws about invading people's privacy. And we didn't have Lazarro's resources. All the same, the more we could find out about people, the more likely we were to uncover someone who might be inclined to kill. As well, I did want to encourage Zack to help me, so it was probably politic to keep on his good side. "Not a bad idea," I said graciously.

Actually, I was amazed that Zack had come up with it. Though, of course, he hadn't really—it was Lazarro who was the genius, and Lazarro was brilliant only because he'd had good writers.

"What should we call this shindig?" I asked. "We don't want to scare people off. A get-acquainted party? No. How about this: a post-earthquake, old-fashioned block party to give us all a chance to get acquainted. I'll make up some flyers. Something about how when disasters strike, people don't always know who their neighbors are and maybe it's a good thing to change that."

I was beginning to like this idea for its own sake. It might foster a sense of community, something that seemed to be lacking nowadays. If neighbors cared more about neighbors, maybe it would be a little more difficult for someone to mug an elderly man and bury him in a public flowerbed without anyone noticing.

"Should we do food?" I asked. "Lunch maybe? And a no-host bar? Dorscheimer's could cater a buffet. We could set it all up in the main corral."

He didn't answer, and I sneaked a quick glance at him. He had closed his eyes.

Time to go, I decided, but couldn't get my body to obey. *It* wanted to sit there admiring the hunk.

"Zack?" I said tentatively. "What do you think? Should I talk to Dorscheimer's?"

He waved a lazy hand in the air. "Why don't you and Savanna decide on the small stuff, Charlie. That kinda thing's women's work."

That got me on my feet. It almost got Zack a left to the jaw. "I'm leaving," I said.

"Later," he responded cheerfully.

That was another thing that irritated me about Zack. He didn't even know when he'd insulted you.

CHAPTER 9

Dorscheimer's, the concession restaurant off CHAPS's lobby, served a chuckwagon buffet—hamburgers, hot dogs, chili, beans and so on—to keep things simple and cheap. Except for the beans, they were all foods I wouldn't eat unless I were hog-tied and force-fed. I'd given up trying to get Dorscheimer's cook, who was Texas born-and-bred, to cut down on fat; apparently men who were men and gals who were gals weren't supposed to pander to their cholesterol levels.

Almost every table in the main corral, including the booths on the raised platforms at either end, was fully occupied. As far as I could determine while floating around and discreetly counting heads, almost everyone had shown up. The exceptions were a few residents of The Granada and a couple of employees at the bank and the arts and crafts shop who had to keep an eye on things but who would drop in when their colleagues returned. Jorge and Maria Blanca had sent regrets; they were serving lunch themselves. As they had opened Casa Blanca after the time of the murder, I wasn't too concerned about their absence. I wondered if Igor was among those present and decided I'd just as soon not know. I'd already used up six days of the month he'd allowed me.

I had been unbelievably busy. (Would Igor accept that as an excuse?) CHAPS had been crowded every night, Tuesday through Saturday. The computer's hard drive had crashed, probably from the strain of playing Zack's golf games, and it had taken me hours and hours to get everything restored and configured. I'd also spent a lot of time coordinating this get-together: arranging the catering, hand-carrying flyers to all the businesses on the plaza and to each resident of The Granada. Savanna had offered to help with distributing the flyers, but I'd hoped someone might start talking about Mr. X and then suddenly blurt out, "Hey, did you happen to hear about the five thousand dollars that blew in my window about the time of the earthquake? What do you think I should do with it?"

Plenty of people talked, nobody blurted.

Most of the neighbors had seemed pleased to be invited, though I'd had a time persuading P.J. to bring her father. He didn't do parties, she'd insisted. It wasn't really a party, I'd countered, just a neighborhood get-together, and he was part of the neighborhood.

It looked as if everyone was signing the guest book. One or two had questioned the state of origin column, but Zack had assured them it was part of a plan we had for later. So far he hadn't shared that plan with me. Zack had also hit on the idea of asking people to fill out name tags so we'd know who everyone was. I supposed Lazarro must have done that at some time or other.

Normally, I abhor name tags. Mostly because I don't like short-sighted strangers staring at my bosom, which isn't all that easy to see.

I noticed that Savanna, who was serving up the hamburgers, had been cornered by Bernie Lightfoot at the buffet table, which had been set up on the main dance floor. She

had a panicky expression on her face, so I started wending
my way between tables, checking out names and trying to
commit them to memory as I went.

Bernie was not one of my favorite people, but he was
hard to avoid. The mini-mart was a handy place to shop for
odds and ends when I was caught short in the middle of
cooking something in my loft. As well, he'd played tennis all
summer just across the border in Condor's city park. Almost every day I'd seen him walking across the plaza in tennis shorts and sneakers, his extremely hairy chest bare. This
particular chest was nothing like Zack Hunter's, believe me.
In Bernie's case any hoped-for macho effect was ruled out
by his sloping shoulders and protuberant belly. I was glad to
see he'd had the kindness to wear a shirt today.

Bernie was around 45 and balding. I've known some
very sexy bald men. Bernie was not one of them. Rob, my
ex, was thin on top, but it didn't affect his impact on the
ladies. And then there was Bristow, who didn't own hair one
but managed to look magnificent.

"Hey, Savanna, you want me to spell you?" I asked.

Savanna's eyes widened with relief. As she edged around
the long table to make her escape, Bernie turned in a half
circle to watch her. "Don't you be such a stranger now," he
said. "I really miss my therapy."

Savanna gave him a stricken look, managed a weak
smile for me, then made a beeline for the rest room.

"So, Charlie, what's new on the body in the basement?"
Bernie asked before I could question his last comment. I
made a mental note to ask Savanna discreetly what Bernie
had meant about therapy. "I heard you nicknamed him Mr.
X," Bernie went on. "I call him Mr. Bones myself—like in
the old minstrel shows. Get it? Mr. Bones?"

He did the hyena imitation that served him as a laugh. A

woman who had been approaching the buffet changed her mind and headed for the bar instead.

I managed to overcome the urge to dump a pan of beans over Bernie's nasty little round head. "Did you know the Watanabes?" I asked.

"Well, not socially," he said. "I seen them around. They came in the store once in a while, though mostly they shopped at the Farmer's Market in Dennison, or the old Oriental grocery that used to be on Santa Domingo Street."

"Did they seem like, well, nice people?"

"You mean did they seem the kind could clobber someone on the noggin and bury him in the flower border?" He screeched again. "Who's to say? My theory is most people are capable of murder if you get right down to it."

"Are *you*?" I asked sweetly.

"Well, my mother often got on my toot," he said, unfazed. "Gotta admit I came close to throttling her."

I was willing to bet Mama Lightfoot had been tempted a time or two herself.

"I have a theory that Mr. Bones was a customer of the Watanabes," Bernie went on. "I expect they served him some of that sashimi raw fish stuff, or one of them poisonous blowfish that if you don't prepare it right kills people off in ten seconds flat. Wouldn't be caught dead eating that kind of garbage, myself." Another screech ascended the scale and tortured my eardrums. "Caught dead. Get it? Caught dead."

Taj was sitting with her golden-haired Josh at a table not far away. She intercepted my glance and grimaced her sympathy. I rolled my eyes, not caring if Bernie saw me. But Bernie had glimpsed Savanna returning from the rest room and was trotting in her direction. I wasn't going to rescue her a second time.

I looked around for Frannie Lightfoot and saw her sitting with Leah Stoneham and a young couple who lived in The Granada. I was about to tell her she should keep her husband on a leash when I saw P.J. and her stout father coming toward the buffet table. He was wearing his tweed cap. Maybe he never took it off.

A couple of times since the police had dug up Mr. X, I had seen Mr. Perry standing under a live oak tree in the Plaza, staring at CHAPS, his spectacles glinting. Both times I had been in a hurry to get to the bank or the post office, and by the time I'd returned he was gone.

"Hi, Mr. Perry," I said brightly.

He looked down at me over his glasses. "Prinny," he said distinctly. "They call me Prinny."

So, I *had* heard right. "Well, Prinny, help yourself to some food. How about I fill a plate and join you? The idea of this shindig is to get acquainted."

"Do I know you, madam?" Prinny asked in his *faux* British accent.

"This is Charlie Plato, Dad," P.J. said patiently. "She's one of the owners of CHAPS."

He gave me a stern look. "I've known some very good chaps myself," he assured me. "Dead now, all of them."

P.J. sighed and started filling plates for both of them. I was glad to see she wasn't wearing her butterfly outfit today. She had on a blue silk blouse and grey slacks that showed her impressive figure to advantage. She didn't object when I settled myself and my salad, beans and cornbread at their table. I thought she was probably glad to have someone to share the burden. "Where's Angel?" she asked, looking around.

"Tending bar," I told her. Actually, Angel hadn't been too revved up about taking part in today's get-acquainted festivities until I'd told him the real reason was to find out if anyone knew about Mr. X's murder. He seemed interested then, and interrogated me at length as to how I would go about questioning people. This was good for two reasons—it meant Angel was getting over his queasiness, and putting my vague ideas into words helped crystallize them.

"Maybe I'll go get a beer," P.J. said, on her feet and moving before I could offer to do it for her. I had an idea she would not have appreciated my offer anyway.

"So, Prinny," I said, seizing the moment, "how come you hang around outside CHAPS all the time?"

"This isn't Oyako Domburi," he said indignantly, peering down at a scoop of beans.

"Excuse me? Oh, is that Japanese? Did the Watanabes serve it when this place was their restaurant?"

"Chicken and Egg," he said, looking at me sternly again. "Oya-ko. Parent and child. Chicken and Egg."

Sometimes he actually made sense. "You knew the Watanabes?" I asked.

He was tucking into his hamburger with obvious relish. For a while he seemed to forget I was there, but then he looked up, his eyes clouded behind his glasses. "I was waiting for Mary," he said.

Disoriented for a moment, I figured out that he was a beat or two behind me and was answering my earlier question about hanging around. "You wait for Mary outside CHAPS?"

"Mary was my mother," P.J. said, returning to the table with a glass of beer. The frown line above her nose was very pronounced. Probably she hadn't had any success with Angel.

I did a little frowning myself. "Was?"

"My mom died of cancer five years ago. Before that, we lived in Laurelhurst, near the top of the hill way west of downtown San Francisco, north of Geary. Mom worked at Sears, which was close by. After he retired, Dad would walk over to Sears to meet her. Most of the time he remembers she's dead, but every week or so he goes off to meet her again. His wandering is my biggest problem. I have a good caregiver for him while I'm at the office. She lives in the same building, so she's usually available. She watches him like a hawk, but once in a while she has to go to the bathroom, or whatever, and out he goes. Has he been bothering you?"

"No, not at all. I just wondered . . . does he have Alzheimer's?"

She shook her head. "Doctors don't think so. They haven't been able to put too precise a label on his condition. Some kind of dementia. He has occasional periods of clarity, but they are getting further and further apart. He's like a child in many ways." She paused, then added heavily, "Except he's never going to grow up."

"I asked him about the Watanabes, but he didn't seem to understand me."

"Sometimes I think he understands things," she said with a sigh. "Sometimes I think he just wants to torment me." She shook her head. "Don't get me wrong. I love the silly old coot; it's just not possible anymore to have a normal relationship with him. Or even a conversation. Everyone feels sorry for him, but he's apparently perfectly happy. I'm the one who needs the sympathy."

Watching Prinny, I could see what she meant. He had both big hands wrapped around an onion-stuffed hot dog now and was gnawing at it with considerable gusto, stopping occasionally to deliver an occasional aside to someone who wasn't there. I put my hand over hers, which were clasped together on the table. She didn't look up.

"Is he ever violent?" I asked softly.

She withdrew her hands. "Never. He may be big, but he's gentle as a lamb. Always polite."

Didn't she *know* about the rock-throwing incident Taj had told me about?

Quite suddenly, she lifted her head and stared at me. She was slightly cross-eyed, I noticed for the first time. "Oh no," she said, "you're not going to lay that *skeleton* at our door. My dad didn't have anything to do with *that*. He wouldn't dream of harming anyone. He just wanders, is all. Mentally and physically." She jumped up. "Come on, Dad, we're leaving."

Dad kept on gnawing. He didn't even look up.

"I didn't mean . . ." I began.

She held up a hand as if she were stopping traffic. "I *know* what you meant, Charlie. Just because you saw Dad staring at CHAPS, just because he has mental problems, you leaped to the conclusion he had something to do with the murder. Well, he didn't. And if he wants to hang out in the plaza staring at CHAPS, that's his business, not yours. It's a free country."

Her voice had risen a decibel or two, and people at neighboring tables were craning their necks. Becoming aware of this, P.J. took a deep breath and crumpled back down into her chair.

"I really didn't mean to sound accusing," I said hastily. "I was empathizing."

She gave a shaky sigh, picked up her glass and drained it. "I get irritable, Charlie," she said. "It doesn't take much for me to reach boiling point these days." She studied her empty glass. "Maybe I need another beer."

"You know, P.J.," I said awkwardly, "Angel's something of a loner, and it's been my experience that men get more interested in a woman if the woman doesn't seem too interested in them."

A flush traveled up from her throat to her scalp, staining her skin crimson. I felt very uncomfortable. "I didn't intend to embarrass you," I said hastily. "It's just that I noticed you were interested in Angel, and I really think . . ." I broke off as she seemed about to leap to her feet again. "Forgive me. I was tactless; it's a congenital weakness of mine. I was trying to help. Next time just tell me to mind my own business."

"Mind your own business, Charlie," she said, but her color had begun to return to normal. Reaching up to her hair, she unfastened the wide bow that held her ponytail back, smoothed her hair carefully and refastened it.

"I'm sorry," she muttered. "Like I said, I have a notoriously short fuse." She smiled wryly. "Your advice isn't much help though—as far as men are concerned, I'm totally invisible. If I were to pretend I'm not interested in them, they wouldn't even notice my supposed lack of interest. They wouldn't even notice *me*. I have to get in their faces if I want any attention at all. Which I do."

Her father was suddenly on his feet, heading back to the buffet table with his plate in his hand. For a big guy, he could sure move fast. "No, Dad," P.J. called after him. "You're supposed to use a clean plate." When he paid no attention, she jumped up and ran after him. Taking the plate from him, she set it down on a side table, then accompanied him to the buffet and helped him to more food.

I wondered how patient I'd be if Prinny were my father. I felt quite sure I'd be happy to have my Dad alive again, whatever his condition, but then it was easy to decide such things from the sidelines.

I wasn't sure if P.J. and her father would rejoin me, but they did. "Do you mind if we sit here, madam?" Prinny asked politely before sitting down.

"Be my guest," I said.

He immediately began wolfing down his second plate of food.

"I have to watch him," P.J. said. "He forgets he's eaten and starts in again. That's why he's getting so heavy. Usually, I won't let him start over, but I don't feel like creating another scene."

She took a deep shaky breath. "You said you'd asked my dad about the Watanabes?"

Obviously, she wanted to change the subject, and I was only too glad to go along. I nodded. "Did you know them?"

"We both knew Joe and Michiko," she said. "Dad seemed okay when we moved here, except he'd get irritable from time to time. Probably the early stage of his condition, according to the doctors. Anyway, he loves Japanese food. He spent a couple of years in Japan with the occupying forces after World War Two. He used to talk to the Watanabes in Japanese, so he was always welcome here."

"*Konnichi wa*," Prinny said, right on cue.

P.J. laughed, looking much more attractive as a result. "You have a great smile," I told her, and she gave me a shy, grateful glance that was very endearing.

"Do you think the Watanabes could have killed the man in the flower-bed?" I asked.

She didn't hesitate. "No way."

"Not all murderers look like Charles Manson," I pointed out.

She grew thoughtful. "Well, Joe was a bit excitable, but I can't imagine him bumping someone off."

"Maybe Mrs. Watanabe bopped Mr. Watanabe on the head and buried him," I suggested.

She giggled. "I don't think that would be possible. Michiko Watanabe was tiny—no more than five feet tall."

"So maybe she hired someone to do the job. How tall was Joe?"

"Probably around five-four."

"There's another theory shot to pieces. The skeleton was tall, Sergeant Bristow said."

I wondered if I should ask her about Prinny's feud with his archenemy Frenchy, but hesitated, not wanting to upset her again, now that I'd got her smiling. Seemed to me she had enough irritation in her life, without me adding to it. Irritation might produce pearls in oysters, but I've noticed people are more apt to get indigestion. I'd make a point of talking to P.J. later, I thought.

About then Zack spoke into the microphone on the stage, and there was an immediate silence.

"Welcome, neighbors," he said in his nice, though fake, down-home drawl.

Everybody clapped as if he'd said something amazing.

"Y'all listen up now," he went on. "Charlie and Savanna and Angel and I thought it would be a right good thing to bring y'all together, so we can get to know each other. How 'bout we get goin' by sayin' how long we've been livin' or workin' on Adobe Plaza?"

He paused, then hooked his thumbs into the waistband of his jeans and segued into his John Wayne imitation.

"Any man who doesn't cooperate, I'll make him wish he'd never been born."

The applause was thunderous this time.

Zack caught my eye and smiled his bad-boy smile. What a ham, I thought. At the same time, all my little red corpuscles were tap-dancing their response to the smile.

"I'll start y'all off," Zack offered. "I'm Zack Hunter, and I'm a California native. I've been involved with CHAPS since January eighth of this year."

"We know who you are, Sheriff Lazarro," a woman called out. "You can't hide your past from us."

Everyone laughed.

Zack smiled a little stiffly and held up the guest book. "It says here that Bart Traskit, who manages the arts and crafts shop, is an Oregonian by birth. How long you been around these parts, Bart?"

A tall, thin young man with a pen protector in the pocket of his short-sleeved shirt stood up to answer. He looked as if he belonged with the Silicon Valley crowd rather than artists. The others at his table also introduced themselves. Pretty soon everyone was impatiently awaiting an opportunity to speak.

"Well, good for Sheriff Lazarro," I murmured, then concentrated on listening, noting that Savanna was sitting at the end of the bar, making notes. Zack must have put her up to that.

Angel was watching from the sidelines. He seemed interested in what the guests had to say, but he kept shifting his weight from foot to foot as if he were nervous. It wasn't until Zack said, "Thank you all, thank you very kindly," that I realized he hadn't called on Angel, although he'd made Savanna and me take part.

Curious. Something to be looked into later.

Now that all the guests had introduced themselves, there was a much more animated feeling in the room. Excusing myself to P.J. and Zack, I started table-hopping, drawing people into a discussion about the Watanabes, the earthquake, the body in the flower-bed. Zack and Angel and Savanna were doing the same thing—we'd agreed on our strategy beforehand.

Like me, many of those present had moved in or come to work in Adobe Plaza after the Watanabes left, but those who had known Joe and Michiko gave identical answers. They were lovely, quiet people. The food had been first-rate. Well, no, they hadn't really known them well. Just as much as you ever know your local restaurateurs.

The only different note was sounded by a young teller from the Plaza Bank who had once seen Joe Watanabe chase one of his kitchen helpers across the plaza with a cleaver. "He was an old man, but he ran lickety split," she said, her eyes rounded with remembered astonishment. It happened a couple of years ago, she thought.

She had no idea what had caused Joe's anger. She'd seen him walking back before she could make up her mind whether or not to call the police. The helper had returned also, a few steps behind. He appeared to be unhurt. As far as she knew there hadn't been another disturbance.

"Was he tall?" I asked. "The guy Joe chased, I mean."

She shook her head. "I don't really—I don't remember."

"Was he Japanese?"

She squinched her eyes up real tight. "I don't think so."

"Did you notice the color of his hair? Or if he had any?"

She shook her head, frowning.

Something else to pass on to Bristow. Maybe she was

wrong about the guy's height. Maybe I hadn't been so far out thinking the Watanabes might be connected to Mr. X. Maybe Joe and his cleaver had caught up with his elderly helper at a later date.

After talking about the Watanabes, it was quite easy to ask about the dead man in the flower-bed. Everyone was anxious to talk about him, but nobody had any theories about who he was. No one remembered seeing an elderly man with grey hair hanging around the Plaza, with or without teeth, dead or alive. Nobody had seen anyone digging in the flower-bed. "Unless you count the gardening syndicate, that is," Bernie the jokester had to add.

I wondered if Bristow had talked to the people at Hoshizaki and made a mental note to ask him.

Bernie followed through with a comment about CHAPS looking pretty bad. "Are you going to leave those mountains of dirt sitting out there forever?" he asked Zack, who had visited enough tables to meet up with me. "I'm pretty good with a shovel. You want me to clean the mess up for you? Wouldn't charge you top dollar. Minimum wage. Looks unsightly, sitting around like that. Do it this afternoon, you say the word."

It sounded as if he *owned* a shovel, I realized. Maybe he had a garden at home. He might even sell spades in his store. But why would he volunteer to replace the soil? I supposed it did look pretty messy from the mini-mart, as all the other flower-beds around the plaza were still vivid with the reds, pinks and whites of geraniums, impatiens and begonias. But somehow I didn't trust Bernie's offer. Did he really need extra cash that badly? The mini-mart wasn't on a main traffic route, but it seemed to get plenty of business.

Frannie was frowning at Bernie as if she were puzzled, too. Was there something in that soil he wanted to look at?

A shiver went through me like an electric shock. Could Bernie Lightfoot possibly be Igor? Was he wanting to look for his money without questions being asked? I rather hoped so. If he were Igor and he found his money, then maybe he'd leave me alone.

"You okay, Charlie?" Zack asked.

I supposed I must have paled. "Something I ate," I said, which brought forth a screech from Bernie and some pointed comments about the restaurant not appreciating my recommendation.

"Can't do nothin' with that dirt," Zack said when Bernie finally wound down. "Police department hasn't okayed it yet. I spoke about it to the detective just last evenin'. Said he'd get back to me on it."

Zack had seen Bristow on Saturday? I knew that he and Bristow and Sheila had met for beers a couple of times, but I'd gone to bed as soon as we closed the tavern the previous night, knowing there was extra work to do today. With all the preparations, there hadn't been time to talk to Zack this morning.

He saw I was staring at him and winked. Did that mean he'd remembered to ask Bristow if the police had found any money? "Don't know what the police're waitin' for," he continued, looking meaningfully at me. "Anythin' was in that hole is gone. Never was nothin' but bones in there anyhow."

I glanced quickly at Bernie, but his round, pudgy face didn't tell me anything. What was I expecting? Signs of disappointment, frustration, anger?

"Nice of you to offer, though," Zack added, mannerly as ever. "Right neighborly."

But somehow Bernie didn't strike me as a genuine neighborly sort.

"How come you didn't get Angel to reveal his life story?" I asked under my breath as Zack and I moved to another table.

Zack shrugged. "He asked me not to call on him."

"All the more reason to do so," I said. "Obviously he's hiding something."

Zack laughed and put an arm around my shoulders, which immediately leaned into him. Sometimes I think my body has no connection to my brain; it's forever wanting to go off and do its own thing. I sent a sharp order down from above. *Straighten up.* I went on leaning.

"All this sleuthin's tellin' on you, Charlie," Zack said fondly. "Angel's just shy about standin' up in front of strangers, is all."

"Sometimes it's hard to distinguish between shyness and secretiveness," I said, but my heart wasn't in it. It was too busy ricocheting off my ribs.

Pathetic, that's what I am.

CHAPTER 10

I noticed that Savanna had pulled a chair over to the buffet table to eat her own meal. Deciding it would be well to separate myself from Zack for a while, I wandered over and brought a chair for myself.

"I'm sorry, Savanna," I began. "Like you said, I'm naturally one hundred per cent nosy. So I have to ask. What on earth did Bernie Lightfoot mean when he said he missed his therapy?"

Savanna had an advantage over me in that if she ever blushed, it didn't show up against her dark brown skin. Mine, on the other hand, could color up like P.J.'s in truly embarrassing situations. Savanna did show discomfort, though. Biting her lower lip, she shuddered slightly, then looked reproachfully at me.

"I've never asked you stuff about *your* past, girlfriend," she said. "Everyone's entitled to a few mistakes."

"Bernie *Lightfoot*?" My voice squeaked.

"Oh, for goodness sake, Charlie, not that kind of mistake. What kind of dummy do you take me for?" She let out a sigh. "If you're going to come up with scenarios that bad, I'd better lay the truth on you."

She looked over her shoulder, then gave a couple of shifty glances to either side. "You know Leah Stoneham?"

"The masseuse? Yes, I've met her," I said.

"She bought the clinic from me."

I stared at her blankly.

"Come on, girlfriend, it's not that hard to figure out. I used to own the physical therapy clinic. I was a masseuse."

"A masseuse," I repeated, not sure whether to be relieved or not. There were masseuses and then there were masseuses.

"A real masseuse," Savanna said, reading me accurately. "Not a prostitute."

"Savanna," I protested, "I never thought . . ."

"Yes, you did, for half a second there. I saw it in your eyes."

I shook my head, but didn't protest any more. "Well, if you were a real masseuse, there's nothing to be embarrassed about, is there?"

She gave me a weak smile. "Nothing at all," she said. "Apart from having to deal with clients like Bernie Lightfoot."

It was my turn to shudder. Then a thought struck me. "Wait a minute. If you owned the clinic, then you were here, working in Adobe Plaza, when Mr. X was killed."

"I suppose so," she said without real interest.

I waited.

She glanced at my face, then away, then back again, then laughed nervously. "What?" she asked.

"Well, did you see anything? Did you ever see a tall old guy with false teeth or no teeth hanging around? Did you ever see anyone digging up the flower-bed?"

"Don't you think I'd have told that nice Sergeant Bristow if I had seen anything of the sort?" she asked, her dark eyes gentle.

"You think he's nice, huh?" I was almost distracted, especially when she nodded and lowered her eyelashes shyly, but I forced myself to continue. "You didn't answer the question," I said flatly.

"Because I didn't see anything, and I don't know anything. I wasn't too happy toward the end of last year and the beginning of this one. I wasn't noticing a whole lot."

This time I let myself be distracted.

"That's when I split up with Teddy," she said.

"Aren't you ever going to open up about that?" I asked. "Was it a problem that he was white? Is that why you don't want to tell me?"

She had finished her meal long since, but now she picked up her fork, scraped it over her plate, then licked it off. I thought she was using delaying tactics, hoping I'd get bored and move on, but quite suddenly she said, "I found him in bed. Teddy. With—with someone. I came home early from the clinic because of a power outage, and there he was. And my baby Jacqueline in her crib in the next room."

The never-to-be-forgotten image of pants-around-his-ankles-Rob on top of Trudi chugged through my memory. "Isn't one woman enough for any of them?" I wondered aloud.

"Oh, that wasn't the problem, Charlie," she said tightly, clattering her fork onto her plate. "Teddy wasn't in bed with another woman. He was in bed with a man. A man who was one of my clients. I would have thought he could find partners in his own line of work—he was catering manager for the Palm Court Hotel in downtown Condor. You'd think there'd be a gay cook or two around, wouldn't you?"

She made a growling sound in the back of her throat. "I had a mixed bag of clients. People with sports injuries, industrial accidents, arthritis, whatever. And I picked up several clients from the ballet school on Water Street. But the guy Teddy chose was not, as you might think, from the ballet school. He was a truck driver. Twenty-two years old. Teddy always did get along well with young folks."

I couldn't think of any comforting words that would fit the situation and not trivialize it, so I wisely kept my mouth shut for once and just put an arm around her shoulders and squeezed lightly.

"It's okay, Charlie. I'm over the shock now. And the bulk of the anger. But that's the reason I gave up the clinic. I discovered that's where Teddy had met his lover. Teddy used to pick me up from work. Often he'd get there early, sit in the waiting room, read a magazine, didn't want to bother me, he said. Didn't want to get in the way. He was just fine sitting out there. Just fine."

She paused, her head cocked as if she'd just now heard the bitter note in her voice, but then she went on even more bitterly. "Seems Teddy was using my waiting room as a bargain basement. Shopping for young studs to take home. The truck driver wasn't the first. Probably wasn't the last."

She shrugged. "Anyway, that's why I put the clinic up for sale. It didn't have the same appeal after that."

"If Teddy was gay, why did he marry you?" I asked.

"My question exactly," she said. "I always knew he wasn't exactly motivated where sex with me was concerned, but that suited me fine. There was a time I loved Teddy, but the sex was never anything to get excited about. He was kind, very sweet really. And there hadn't been much kindness in my life until then. I had this need for affection. Pathetic."

"Everybody needs affection," I said. "It's just that

some of us get in the habit of pushing it away because it hasn't done us much good so far."

She glanced at me curiously, as though wondering if my comment were autobiographical, which of course it was, then sighed deeply. "Teddy told me he'd always thought of himself as bisexual, but he had to admit as he grew older his preference was for men. As for why he married me, his mother kept nagging at him: 'Get married, get married, get married, give me grandchildren for my old age.' " He didn't have the courage to tell her he was gay, and he was angry with her for going on about it, so I was some kind of revenge. 'Okay, Ma, you wanted me to get married, guess who's coming to the church.' "

I wanted to hug her again, but she was holding herself very stiffly, and I was afraid she'd either reject me or break down and cry.

"Where is Teddy now?" I asked gently.

She shrugged. "Who knows? I threw him out of the apartment that day, and he disappeared from my life. Couldn't even find him to serve divorce papers. Didn't really care."

"He's not paying child support?"

"No. And don't you go putting on that do-gooder face of yours, Charlie Plato. I cleared out our savings account the minute he was out of the house. That's what I used to buy my share of CHAPS. He never came back at me about that. I'm afraid if I was to go looking for more money from Teddy, he'd try to get custody of Jacqueline. He might win, too. The courts are coming out with strange verdicts nowadays."

She sighed. "I don't mean to sound bitter, Charlie. I wasn't all that broken up, to tell the truth. It wasn't that great a marriage. How could it be? Anyway, besides my sixth share in CHAPS, I got Jacqueline. Any time I look at her sweet face, I get over feeling bad about being married to Teddy."

"Didn't you say Teddy worked in Condor?" I asked.

She bit her lower lip. "He quit his job right after we split. He told the people there he was going to remake his life."

Having done the same, there wasn't much I could say to that.

About then Bernie Lightfoot gave out with one of his shrieks of laughter. Savanna shot to her feet. "Why don't you ask Bernie where Teddy is?" she said in ringing tones.

As luck would have it, she spoke into one of those sudden silences that come over crowded places at entirely the wrong moment. A lot of people had drifted out, but everyone who was left in the place heard her.

All of us froze in place. Bernie was standing. He had a funny, sick look on his pudgy face. "You ought to know where Teddy is, if anyone should, Bernie," Savanna said, still speaking loudly. "You were forever bopping over to my clinic soon as Teddy showed up, looking around, cracking jokes about the best therapy in town. I should have known about Teddy then, but I didn't pay attention. I didn't want to pay attention to you, Bernie, because I knew why you were hanging around when you didn't even have an appointment. You liked Teddy, didn't you, as well as those guys from the ballet company? I may not have been as worldly as some. I may not have suspected Teddy was queer, but I always knew *you* were."

Savanna spun on her boot heel and headed for the door, head held high. Halfway there, she turned back. "Well," she said, with an air of surprise and one of her killer smiles, "I should have done that months ago. I feel much better now."

Everybody turned to look at Bernie. I must say, he held up very well, though his round face was almost purple. "It's true that I'm gay," he said, with compelling dignity. "But I assure you all, I know nothing about Teddy Seabrook's whereabouts."

Savanna had left by the front lobby that led to the parking lot. Bernie stalked over to the plaza exit.

Everyone looked at Frannie Lightfoot, who appeared totally dejected. She was crouched down in her seat, looking more birdlike than ever, clutching her handbag to her chest as if it were a life preserver and she was afloat at sea. I walked over to her table. "I'm so sorry, Frannie," I said. "I'm afraid I stirred all that up. I had no idea . . ."

She didn't look at me. "It's all right, dear," she said quietly. "It's not as if I didn't know. We always knew, Mother, Father and I."

Frowning, I sat down in the chair Bernie had vacated. "I don't understand," I began, but she interrupted me, darting one of her birdlike glances at my face.

"They can't help it, you know. People are born one way or the other, and they can't do anything about it."

I nodded. "I didn't mean that—I meant, well, I guess I don't understand why, if you always knew, you married him. Surely you didn't think you could change him?"

Her head came up, and there was no mistaking her astonishment. "Oh my," she said. She made a funny little choking sound that was halfway between a laugh and a cry. "I'm not married to Bernie, dear. Whatever gave you that idea?"

I stared at her. So did everyone else within hearing range. Taj's eyebrows had almost disappeared into her hairline. "The sign on the mini-mart," I stammered. "Bernie and Frances Lightfoot."

She shook her head on its little bird neck. "I'm his sister, dear."

This was turning into some party.

Frannie patted my arm. "Don't you go thinking I'm like that—like Bernie, I mean, only female. The reason I've never married is due to a disappointment in love when I was in my twenties. I never got over it. Bernie wanted to buy the mini-mart after our father died, so it seemed natural to go into business with him. We've been here several years now. Our mother died here. I had no idea anyone would think we were married, but I quite see now why they would."

She sighed. "Poor Bernie. He didn't want people to know he was homosexual. It never did sit easy on him. But now he's been—what is that word?"

"Outed?" I suggested. I still hadn't recovered from the shock of this whole glut of information about Teddy and Bernie and Frances, but at least my voice was operating.

Frannie nodded, looking pleased. "I think Bernie will be much happier now," she said. Then she frowned. "That young woman, Savanna—that wasn't nice, blurting that out about Bernie. But then I've never thought too highly of her, so I shouldn't be surprised."

"You don't like Savanna? What's not to like?"

"Well, I knew Teddy best. And liked him best. He used to come in the store for cigarettes before going to the clinic to pick up his wife. He and Bernie would exchange recipes. Bernie's always enjoyed cooking. His lasagna is. . . ." She broke off, then looked around as though to check if anyone was listening. Everyone had gone back to their own conversations. Judging by the buzz, they were all busily discussing recent revelations.

I waited.

Frannie gave herself a little shake as though to settle herself in place, then leaned closer to me. She smelled rather musty, as though she'd lived in a damp place for too long. "Teddy was a gentleman," she said. "Very good-looking. Very nice. Very nice indeed."

There was a yearning note in her voice. I remembered that one time when I was in the store, and Bernie was sounding off about something, she'd commented that he should know better, even if he was younger than her. I happened to know Bernie was forty-seven because he'd told me so without my being the least bit interested. So Frances could be pushing fifty from one direction or the other. So could Teddy, for that matter. Savanna had said "as he grew older . . ."

"How old is Teddy?" I asked.

Frannie blinked. "Oh, my dear, I can't say, I'm sure."

"Have a guess," I suggested.

"Well, he did have grey hair," she said. "He told me it started turning before he was forty. Lovely it was. Thick. Like Phil Donahue's."

Grey hair.

"A tall man, was he?"

"A fine figure of a man," she replied.

"How were his teeth?" I asked.

She looked surprised. "He had a lovely smile."

"Even teeth?" I proposed.

She nodded.

False teeth? I wondered, but couldn't bring myself to ask.

"I never did understand why he married that woman," she said with an acerbic note in her voice.

"You mean because he's white and she's black?" I asked flatly, ready to take offense on Savanna's behalf.

"Oh my, no, dear, there's not a prejudiced bone in my body," she said. "We're all children of Adam and Eve, I always say. The only reason for blackness was to protect people who lived near the equator. I just meant that she was such a child compared to Teddy. Now that I think about it, I believe he told me one time he was a quarter of a century older than his wife. He was making a joke, you understand."

Savanna was thirty-six. A quarter of a century would make Teddy sixty-one. According to the coroner, Mr. X was probably early to mid-seventies, but nothing was absolutely certain because he'd deteriorated . . .

I felt nauseated suddenly. I didn't want to hear any more. I couldn't bear to think that Savanna might turn out to be Mr. X's widow. That it might have been her ex-husband's foot, Jacqueline's father's foot, she'd looked at in our flower-bed.

"Do you know where Teddy is now?" I forced myself to ask.

Franny pursed her lips, causing wrinkles to spread to her chin. "I haven't seen Teddy since he left that woman," she said. "Nor has Bernie. He's asked Savanna several times for Teddy's address, but she always says she doesn't know where he is. Hmph!"

"Did you ever think she might be telling the truth?" I asked. "Did you know she came home from work and found Teddy in bed with a man? A truck driver. Can you imagine what a shock that would be to a loving wife?"

"*If* she was a loving wife," Frannie said.

"There's some doubt? Did Teddy ever indicate she wasn't?"

She frowned over that thought for a while, then sighed. "No. I can't say he did," she said at last. "He was such a gentleman, as I said."

I realized with a sinking stomach that I was going to have to tell Bristow all this.

Afterward, I couldn't remember actually getting up and leaving Frannie Lightfoot. I may have excused myself; I may not. All I remember is heading toward Taj's table as if it were an oasis of calm.

Josh popped his eyes at me, and I managed a smile that didn't feel too genuine. Josh had kept a pretty low profile today, I realized.

"Are you okay, Charlie?" Taj asked. She had the most soothing voice, husky and warm. I kept meaning to ask her if she was a good singer, sure that she would have to be. But this hardly seemed the time.

"I'm fine," I said. "Sorry the party turned out to be such a bust."

"The party was great," she assured me. "It was a sweet idea, getting the neighbors together. Disasters like earthquakes make you realize how much you depend on other people being there." She laughed her wonderfully infectious laugh. "Zack said we should get to know each other. We certainly did that, wouldn't you say, what with Bernie and Teddy Seabrook and P.J. and her dad?"

I had to laugh too, if a little more wryly.

"Did you know Teddy Seabrook?" I asked.

She shook her head. "He came in the bank a couple of times to cash a personal check, but I didn't know him. Nice-looking man. Seemed friendly. I didn't know he was gay, but then I don't ever concern myself with such things. To each his own."

"I didn't even know Savanna used to be a physical therapist," I confided.

"I'd forgotten that," she said. "I never did consult her, don't know if I ever actually met her before she showed up at CHAPS, to tell you the truth." A glint of humor showed in her dark eyes. "She and Teddy are no longer together, I take it."

"Separated, but not divorced." I didn't really feel right talking about Savanna, even to Taj. "She doesn't know where he is."

She shook her head, looking sad. "Poor thing. She has a child too, doesn't she?"

"Jacqueline. She's two."

Evidently it hadn't occurred to Taj to wonder if Teddy could be Mr. X. It was a wild idea at best.

A few more people had drifted out. The latecomers from the arts and crafts store were almost through eating. From the corner of my eye I'd seen Zack and Angel talking to them. Before CHAPS opened for the evening, we'd need to get together and compare notes. I hoped Savanna would come back. Sunday evenings were usually fairly slow, but I didn't want her brooding in her apartment.

Personally, I was ready for this party to end. I didn't think I could stand too many more surprises.

Luckily there weren't any more—at least not that day.

CHAPTER 11

It was Monday, September 18th. I had three weeks to come up with Igor's five thousand dollars.

"Are you sure you know where you're going?" I asked as Zack swung his pickup into yet another residential street. "Aren't we supposed to be heading for downtown Condor? The Bagel Barn? Next to Long's Drug Store? Why didn't you take the freeway? And why do you keep slowing down and speeding up? Do you always drive this erratically?"

"Chill, Charlie," Zack said with a sideways grin. "You're the one was scared of meetin' with Sergeant Bristow at the police station. You're the one said your friend Igor might be watchin' you. I'm usin' evasive drivin' techniques to make sure we aren't being followed, that's all. I made three consecutive right turns. Odds are pretty high against someone accidentally followin' you through three consecutive right turns."

Sheriff Lazarro was on the job. About to make some smart remark to the effect that if Igor were following he'd be suffering from motion sickness, I zipped my lip. Zack was showing concern for my welfare. How could I complain about that?

Bristow had agreed by telephone to meet with us away

from Bellamy Park so we could tell him the results of the party. I'd used the excuse that if any of CHAPS's clients saw us hanging around the police station, they might wonder if we were suspects.

"Don't think for one minute I'm encouraging your amateur snooping," Bristow had told me. "But if you feel you've really got something useful, least I can do is listen."

While Bristow demolished three sesame bagels to my one, and two mugs of coffee, I told him about Mr. Perry, who liked to be called Prinny and who stood around staring at CHAPS. About Bernie Lightfoot and Teddy Seabrook picking up partners at Teddy's wife's clinic, and about Teddy disappearing after Savanna kicked him out.

"You're not suggestin' Savanna had somethin' to do with that skeleton in our flower-bed," Zack interrupted around a mouthful of bagel.

"I'm not suggesting anything. I'm just telling what I know. What Sergeant Bristow does with it is up to him."

Zack narrowed his eyes at me. So, okay, he was fond of Savanna. So was I.

"Do you think the M.E. could be wrong about Mr. X's age?" I asked Bristow. "Apparently, Teddy would be sixty-one now. That's not too far off seventy, and he had grey hair and was tall. Plus, according to Savanna, he's gone missing."

"That's not what you told me originally," Zack pointed out. "You said she doesn't know where he is."

"If it's not possible the M.E. was off a few years," I went on, "then maybe Teddy was the murderer. Maybe Mr. X was his sexual partner, or maybe Mr. X was blackmailing Teddy, and Teddy bopped him and that's why he disappeared. Teddy, I mean." I warmed to this possibility. If there was blackmail involved, there'd be money involved. Igor's money.

Bristow thought that over for a while, munching tidily on yet another bagel. "I'll talk to the M.E." he allowed finally. "Might also look into Teddy's whereabouts." The corner of his mouth twitched in a crafty-looking smile. "Might talk to Mrs. Teddy, too."

"Be kind to her," I said. "She's the injured party in their parting of the ways." I couldn't resist adding. "She thinks you're nice."

"Does she?" He definitely looked interested.

"You'll want to talk to Bernie, too," I suggested. "Evidently, he fancied Teddy. Savanna said he was always, quote, 'bopping over to the clinic,' when Teddy came by."

"Bernie Lightfoot. Yes, ma'am, Ms. Plato," Bristow said, making a note. "Wasn't there something said early on about you just telling and me deciding on police procedure?"

He accompanied this with his terrific smile, which took any possible sting from his words. He and Savanna really would make a dazzling couple.

Noticing him glance at his wristwatch, I launched into the story of Joe Watanabe and his cleaver, which Zack had also heard from another of the Plaza bank's tellers. According to Zack's source, the kitchen helper was a tall, skinny white man.

"Did you talk to the people at Hoshizaki?" I asked Bristow next. "Several people commented on them being the only ones to dig up the flower-bed. I know it's a long shot, but . . ."

Bristow was holding up a hand, palm out to stop the traffic. "I talked to them already, best I could. Not too many of the employees speak English. Far as I could determine, none of them knew anything about a body in the flower-bed. The beds are tidied and weeded every month, with special attention in the fall and spring. Old bulbs divided and new bulbs planted last fall. Annuals put in this spring. No deep digging. Nothing unusual noticed."

"Speakin' of diggin'," Zack said, "what's goin' to happen to all that dirt? People round the plaza complainin' it's unsightly."

"Corp yard's been occupied since the earthquake," Bristow said. "Might possibly be able to get something done in a week or so."

"How about we get Hoshizaki to put the flower-bed back the way it used to be and send the city the bill for the work and the new bulbs?" I suggested.

Bristow was sipping a fresh cup of coffee and snorted so hard he began choking. I thumped him on the back until he recovered. "Worth a try, I guess," he said finally, his amber eyes glinting.

"But you're not holding out much hope?"

He grinned, then stood up.

"You'll keep in touch?" I asked.

He grinned again, but didn't answer.

"This is okay, I guess," Zack said as we drove back to Bellamy Park. "Talkin' to Hoshizaki 'bout repairin' our landscapin', I mean. But what if the city doesn't pay up? Y'all gonna split it four ways?"

"You pay half; Savanna, Angel and I pay one-sixth each. That should be fair."

He looked at me sideways.

"While we're at Hoshizaki, *we* can ask if they noticed

anything funny," I said before he could launch into an argument about financing. "Some people don't like talking to the police."

Zack settled his cowboy hat at its proper angle and nodded wisely, harking back to Sheriff Lazarro, I suspected.

Jiro Hoshizaki was the tallest Japanese man I'd ever seen. He must have topped six feet by a couple of inches. He was around thirty. I remembered a TV documentary about Japanese schools that said the younger generations were so much taller than their parents, the desks and chairs had to be replaced.

Zack explained our mission, and Jiro agreed to get the flower-bed cleaned up and replanted in the next couple of days. His English was formal, but as understandable as mine. "Detective Sergeant Taylor Bristow of the Bellamy Park Police Department told us few of your employees spoke English," I said, trying not to sound accusing.

"Ah, yes," Jiro said. "My employees told me of his visit and the reason for it. Very sad. I was in San Diego at the time. My father, who began this company, has retired there with my mother. I regret I was not present to help the detective."

"The sergeant was worried that perhaps your people didn't understand what he was asking. He wished to know if they had noticed anything strange about the flower-bed in the months before the body was found."

I ignored the sudden glance this convoluted, not-quite-true statement brought me from Zack. I was watching Jiro's face, which was a perfectly nice-looking face. All the same, though he might have been away when Bristow came investigating, where was he when Mr. X was killed? Maybe he'd helped Joe Watanabe out by planting the kitchen helper along with the azaleas. Anyone from Hoshizaki could have dug in the flower-bed without attracting any attention or curiosity. Who notices the gardener when he's there on a regular basis?

Jiro shook his head. "I think they understood very well," he said. "They explained everything to me. The officer wished to know if they had noticed any change in the soil or flowers or plants between November first and the end of January. They had not."

Oh well, it had been worth a try.

"One thing has occurred to me," Jiro went on.

Aha!

"What's that?" Zack asked, looking officious all of a sudden. Sheriff Lazarro stepping in.

Jiro turned to him. "One of my employees did not work out. I had to dispose of him."

His choice of wording gave me pause. "I hope you mean you had to let him go?"

He nodded. "He was inclined to drink too much sake, and was undependable."

"When did you fire him?" Zack asked.

Jiro squinched his eyes almost shut while he thought. "On March seventeen. I remember because it was Saint Patrick's Day."

Zack and I both stared at him blankly. "You sell shamrock?" I asked finally.

"This particular employee celebrated all holidays, American and Japanese," Jiro explained.

"How long did he work here?" Zack asked.

"Six months."

Zack and I exchanged a glance. "Could we get his name and address?" Zack asked.

"You wish to give this information to the sergeant? Yes, I would be pleased if you would do this. I do not wish to get Sato-san in trouble, but it is always possible he has noticed something." He nodded twice. "He worked at Adobe Plaza several times."

Jiro's handwriting was angular, but legible enough. The man in question now worked for a nursery on the road to Half Moon Bay. Zack and I decided to drive over there on the chance of catching him on the job. Fortunately, CHAPS was always closed on Mondays, so we had plenty of time.

The two-lane road to Half Moon Bay twists through wind-swept highlands densely covered with thick chaparral. As we descended into the lowlands closer to the coast, we could see large pumpkins in the fields. "Give it another month, the farms'll be crowded with munchkins lookin' to make the perfect jack-o'-lantern," Zack told me. "Farmers here put on pony rides, games—all kinds of doin's. Town has a festival—food, entertainment."

I looked across at him. "You were in the area last year this time?" I asked.

After a slight hesitation, he nodded, but his face tightened up as if he wished he hadn't given himself away. What *had* he done in that sixteen-and-a-half month hiatus between departing *Prescott's Landing* and transforming a Japanese restaurant into a country-and-western bar? I wondered. One commercial shouldn't have taken that long, should it? Looking at his closed face, I decided not to ask. Not at the moment, anyway. Maybe I'd find out some other way.

He had brought up the subject of children, however. "You don't have kids, do you?" I asked, never one to miss an opportunity to broaden my knowledge. Judging by the

shudder that accompanied Zack's negative headshake, he
was far from being a frustrated parent.

I could understand the shudder, having put my own biological urges on hold. Rob hadn't wanted me to have children—he'd had two by his former wife, and Brittany and
Ryan were two of the brattiest kids you'd ever want to
meet. We'd had them for summer vacations. I qualified for
sainthood those summers.

The nursery where Hoshizaki's ex-gardener worked was
almost into Half Moon Bay. I could smell the Pacific as I
climbed down from the truck. The sky was overcast, the
breeze off the ocean chilly.

The nursery was small, but tidy, bursting with bare root
trees and sunflowers and all manner of shrubs in pots, as
well as a few hundred pumpkins. A fair sized field was
planted in precise rows of healthy-looking Christmas trees.
I made a mental note to come out here to get a couple for
CHAPS in December.

The man's name was Tak Sato, and he was very short
and wiry and dark. Fifties maybe. Gold winked in his mouth
when he smiled. Zack explained our mission, stressing the
importance of a truthful answer, hinting at a reward if
Sato's information led to an arrest. I hoped my inventive
partner would remember that his percentage of any reward
would follow the usual proportions.

The man thought for a few minutes, then his lips moved
as he murmured to himself, apparently counting. After a
while, he nodded. "In September I planted bulbs. Anemone,
crocus, daffodil, tulip, hyacinth, ranunculus. October, November, I did the weeding. Everything was okay. In December I did the cleanup, more weeding. Everything the
same. Very tidy. Then in January I did another cleanup.
Something in CHAPS flower-bed was not okay."

"January the what?" Zack asked at the same time I queried excitedly, "What didn't look right?"

Tak's eyes hooded as he thought. "January thirty-one," he said firmly. "It was the day after my birthday, so I remember." He smiled broadly. "I remember the headache I had from meeting with my friends the previous night."

"A sake headache?" Zack queried.

Tak nodded, smiling man to man. Then he turned to me. "Bulbs," he said. "I planted bulbs in September, like I said. In December there were many sunny days, shoots coming up everywhere. In January, there was one whole big place in front of CHAPS that had no daffodils, no tulips, no flowers at all. The beauty bark was not in the proper place. I thought maybe somebody's dog dug up the bulbs, scattered the bark, maybe the dog's owner picked up the flowers. I made good with plants that were already in bloom and with new beauty bark."

"Was that empty place to the right of the steps as you're looking at CHAPS?" I asked.

He nodded.

"You're sure the bark was in place in December?" Zack asked, sounding irritated. Stood to reason he'd prefer to hear that the flowers had been dug up before he bought CHAPS.

"Did you work on the plaza at the same time in December? End of the month?" I asked.

Tak began to nod, then shook his head instead. "The middle. There was a change in the schedule to make everything pretty for the holiday time."

"And everything in CHAPS's flower-bed looked okay in the middle of December, but not by the end of January?"

"I am sure, yes. If there was anything out of place before, I think I would have noticed."

"You didn't happen to have sake the night before the December schedule, did you?" Zack asked.

Tak grinned. "Possibly," he said.

"Not one of your more reliable witnesses," Bristow said when I called him from my loft to pass on what Zack and I had learned from Tak. "If he's right, though, then the body was buried sometime between mid-December to late January, which is entirely possible and would let out the Watanabes, seeing they left the country November twenty-third. But sake has been known to affect a man's judgment, and memory. He just may not have noticed anything out of place in November or December."

"So what do we do now?" I asked.

"What we do now is hand the detecting back to the experts and let them think about what to do." His speaking voice was just as beautiful when it was decisive.

"Bristow's not overly impressed with our detecting," I told Zack after I hung up the phone and went back into the kitchen area. "He says it might seem to narrow the window of opportunity so to speak, but it might also be that Tak simply didn't notice the beauty bark was messed up in November or December. Tak did get fired for being undependable."

I sighed as I finished washing my hands and picked up a towel. "The sergeant did sort of say he'd take Tak's evidence into consideration, though, and he didn't chew me out for following up on Tak."

Zack had come up to my loft because I'd invited him to dinner to show my appreciation for his help. On the way in, we'd stopped at Lenny's Market to buy salmon and vegetables and freshly made pita. I'd already blanched the vegetables and brushed a couple of pita with olive oil before putting them on my electric griddle. The water in the deep skillet had boiled while I was on the phone, and I placed the salmon fillets and herbs in and set the clock timer.

Sitting in the overstuffed recliner I'd picked up at a Condor garage sale, Zack had eyed these preparations with suspicion. He wasn't used to eating healthy. He appeared to feel at home, however. He'd removed his cowboy hat and was leaning back with his feet up, hands laced behind his head.

I felt quite at peace myself as I set place mats on the round table by the window. Our inquiry had produced something useful, whatever Bristow thought of our interference, and it had felt good to get out and about. It also felt good to be here in my loft with some company so I didn't have to think about Igor.

What a cliché. Little woman puttering around in kitchen. Man in chair, taking his ease, watching, keeping her safe.

"Where's the beef?" Zack demanded with a grin when I invited him to the table.

I ignored him, served my own usual four ounces of fish, gave him the rest and stuffed half a pita. There is nothing tastier than a grilled pita stuffed with barely cooked asparagus, broccoli, cauliflower, and sautéed mushrooms drizzled with no-fat honey-mustard dressing.

I'm not altogether sure Zack agreed with me—men I have known seem to feel there's something unmasculine about vegetables—but he ate without further complaint. We both made inroads into a superb Napa Valley chardonnay. Benny nibbled kibble in his cage.

Afterward I made a couple of tall lattés. I caught the espresso habit when I lived in Seattle, and Zack allowed as how he wouldn't mind tryin' one to see what the fuss was about.

I felt comfortable with Zack. Well, let's be honest here, who's going to be entirely comfortable when one of the major sex symbols of the past decade is lounging next to her on her second-hand sofa, glancing her way every once in a while with his well-known devilish grin?

But it felt sort of relaxed, all the same, sitting there discussing CHAPS and some of the upcoming programs, rather than skeletons and possible suspects.

So relaxed in fact that I was beginning to be aware of an underlying sizzle in those sideways glances of Zack's. Probably, I thought, this would be a good time to get up and start clattering dishes into the sink.

But I didn't move.

Benny was hip-hopping around his cage, looking for action. Zack leaned over and let him out then scooped him up. There is something about a man's big hands holding a small creature—whether it's a human baby or a small animal, that tugs at the heart. Benny seemed fairly content to be held, though usually he's wary of strangers. He wasn't totally relaxed—his ears were alert—but he was vibrating happily.

I reached over and stroked his fuzzy back. Somehow my fingers got tangled up with Zack's. There was a moment when I focused on warm hands, blood pulsing, fingers—mine—trembling, and the room seemed to empty out of oxygen.

A heartbeat later someone punched one of the downstairs doorbells, which makes the plug-in extension in my loft sound off like a klaxon.

Zack and I both jumped. Benny leaped straight up in the air and came down hard in my lap, where he tried to get his whole quaking body under my hand so he could pretend he was invisible.

I glanced at the kitchen clock as I scooted him back in his cage where he always felt more secure. Nine o'clock. Who on earth . . . ? Except, possibly, Igor.

Zack went down the stairs with me, and I peered out of the peephole in the lobby door. Nobody there. We jogged through the tavern to the plaza door, turning on lights as we went. That door has a glass panel on either side and a light above it on the outside, so we could easily see the elderly Japanese couple at the foot of the steps.

The man and woman appeared to be engaged in an argument. The man was gesticulating wildly at the mounds of soil while the woman—who was very short indeed—tugged at his arm and shook her head.

Hoshizaki had sent people out at *this* time of night?

Zack unlocked the door and flung it open. "What do you . . . ?" he got out before the man turned and directed a torrent of Japanese at him.

"Whoa!" Zack said, but the man went right on.

Surely it was unusual for people who were planning to work in dirt to get so dressed up, I thought. The man had on a nice suit, a white shirt and dark tie—the woman a well-cut skirt and jacket and what looked like a silk blouse. She had wonderful posture. Her black hair, barely shot with gray, was beautifully arranged around her lined face. The man's hair was just as thick, but had more white in it.

Evidently realizing that he wasn't getting through to us, the man abruptly stopped talking. He might have run out of breath; his face was very red. The woman was calmer. Very dignified. "We are Joe and Michiko Watanabe," she said, with a slight bow. "I am sorry for my husband's behavior. He is distressed by so much disorder. I tell him it is nothing to do with him anymore, but he will not listen."

Watanabes. The former owners. Zack invited them in. Mr. Watanabe seemed hesitant, but his wife shot a few terse Japanese phrases at him and he entered slowly. Zack waved them to one of the tables, and we all sat down.

"What has happened here?" Mr. Watanabe asked after a worried glance around the main corral.

"I turned the place into a country-and-western tavern," Zack told him. "Place looked real nice the way you folks had it, but it wouldn't have worked. . . ."

"No, no, I am asking about outside," Watanabe interrupted.

"Police dug it up," Zack said bluntly. "Account of we had a dead body turn up there after the earthquake. Not so much a body as a skeleton. Right out there in the flowerbed. Coroner says it might have been put in there early as last November, but the Hoshizaki dude placed it in December."

He eyed Mr. Watanabe with deep suspicion. "When exactly did you leave the U.S. anyway?" he asked in his best Sheriff Lazarro fashion. "You wouldn't happen to know anythin' about that body, would you? We heard tell you chased one of your kitchen honchos with an ax one time."

"My husband never chased anyone with an ax," Mrs. Watanabe said firmly. "It was a kitchen knife. A big kitchen knife. And we left here in November because of Joe's parents. They died. We traveled the Inland Sea for our vacation. Came back now because of bad weather. Typhoon. We do not like typhoons."

"A body? A dead body?" Watanabe gasped. "What is this about a dead body?" Quite suddenly, he clutched his chest and toppled sideways to the floor. His face wasn't red anymore. It was buttermilk white.

Mrs. Watanabe followed her husband down, her small hands fluttering like a ballerina's. "Oh my goodness, please call 911," she said, and I dashed over to the main bar to do just that.

When I returned, Zack had the old man stretched out on the floor, one hand supporting his neck while he gave him mouth-to-mouth resuscitation. "Joe has stopped breathing," Mrs. Watanabe wailed, clutching herself with both arms.

I had taken a CPR course myself when I was married to Rob, so I tapped Zack on the shoulder and indicated I was there to help. I began pressing on Watanabe's chest, and Zack blew air into him on the count of five.

We had Joe breathing by the time the medics arrived. As they got him onto a gurney, Mrs. Watanabe clasped our hands and expressed her gratitude, bowing over and over. At the last minute she asked Zack to please come with her, so he hoisted her bodily into his pickup and took off after the ambulance. The next thing I knew I was standing shivering in the parking lot, all alone, watching taillights disappear around the corner. As the sound of the ambulance siren faded, I managed to get myself inside and lock up. Stumbling up my stairs, I wondered what had happened to my peaceful evening.

CHAPTER 12

Most days the four of us assembled around a pot of coffee in the office at 3 p.m. to check what needed to be done before we opened CHAPS for the evening.

Tuesday, the day after Mr. Watanabe's heart attack, Zack and I apprised Savanna and Angel of the new developments with Hoshizaki and the Watanabes. I'd called the hospital that morning and learned that Joe Watanabe was "resting comfortably."

"Joe's the second person to collapse here in the last month," I said, looking directly at Angel.

A blush highlighted the edges of Angel's high cheekbones. His mouth tightened under his drooping black mustache as if he were literally sealing it shut.

"Come on, Angel," Zack said. "We're your partners. Charlie's worried about you. How 'bout givin' us an explanation of that faintin' fit?"

Angel's mournful gaze switched to me.

"Seems to me in a situation like this we all need to avoid kicking up trail dust," I said. Sometimes I sound as pseudo-Western as Zack. Maybe wearing a cowboy hat affects me, too. "We need to be honest and truthful so we don't complicate things," I translated.

Savanna made a small sound and looked at each of us in

turn. "Can I start us off by apologizing for the way I behaved on Sunday? Lighting into Bernie like that. I was mortified when I calmed down and thought about it."

"No need to be sorry, darlin'," Zack said. "Pudgy dude had it comin'."

Savanna rewarded him with her killer smile. "I want you all to know that I genuinely don't have any idea where Teddy is—I didn't make that up."

Zack and I exchanged a glance. Probably he was thinking, as I was, about our idea that Teddy might be the body in the flower-bed. Obviously this possibility hadn't occurred to Savanna. I wasn't going to be the one to bring it up.

"Speaking of pudgy dude," I said, feeling awkward. "After you left, Savanna—and that was a magnificent exit, by the way—we discovered Bernie and Frannie are brother and sister, not husband and wife."

"I knew that," Savanna said. "I always knew that. Hoo, girl, you thought they were *married*? Who would marry Bernie? Or Frannie either, come to that?"

Zack and I laughed. Then we all looked at Angel, who was sitting on one of the desks and had still not answered our question about his temporary blackout. He kept his gaze averted and scuffed his boot toe on the wooden floor. "When I was a kid," he began, then stopped and swallowed. "Someone I . . . knew . . . was murdered." Each word seemed to be dragged out of some secret recess through a narrow aperture. After a long pause, he added, "I discovered the . . . body."

We sat in silence, staring at him, waiting to see if there was any more. I built a picture in my mind of Angel as a little kid. Short black hair, no ponytail, little solemn face, dark eyes, sturdy body.

"Was the murderer caught?" Savanna asked, her voice

ripe with sympathy. Earth mother coming through as usual.

"Police knew who did it right from the start."

That didn't quite answer Savanna's question, and she kept her always-compassionate gaze on him. "No," he said at last. "Far as I know, he was never arrested."

He shook his head, still without looking up. "I'd as soon not talk about it."

Big-eyed, Savanna reached over and patted his arm. He managed a sickly-looking smile. "I guess the shock of seeing that foot reminded me," he said. "Freaked me out."

I could feel grief vibrating out of him all over again. On top of that, there was so much pain in his voice, it made my throat ache. As far as I was concerned, the subject was ended. Though I couldn't help remembering what Savanna had said at the time. *Angel was sad. Not shocked. Sad.* Not freaked either, my own internal voice added.

"Your turn," I said to Zack.

He gave me the long, steady look he'd learned from Lazarro's director. "Nothin' to tell, darlin'," he said easily. "Whoever killed Mr. X and buried him did it before I bought this place, or at least before I took possession."

I persevered. "What *about* the time before you bought the building? Where were you then? You said you were written out of *Prescott's Landing*. What did you do after that?"

"I rested," he said. His green eyes were harder than I'd ever seen them. Like unpolished jade. His body was stiff, his right hand curved as if he were about to reach for the gun he used to pack on the show. I wasn't going to get any more answers from him *or* Angel, I could tell. And if I kept on, I was going to risk my friendship, *and* my partnership, with both men.

"Well, as I wasn't even in the state when Mr. X passed on, I've nothing to add," I said lightly. "So it looks as if it weren't one of us did the old man in."

The tension in the room lifted as though someone had opened up the roof and sucked the stress out with a vacuum cleaner.

Zack took off his cowboy hat and massaged his scalp through his hair. Leaning his chair back at a dangerous angle, he put his booted feet on the desk and balanced his hat on his knees. "Lazarro and his deputies used to toss out theories after a homicide," he said. "No one worried how wild they might be—it was a sorta brainstormin' session."

"Why don't you start us off?" I suggested.

He looked at the ceiling for a while, then nodded. "I reckon maybe a couple of swacked bums broke into CHAPS while it was standin' empty, some time between Watanabes leavin' and me takin' over. Probably they got in a fight, and one bopped the other. With a bottle maybe. Maybe the fight was *over* a bottle."

"Not bad," I said. "Except would the remaining drunken bum stick around long enough to take the other one's clothes off and bury him in the flower-bed?"

"Maybe his clothes were already off," Savanna said flatly. "Maybe they were *gay* drunken bums."

And maybe her subconscious mind was picking up on the idea that Teddy might be murderer or victim. She just hadn't put it together yet.

"*I* think the murderer is most likely to be someone who lived or worked around here or had some kind of social or business life in the neighborhood," I said. "Someone who *knew* this building was empty and about to change hands, so nobody would interrupt whatever they came here to do."

"What were they plannin' to do?" Zack asked.

"How would I know?"

"Maybe the old dude—Mr. X—brought a lady friend in for some party-time," Zack said.

"He was in his seventies," I reminded him.

His eyes glinted. "I mean to party into my nineties, God willin'," he said.

Angel, who had seemed distracted, made an exclamation under his breath. "Something I forgot to tell you, Charlie, something someone said at the party Sunday."

We all regarded him with interest.

"Your friend with the funny name. The big lady. You were sitting with her Sunday. Works at the bank next door."

"Taj? Taj Krivenko? What did she say?"

"Not something *she* said, something about her." He tugged on his mustache a time or two. "I'm trying to think who said—oh yeah! That nice little lady—" He stopped himself short and gave me a sideways glance before I had time to protest; he was getting to know me pretty well. "That nice young woman who started working in the store in the lobby—Buttons and Bows—a day or so before the earthquake. The one with the hair cut kinda punk—short and spiky on top and long in back."

He'd really noticed this young woman, I realized with interest.

"Gina," Savanna supplied. Earth mother knew everybody.

Angel nodded. "Yeah. Gina. Anyway, when Charlie's friend Taj stood up and introduced herself, Gina said that was funny, she'd known that lady—woman—years ago in San Diego—they lived in the same street—only she had a different name then."

I stared at him, feeling confused. "*Taj* had a different name?"

"Enid something. No. Edith. Edith Jones."

"Probably Gina's got her mixed up with someone else."

"She said not. She said the big woman hadn't changed any since she knew her, 'cept to look older. Said her mom's name was Delly Jones, and the neighborhood kids were all scared of her—the mother. She had a mouth on her had to be heard to be believed, Gina said."

"How come you didn't tell me this on Sunday?" I asked.

Angel looked apologetic. "I'm sorry, Charlie. After Savanna said—well, after all that stuff about her husband, it went out of my head. There was other stuff, too. I mean, other people told me stuff about each other, and I got it mixed up when we talked, remember, so it was only after that I thought about Gina again and got it straight in my mind." He nodded again. "Gina said she was real sure, but she'd never said anything to the big lady about it because there was maybe some good reason why she'd changed her name."

I started to comment, changed my mind about what I was going to say and stammered. "Why the—what on earth *would* be a good reason for someone to change her name?"

Angel shrugged. "Gina didn't say."

Zack raised quizzical black eyebrows. "You gonna tell Bristow?" he asked.

I was still feeling confused. I'd only known Taj for five months, but I'd talked to her pretty often and I'd thought of us as friends. Of course, if you had changed your name before you even *knew* someone, it's not the sort of thing you'd suddenly bring up in the middle of a conversation. *Hey, by the way, I'm not who I used to be.*

"I'll talk to Taj," I told my partners. "No point mentioning anything to Bristow until I do that."

The others agreed and went on throwing out some fairly far-fetched theories, but I wasn't able to concentrate. There was no real reason to think there was something sinister about someone changing their name, of course. Except that Taj worked in a bank.

I thought it best to talk to Gina at Buttons and Bows first and struck up a conversation after trying on a couple of cowboy hats and a fringed jacket. She turned out to be just as nice as Angel had said and quite attractive in a brash, punkish way—petite, spiky-haired with a dash of burgundy among the brown, slashes of maroon blusher in lieu of cheekbones.

She wished she hadn't said anything to Angel. "I don't want to get the big lady into trouble," she insisted. "It just struck me odd that Edith had changed her name so drastically." She hesitated. "After I talked to Angel, I thought maybe Krivenko is her married name."

I shook my head. "She told me she'd never married. You didn't say anything to her about knowing her before?"

Gina shook her head. "She didn't recognize me the one and only time I saw her in the bank. No reason why she should. I was just a little kid when I lived on Catamaran Street."

I stopped in at the bank on Wednesday morning. "Any chance you can have an early dinner with me?" I asked Taj.

Seated behind her desk, she shook her head. "I'm babysitting right after work. I've been taking care of a three-year-old boy off and on for a while. This week I have him evenings. Josh and I won't even make it to CHAPS this week. The little guy's mother's getting some intensive drug counseling."

She sighed. "Well, at least she's in there trying. Social worker drops Mikey off at my house. No way I'd go to the neighborhood he lives in. It's bad enough that *he* has to live there."

Her smile was regretful. "Sorry, Charlie, I'll have to take a raincheck."

"You're really something," I said. "I never knew anyone to get so involved in so many causes."

She made a dismissing gesture. "My uncle Harley, the family do-gooder, passed his genes on to me."

I thought for a minute. "Sun's shining," I pointed out. "How about I have Dorscheimer's make us a couple sandwiches and we have lunch in the plaza?"

She looked up at me and shuddered slightly. "My stars, Charlie. I don't ever want to sit on those steps outside CHAPS again."

I winced. "Me neither. Besides, Hoshizaki's people are working there today. It's a regular dust storm. How about we sit on that bench at the other side of the plaza?"

She smiled. She looked very pretty today in a mustard-colored suit that brought out golden glints in her brown eyes. I wondered how long it took her to get her hair up in that topknot, and whether there was any possible way I could do mine like that. Hers always looked so neat. Taj never had odd tendrils hanging around or down like most people. "Sounds great, Charlie," she said. "I should be free around twelve-thirty."

The sandwiches were composed of turkey and onion, two kinds of lettuce and a leaf of radicchio. The turkey was real, not that revolting processed turkey loaf so many places pass off on their customers nowadays. The assistant cook at Dorscheimer's had filled a thermos with hot tea and cut up fresh fruit into a couple of plastic containers. The bread was multi-grain, with sprouted wheatberries in it. No butter or mayonnaise, just a smear of Dijon. The assistant paid more attention to my lectures about fat than the cook did. Sitting in the sunshine, I was as happy as a health-food nut can get. I realized I hadn't even thought about Igor this morning, which was a first. He'd hovered somewhere behind my left shoulder every day since he'd given me a month to come up with his money. The time line now said that I had nineteen days left to come up with answers for Igor. Or face consequences I wasn't inclined to dwell on.

Taj ate slowly, savoring every mouthful. I munched along with her, my brain racing the whole time to find a way to ask the really nosy question I had to ask.

My dad used to say if a job is hard to do you should just plunge in and get it over with. "Somebody said something really weird at the party the other day," I began.

Taj's big brown eyes regarded me fondly. "There were several weird things said at that party, Charlie."

"Yeah, well, this wasn't quite that weird." I took a deep breath. "Some woman said she used to know you a long time ago."

"Who?" she asked, her smooth brow puckering.

"I don't remember," I said, protecting my source. "She said you had a different name then. Edith Jones."

Taj's eyes filled first with shock, then with moisture. Putting what was left of her sandwich neatly back in its baggie, she set it aside on the bench and looked at me, her eyes glistening, expressive mouth trembling slightly.

My own eyes smarted in sympathy. "Gosh, Taj, I'm

sorry. I shouldn't have brought it up. It's just, well, I thought if the police heard about it, they might wonder and . . ."

She lowered her head and started crying hard, her big shoulders heaving. I felt like some kind of monster. "I'm sorry," I said again, patting her back gently.

It took a while for her to stop. Then she said, in the saddest voice imaginable. "It's okay, Charlie. I guess it was bound to come out some day." Sniffling, she fumbled in her jacket pocket and brought out a folded tissue and wiped her eyes carefully with the edge of it, the way women do when they're wearing mascara.

"Krivenko really is my name," she went on after blowing her nose and generally getting herself calmed down. "I wasn't born with it though. I had it changed from Edith Jones legally."

"But the Russian great-grandparents, the escape from Moscow, the balalaika?"

"All lies." She looked on the verge of tears again. "Taj isn't even Russian. It's not even a person's name. It's what kids in junior high used to call me. Taj Mahal. That's a mausoleum in India with a big round top. We had a question in a quiz one day along with a picture of it. 'What is this shape called?' the teacher asked. The answer, of course, was 'a dome.' But the class comedian, a kid called Geoffrey Messenger, said 'That shape is called Edith Jones,' and everyone laughed. For a while, they all called me Taj Mahal, the great white dome."

Having put up with a certain amount of teasing for my orange hair, I could imagine her feelings of humiliation. "There ought to be a way to make birth control retroactive for certain kids," I said.

She reached over and patted my hand. Her rings glinted

in the sunshine. "Kids love to have a butt for their jokes, Charlie," she said. "It seems to be human nature to pick on someone. Because I was fat they saw me as the weakest one in the herd."

She sniffed a couple of times more, then gave a shaky sigh. "It turned out okay. By the time we got to high school, nobody called me that anymore. But I'd gotten to where I liked it—it seemed more distinctive than Edith. I always thought of myself as Taj after that."

"Well, I admire you," I said stoutly. "You took a name that was applied to you in a pejorative way and made it your own. That took a lot of guts."

She smiled at me gratefully.

"And the Krivenko?" I asked. Okay, so I probably shouldn't have pushed it. She'd explained the Taj part; I should have left it alone. What can I say? I've already confessed I'm nosy. I can't help it. "Don't tell me you made that up, too? And what about Pavel and Irina? Your great-grandparents?"

"Krivenko *is* Russian," she said. "I added it about the time I moved up to this area. Nobody knew me. It seemed a good time to start over. Krivenko just sort of came to me one day—I was walking on the beach over in Half Moon Bay, and it was like when Native American kids go into the woods or mountains to get their names. As if a voice said it in my mind. It sounded like a name you'd have if you were somebody. I looked it up and found out it was Russian and decided to make it legally mine, along with Taj. The story of my background just sort of developed from there."

She was looking straight ahead now, as if she were vitally interested in the nearest live oak tree. "When people ask you your name in a store or an office or whatever, and you say Edith Jones, they don't even look at you. It's yawn time. You say Taj Krivenko, they do a double take. They have to ask you how to spell it, and it sounds interesting to them, and they look at you and ask you what nationality it is and you've become an interesting person."

She produced a brave imitation of her musical laugh. "I thought it would be a good name to use when I became famous."

"Famous for what?" I asked.

Her mouth quivered. "It didn't much matter," she said, looking wistful, her dark eyes misting over again. "I used to tell myself when I was growing up that one day I would be so famous, nobody would laugh at me anymore. I didn't even consider what I'd be famous for. And it didn't happen anyway."

She looked at me with such sad eyes I reached over and hugged her. She hugged back. I think I've already mentioned that she hugged good. As if she meant it. Not like people who just pitty-pat their hands against your back.

"I'm sorry, Charlie," she said as we separated. "I've been telling that story for so long—about Pavel and Irina and how they fled Russia—I've reached the stage where I don't even remember it's all made up."

"Well, you do it real well," I said, trying to lighten us both up. "I could hear the balalaikas playing in the background when you told it to me."

"I truly did learn to play the balalaika," she said. I was glad to see the twinkle had returned to her brown eyes. "Are you going to report me to the police?" she asked.

"For what? Legally changing your name? Even if it weren't legal, I wouldn't tell anyone—especially now that I know why you did it." I hesitated, my curiosity not yet totally satisfied. "Does Josh know you changed your name?"

"Oh, my stars, yes, I don't ever keep anything from

Josh. He knows everything I know, soon as I know it." Her face dimpled attractively.

I let my affection for her show. "I'm sorry you didn't get famous, Taj."

She made a face. "Me too."

Then we both laughed and went back to eating our lunch.

CHAPTER 13

Two things happened within the next twenty-four hours. Michiko Watanabe came by, and we learned who Mr. X was. Not from Mrs. Watanabe. I don't always get my stories in logical order. You've probably noticed that.

Mrs. Watanabe arrived at CHAPS a few hours after my lunch with Taj, about the time the first few patrons were drifting in to the main bar. Zack was present even though it was a Wednesday, because one of his poker playing buddies was sick and the game had been called off. He took Mrs. Watanabe into the main corral area, and called Angel and Savanna and me over to a booth.

Mrs. Watanabe told us to call her Michiko, which wasn't easy for me. She was a dignified little person, and calling her Michiko seemed frivolous. "I came to say we are leaving Bellamy Park already, Joe and I," she said in her sweet sing-song voice. "Joe must have an operation on his heart. The doctors here say the best place for this operation is a hospital in Texas. Some famous specialist is there, so we must go there."

She looked at Zack, who had carried a chair over to the end of the booth. "I wish to thank you, Mr. Hunter, for saving my husband's life. And you also, Miss Plato," she said to me. "You must not blame yourselves, thinking you have some responsibility for Joe's heart problem. He had three times chest pains while we were in Japan, but he refused to see a doctor. I think it is best for you to remember only that you saved him."

We both made demurring noises. I probably looked as pleased as Zack did at the thought that we had really helped save someone.

"Do the police say it's okay for you to leave?" Zack wanted to know.

I scowled at him, thinking he was being even more tactless than usual, but then he explained that when he'd taken Michiko to the hospital they'd run across Bristow who was visiting a fellow officer. While they awaited word on Joe's condition, Bristow had questioned Michiko about the body in the flower-bed and had told her he'd need to talk to her again.

Michiko nodded. "The sergeant visited with Joe and me two times today," she told Zack. "We assured him we knew nothing of this man who was found here dead."

"Did you leave a spade behind when you cleaned out Tomodachi?" I asked.

Michiko, Savanna, Angel, and Zack all looked at me blankly.

"It just occurred to me," I explained. "Mr. X was buried. The murderer had to use a spade. Where did he get it from?"

Michiko was shaking her head. "No spade. What use would we have for a spade? Hoshizaki took care of everything."

"Everyone in Adobe Plaza could say that," I pointed out.

She nodded again, looking solemn. "This is true. But it is

not for me to worry about. Sergeant Bristow was able to discover Albert—the man Joe had the argument with. So all is clear there. Albert is working at a fish and chip place in Dennison."

She looked at each of us solemnly. "Do not eat there. The reason Joe was mad was that Albert did not put in clean fat for cooking tempura. Risking customers' health is a very bad thing."

She frowned, then nodded. "Sergeant Bristow will know where we are if more questions are needed about the dead man." She smiled sweetly at Zack. "I am sorry that you have this problem. It reminds me of an ancient Chinese curse: 'May you live in interesting times.' Sometimes it is not so good to do so."

Zack smiled at her in the affectionate way he sometimes smiled at me. The similarity was depressing to my hormones.

When Mrs. Watanabe left, Sundancer began checking out his sound systems, and people were starting to pile in to CHAPS, so none of us had time to talk about her visit. Wednesday evening is one of our busiest.

The next morning I decided I needed to get back to my workout routine, which had suffered from all the cleaning and patching up and general disorganization we'd gone through since the earthquake.

I use a gym in Condor rather than Dandy Carr's in Bellamy Park. Dandy was the currently sick member of the Bellamy Park Irregulars, as Zack called his Wednesday night poker-playing buddies. His gym was state-of-the-art and was usually crowded with perky young things in spandex, swigging designer water, and macho guys grunting and spattering sweat all over the floor and mirrored walls.

The gym in Condor has out-of-date equipment—separate bench presses with long handles, old-style leg extension and leg press machines. I especially like the rowing machine and the treadmill, which don't have any plastic clips to fasten on your ear to check your heart rate or digital displays that tell you how fast and far you've gone.

At nine o'clock in the morning, I usually have the place to myself, and if anyone does wander in, they wear sweats that look as grungy as mine.

I was flat on my back doing bench presses when Zack and Sergeant Bristow arrived, both of them looking solemn. I sat up so fast I got jammed between the levers and had to wriggle free. "What's up?" I asked, concerned.

Zack leaned his elbows behind him on the barre that ran the length of one wall. He could usually manage to position himself in a way that set his lean body off to best advantage.

Bristow settled himself on the seat of the leg press machine and put his feet on the pedals, which brought his knees almost to his chin.

I stared at him.

"I called Zack to suggest the two of you join me for a bagel again," he said. "Zack stopped at CHAPS to pick you up. He guessed you might be here. I wanted to bring you up to speed on the latest development before the media gets into the act, which will be by tomorrow morning, probably. I've found out who your Mr. X is. Figured since you discovered him, you had a right to know first."

They had gone by CHAPS. What if Igor had seen them? What if Igor knew Bristow was a police officer?

About to shoot Zack a look, I suddenly absorbed what Bristow had said.

"Condor P.D. finally got their equipment going," Bristow said. "Computer came up with a missing persons report from December. Seems like your Mr. X was a crazy old guy known only as Walter—a panhandler, a drunk, a homeless person."

"He really *was* crazy?" I asked. "Or was that just an expression?"

Bristow smiled. Much as I hated to admit it, Zack was right; he did look like Michael Jordan when his face lit up like that. "You be the judge," he said. "Here's this old man wears ragged, dirty clothes, boots with holes in them. He's totally unkempt, unshaven. Used to hang out in Condor Library, people complaining he smelled like a goat—a goat pickled in alcohol, one guy said. Told everyone he was rich. Kept his nose buried in newspapers, pretending to read the stock reports, scribbling in a notebook, muttering about needing to transfer his funds. Sat in a corner. Even complained about the poor lighting. Sipped out of a bottle-shaped paper sack when he thought nobody was watching. Seems one of the volunteers who works at the library felt sorry for the old guy, made everyone else let him be. Soon as she was off-duty, the others would throw him out."

He pushed on the leg press pedals, wincing when they squealed their thirst for WD40. "Woman who felt sorry for him was the one reported him missing. Olivia Emmett. Nice old lady. Nobody else paid a whole lot of attention except to complain about the aroma. Homeless people come and go. Fact of life nowadays. Anyway, when Miss Emmett reported to Condor P.D. that Walter hadn't shown up in a month or so, she included in her description that he sometimes left his false teeth out. The report surfaced yesterday, and an officer remembered I was checking on a victim who had shown up toothless."

"Miss Emmett doesn't know Walter's full name?" I asked.

Bristow shook his head. "Walter's all she knows." He

chuckled. "Seems like he told her he was going to remember her in his will. Told other people the same thing. Old lady made me promise I'd let her know if we came across a will. We found the shack he lived in under the bridge that goes over the disused railroad in Condor. Nothing in there with a name on it. No will. Surprise, surprise."

"How can he be homeless if he lived in a shack?" I asked.

He turned to face me, stretching his legs, his hands dangling between his knees. "Shack was made out of cardboard," he explained. "All we found in it were dead soldiers—empty bottles. Wine, beer, whisky, rum, gin—not a discriminating drinker, old Walter. Found some hairs stuck in a ratty old hairbrush. Matched Mr. X's."

Relief drained some of the residual tension from my body. Mr. X was not Savanna's Teddy. Almost at once, my muscles tensed up again. Teddy was still missing. He might not be the victim, but he could still be the murderer.

"Seems like maybe my theory about a couple bums breakin' into the buildin' and gettin' in a fight might not have been out of line," Zack said, looking as pleased with himself as Sheriff Lazarro had when the camera zoomed in on him at the successful conclusion of yet another case.

"Except that the real estate woman never did see any sign of a break-in," Bristow put in.

"And one of the bums would have to have brought a shovel along," I added.

Bristow raised his eyebrows, and I explained that Mrs. Watanabe had told me they hadn't needed a spade at the restaurant and certainly hadn't left one behind.

"The analytical philosopher scores again," he said approvingly.

"So what happens now?" I asked, pleased at the compliment.

"We wait to see if there's any report from a dental lab or dentist. Find out more about Walter. A last name, for instance."

"You're just going to wait?" I protested. "Nobody's going to investigate?"

"I told you I'd keep an eye on the case," he said mildly, getting to his feet. "Condor was happy to give me all the information they had on the missing individual—they've got enough going on. And, of course, Walter was killed and buried in our city limits. But as I explained to you earlier, I have a pretty heavy caseload. I've at least a dozen cases pending. I also have to think about operating expenses and all that boring stuff."

"Would it be the same story if you'd found out Mr. X was an eccentric bank president or mayor or Supreme Court Justice who really *was* rich?" I asked. "The shortage of staff has nothing to do with Walter not being important, not having anyone who cares enough to lean on the authorities?"

Bristow regarded me steadily for a moment, then turned to leave, shaking his head. Almost to the door, he stopped and half-turned, one hand holding the doorjamb. Without so much as glancing my way, he said, "According to the gentleman who worked at the library, the same one who said Walter smelled like an alcoholic goat, Walter used to wear a key on a chain around his neck. Said it was the key to his fortune. He also carried an old-fashioned briefcase—like the black bag doctors used to take with them on house calls. Seemed very protective of it if anyone came near. Not that many people came near. We didn't find any key or briefcase at his shack."

"Did you ask the woman about it?" I asked. "The woman who reported Walter missing?"

Bristow nodded, hesitated as if he were going to say something else, then went through the exit into the main part of the gym. I could hear his footsteps echoing all the way across the basketball court.

Zack was still leaning against the barre. "Why d'you suppose Bristow told us all that about the key and the brief-case?" I asked.

Zack frowned.

"I'll tell you what I think," I said without allowing time for his thought processes to click in. "I think he told us all that so we could look into it. He doesn't have time to investigate, but he thinks we might dig something up." I shuddered over my choice of words. "So to speak," I added lamely.

The more I thought about it, the more convinced I was that Bristow had told me, in effect, to go for it, to find out what I could.

Quite suddenly another thought occurred to me. I shot to my feet and stared at Zack.

"What?" he asked.

"Igor has to be the murderer," I exclaimed.

Zack squinted wisely at me, which meant he hadn't the foggiest idea of what had led me to that conclusion.

"Stay with me, okay?" I said. "Igor told me to find his five thousand dollars or he'd . . . dispatch me. Now Bristow says Mr. X—Walter—told people he was rich, he was going to put them in his will. So maybe Walter was talking about the money Igor says he stole from him."

"Five thousand dollars doesn't make anyone rich, Charlie."

"If you're a homeless person it might seem like a lot."

"So maybe you ought to tell Bristow about Igor?"

A chill went through me. "I probably should." I glanced over my shoulder as if I expected to see Igor lounging in the corner. I imagined him with little lizard eyes. I don't know why. The specific nature of his threat was still deeply engraved on my memory. "I'll think about it," I hedged. "In the meantime, I might consider taking a look around for the stuff Bristow talked about. There's a good chance Igor's money is in that missing briefcase."

Zack straightened up and settled his cowboy hat in place. As he looked around the room with that quizzical glance of his, I could almost hear him comparing its worn equipment to the top-notch stuff in Dandy Carr's gym where *he* worked out. "Where would we look?" he asked.

A good question. "I'll think about that, too," I said.

The phone was ringing when I let myself into the loft. I waved hello to Benny in his cage, snatched up the receiver and heard the loud breathing that had heralded the last call from Igor.

Life is so often predictable. Why should I be surprised that just when I had begun thinking I might tell Bristow about Igor and his threat, Igor would call me again?

"It hasn't been a month yet," I protested. "It's only been ten days."

"You talked to the cops," the robot voice said.

The blood in my veins mutated into ice water and made me shudder. "I did not," I squeaked.

The asthmatic breathing returned.

"It was the other way around," I said when I couldn't stand the sound any longer. "Sergeant Bristow talked to me."

In, out, in, out. The robot had to be elderly to breathe

that noisily. Who did I know who was elderly? Mr. Perry. Prinny. I kept coming back to Prinny.

"Is this Mr. Perry?" I asked.

Did the breathing sound get raspier, as if I'd worried him?

In, out.

Bristow had said the media would have the story by tomorrow, so why should I be a hero? "The sergeant told me he found out who the body was," I said cravenly. "That's all he wanted to talk to me about. I didn't tell him anything about you. I won't. Honestly. And I'm trying to find out what might have happened to your money." I wasn't going to mention anything about the briefcase, I decided. Not until I knew Igor's money was in it or until the last possible minute of my month, whichever came first.

In, out, in, out.

"His name is Walter," I babbled on. "He was a homeless man. Used to hang out at Condor Library. He didn't *have* any money."

Igor hung up.

I took the phone away from my ear and looked at it. I didn't know whether to feel relieved or frightened.

I decided on frightened.

CHAPTER 14

The directory in the lobby of The Granada listed P. Jenkins's apartment on the third floor of the four-story building. I decided to go up the stairs, rather than take the elevator. After hearing from Igor again, I was uneasy about small, enclosed spaces.

A tall, bony woman with cropped grey hair and a flattened nose opened the door when I knocked. The caregiver, I supposed.

"I'm Charlie Plato," I told her. "I'm part-owner of CHAPS across the plaza."

"Noisy," she said.

"I beg your . . . oh, yes, well, I suppose it gets a little out of hand when people leave at closing time but . . ."

"You selling tickets to sumpun?"

"No, I . . ."

"Good, 'cause I ain't innerested."

She began closing the door, and I stuck my foot in it as assertively as a door-to-door salesperson.

"I came to see my friend Prinny, Mrs. er . . ." I said.

"Garrity," she said. "Dee-Dee Garrity."

She looked less like a Dee-Dee than anyone I'd ever met. But then I suppose even someone named Tiffany will get old one day.

Blue eyes showed suspicion more clearly than any other color, I decided. Considering the color of my own eyes, I needed to remember that.

"George don't have any friends I know of," she said. "Nobody ever comes to see him."

"Well, *I'm* here," I said, getting exasperated. "Do I need a search warrant to get in?"

She glanced nervously from side to side. Maybe she'd had trouble with the police at some time. Whatever the reason, she finally opened the door and waved me into the kitchen.

Prinny was sitting by the window at a lovely antique gateleg table that gave me a moment's nostalgia for my old furniture. He had a cup of coffee in his big right hand, but he was just sitting there, nodding gently, the metal rims of his glasses glinting in the sunlight. He kept on nodding as I slid into the opposite chair.

"Hi, Prinny," I said cheerily.

"Well, hello." His voice was so intimate, it took me aback. It evidently satisfied Dee-Dee. She gave a couple of nods herself—maybe it was contagious—and disappeared into the next room.

I was surprised to see that Prinny had a good head of grey hair; I hadn't seen him without his cap before. He was actually quite a handsome man, even if he did look supercilious.

He could see CHAPS from here, I realized, looking out. Everything looked orderly over there now. Hoshizaki had done their usual neat job—apart from the orangy newness of the beauty bark, the flower-beds looked as if they'd never been disturbed.

"Did you call me a couple of hours ago?" I asked Prinny.

The coffee cup wobbled, and I hastily took it from him and set it down. He didn't protest. He didn't even seem to notice. He leaned forward in such a conspiratorial way my heart rate accelerated to Mach one. I wouldn't have been surprised to hear a sonic boom.

"Who is that woman who let you in?" he asked. "She's always bossing me around. Do you know who she is?"

"Isn't she your caregiver?" I asked, suddenly alarmed. Had I surprised a burglar?

"There's another woman comes on duty in the evening," he went on. "A younger one. Blonde hair. She gives me orders, too."

This was evidently not one of the periods of clarity his daughter P.J. had mentioned.

"You going to be here a while?" Dee-Dee asked from the doorway. "I need to scoot over to the mini-mart, get some milk."

A golden opportunity to snoop. "Sure," I said. "I'll be happy to keep an eye on my friend Prinny."

"Don't turn your back," she said. "He's faster than he looks, be outta here before you know he's on his feet."

"I'll stay alert," I promised.

"Did one of the Frenchies send you?" Prinny asked, narrow-eyed, the minute she was gone.

There was more than one? "Why don't you tell me about these Frenchies of yours?" I suggested.

That was probably a mistake. Sitting up very straight, Prinny launched into a tale that seemed destined to rival one of Scheherazade's, for length if not interest. To tell the truth, I didn't really listen for the first five minutes. I was trying to detect any note in his voice that sounded like Igor's, and when I couldn't make up my mind one way or the other—except that Igor hadn't spoken with a phony English accent—I started wondering if Prinny would notice if I got up and looked around for a briefcase and a key.

"Arthur Wellesley, first Duke of Wellington," he was saying when I tuned back in.

I blinked. And quite suddenly it all fell into place. The Duke of Wellington. Waterloo. 1815. The Napoleonic wars. Frenchy. Prinny. The phony English accent.

I've always been a compulsive reader. Mystery novels, literary novels, science fiction, romance. In my early twenties I was especially fond of Regency Romances—entertaining and mannerly tales that are set during a certain period of English History—1811–1820—after George III of England had lost America and supposedly gone mad, though not necessarily in that order. His oldest son, destined to become George IV, had been appointed Prince Regent. Nicknamed . . . you guessed it . . . Prinny.

The wall telephone next to the refrigerator rang.

Prinny went right on talking as I stood up and took the receiver off the hook.

So disoriented was I by my sudden insight into the world Mr. Perry was living in that I wouldn't have been surprised to hear Igor on the other end of the line.

But it was P.J.

"What are you doing there, Charlie?" P.J. demanded as soon as I identified myself. "What happened to Dee-Dee? Is something wrong with my dad?"

"Everything's cool," I assured her and repeated my fiction about making a neighborly visit to my friend Prinny. "I've just this minute figured it out," I said. "He thinks he's the Prince Regent of England, right?"

She sighed. "Did he tell you how he defeated Napoleon in the Battle of Waterloo?"

"More or less."

"The funny thing is, Charlie, when he first started on this kick, I looked it up. The *real* Prince Regent used to try to convince people he was at Waterloo, but he wasn't."

"Where on earth did your father come up with it all?" I asked.

"He used to be a history professor, Charlie. A very popular one. He made history come alive for hundreds of students. He was a wonderfully vivacious man, a terrific teacher, charismatic."

There was a silence. "That's so sad," I said.

"Yes, well, I sure appreciate you visiting Dad," P.J. said, which deposited all kinds of guilt on my spirit. From now on I would visit Mr. Perry regularly without any ulterior motive, I determined. I would be extraordinarily nice to P.J. I'd even talk her up to Angel.

"I heard Zack Hunter was asking around about me," P.J. said after another silence.

Uh-oh.

"Do you know why?" she asked.

"No idea at all," I said without even blinking. Well, I was hardly going to tell her it was my idea to find out her real name because I was well on the way to thinking her father might have committed murder.

"You don't suppose . . ." She broke off, then started in again. "You think there's any chance Zack might be, well, interested in me?"

"I suppose that's possible," I said. With Zack, anything was possible. And he was perfectly able to protect himself.

"Wow!" P.J. exclaimed.

She hung up before I got through explaining about Dee-Dee taking off. I decided she either didn't want to take responsibility, or she wanted time alone to speculate on Zack's interest.

When I turned around, Prinny was gone. I panicked for all of thirty seconds until I dashed into what was evidently his bedroom. He was napping in a wing back chair.

In sleep his face was wiped clear as a baby's. His glasses had slipped to the end of his nose. I gently removed them, then covered him with an afghan that had been draped across the foot of the bed. People always look vulnerable in sleep. Studying his slack face, I tried to imagine him threatening to make tentative slashes in my throat, cutting deeper and deeper until the blood spurted out.

I'd really fancied Prinny as the murderer, but right now he didn't fit the picture at all. Though Taj had said he could get teed-off from time to time and P.J. had said he could be irritable.

Just to be on the safe side, and rationalizing that Bristow had come really really close to deputizing me, I took a quick look through Prinny's drawers and closet, then whisked myself into the adjoining room. There was a small mountain of clean laundry on what must be P.J.'s bed. I would be a good neighbor and fold it for her. And figure out where the undies and tee-shirts and socks belonged.

Somehow I managed to rationalize my way into every cabinet and drawer in the apartment. I got through minutes before I heard Dee-Dee's key in the door. She'd been gone an hour, which was really taking advantage of me, but I smiled sweetly at her when she half-heartedly apologized and left before the blush I could feel coming up from my conscience made it to my face.

I hadn't found anything of interest except for a diaphragm in a cute little flowered case in P.J.'s nightstand. It was accompanied by a half-used tube of jelly, which seemed to indicate at least occasional action. Oh, there were keys around, and even a briefcase, but nothing like Bristow had described.

So much for Prinny. So much for Thursday.

Friday night, when Zack showed up, I told him Prinny didn't seem to be a possible suspect after all, then went on to tell him about Igor's second call. "Both dudes are nut cases," he said. "Not worth worryin' about."

So much for any concern for my safety. I decided not to acquaint him with the plans I was busy formulating. Nor did I warn him P.J. had heard about his interest in her and had added two and two to make half a dozen.

The entire evening, she stalked him. By closing time he had a lean and hunted look. Served him right, I thought.

The following Monday—two weeks into Igor's month—I approached Frannie Lightfoot with the phony confession that I'd overextended my credit card and needed to make a few bucks on the side. She accepted my offer to clean the living quarters over the mini-mart with so much pleasure, my guilt feelings became almost, though not quite, unbearable.

I used the same tactics at Leah Stoneham's clinic. So what if she didn't move into Adobe Plaza until after me? I was through trusting anyone.

Jorge and Maria Blanca let me clean the restaurant. Maria usually did it herself, but she felt sorry for me.

To my subconscious, I excused myself from all responsibility by laying the blame on Bristow. He had told me about the briefcase and key. For good measure I reminded myself that I hated cleaning, so I was really martyring myself in order to help out the police department track down Walter's killer.

If I'd explained all of this to my mother, she would have

looked at me the way she used to when I was a little kid
trying to wiggle my way out of trouble—the way that always made me feel ashamed and vow never to do anything
to offend her again.

On Friday, I looked Taj up again, ready to offer to clean
her and Josh's place, but out of the blue Taj invited Zack
and me to dinner and we made a date for the next Monday.
Fate was intervening, I decided. After several consecutive
nights of Mikey, she and Josh always needed adult company, Taj said. She invited Angel and Savanna too, but
they both pleaded other engagements.

Savanna I could understand—her time with Jacqueline
was precious. But I was consumed with curiosity about
what Angel was doing that couldn't be postponed. Because
of the rich vein of curiosity that lives inside me, which
Savanna had already brought to everyone's attention, I
couldn't resist asking him, "You have a date?"

I watched his sculptured cheekbones, which were not
only a pleasure to look at, but were always dead giveaways.
Sure enough, a line of red streaked across their crests.
"Gina," he muttered. I felt pleased. Adamant as I am about
remaining uninvolved myself, I find vicarious pleasure in
other people's romances and I'd liked Buttons and Bows'
young manager.

"Good," I said.

On the way to Josh and Taj's townhouse, which was at
the other end of Bellamy Park, I acquainted Zack with my
activities of the previous few days. He laughed himself silly.
If he hadn't been driving, I'd have kicked him in the shins.

"I'm worried about Igor," I admitted. "Worried being a
euphemism for scared to death. It was three weeks ago
today he called me the first time. We're into October, Zack.
Igor's probably sitting around somewhere checking off days

and telling himself that in just one week he can take out his frustrations on my larynx."

"He call you again?"

"Not since the last time I told you about. I'm not sure if that's a good sign or a bad one. He may have decided not to give me any more warnings. He'll just show up next Monday with a knife in his hand and. . . ."

"Next time, press the record button on your answerin' machine," Zack interrupted.

"Isn't that against the law?"

He sighed explosively. "You goin' to worry about bein' legal when the dude's threatenin' your life, Charlie?"

If Zack was figuring things out better than I was, my brain was obviously dead.

"You going to snoop around tonight?" he asked.

Might as well confess. "I was just about to ask if you thought you could keep Josh and Taj occupied while I took a look here and there."

He laughed again. "Then what, Charlie? You gonna clean every apartment in The Granada? Have you volunteered to clean the bank yet? They gonna let you scrub out the vault?"

"The bank's not my only problem," I said. "There must be a dozen employees, all of whom have homes they could've hidden that briefcase in. Which might or might not have Igor's money in it. The same goes for Jorge and Maria and Leah Stoneham—how do I find out where their houses are? How do I get inside them? So far I've concentrated on people who have some connection to CHAPS, no matter how tenuous, people we know something about. I haven't found a single suspicious thing. You have any ideas how I can approach the others?"

He gave me the fond look that always used to turn me on

until I saw him look at Michiko Watanabe the same way. "Igor's threats aside, why do you *care* so much, Charlie?" he asked.

"Walter was a human being," I reminded him. "He must have had a mother, a father, a childhood. He could read—at least you wouldn't think he'd sit around in the library studying newspapers if he couldn't. So he'd had some education. He wasn't always a homeless person. Even if he was, he still didn't deserve to die that way. At least we don't know that he did, so we ought to try to find out what happened."

"You want to be a do-gooder, Charlie, there're plenty more transients livin' under that bridge."

I stared at him as I absorbed the significance of that. "So there are." Elated, I gazed at him with gratitude. "What a brilliant idea." Words I never thought to hear myself say to Zack Hunter. "We can go there, talk to the people, find out what they know about Walter."

Zack groaned. "Now hold on. Don't you suppose Bristow already did that?"

"Sergeant Bristow keeps telling us how busy he is," I said irritably. "All he's doing is waiting around . . . Walter was killed *inside* CHAPS, Zack, don't you feel some sort of responsibility?"

Without warning, he pulled the pickup to the side of the road and switched off the ignition. His mouth had set in a tight line. My heartbeat made itself known. Sheriff Lazarro was about to get dangerous. "Is that supposed to be an accusation? I may have had a problem or two in the past, but that hardly makes me homicidal." He'd forgotten to drawl. Every word was clipped and precise.

I stared at him. "Of course I wasn't accusing you," I said

sharply. "I just meant that as long as Walter died on our property, we should surely be concerned about what happened to him. Why on earth would you think I was accusing you of something?"

"Guess I overreacted, darlin'. Sorry." The drawl was back, along with the tight smile.

Why had he overreacted—that was the question. And what were the problems he'd brought in out of the blue? Did they have something to do with that time period he hadn't wanted to account for?

Sometimes it seemed that everyone in the world had secrets. Certainly all three of my partners had; Angel with his discovery of a murder that he didn't want to talk about, Savanna's gay husband, Zack with his missing year or more.

It occurred to me that I had a couple of secrets myself. I'd had murderous thoughts about my stepchildren on occasion, and I'd had a slight psychological problem with eating. Okay, a fairly *severe* problem. Well, both experiences were over. There was no need to think about either one ever again. All the same, I wouldn't want anyone delving around in my psyche to find out what was in there.

Savanna's secret was a secret no longer, so I didn't have to fret about that one. Angel might feel like telling more about his secret when he knew us better, in a year or two. Zack, however, being a public person, was surely fair game.

I had my mouth open to demand answers when a voice hailed me through the pickup's open window. "My stars, Charlie, are you going to sit in that truck all night?" Taj asked.

I hadn't even realized where Zack had parked.

The condo was one of a complex of six townhouses on a quiet street. Mansard roofs, flower-filled window boxes and painted shutters gave them European flair. Zack and I stopped dead in the small entry hall. The fluffy carpeting was white. We both yanked off our boots before going up the stairs to the living room.

Taj's taste ran similar to mine—to simple elegance rather than frou-frou—furniture upholstered in muted pastels, severely tailored. The one splash of color was the painting over the fireplace that she'd told me about—the one that had fallen down in the earthquake—a lively abstract that suggested sailboats at sunset.

Josh was in the kitchen, scraping minced garlic off a cutting board into a deep wooden salad bowl. He had a butcher's apron on over his usual blazer, shirt, tie and slacks. A niche at the end of the counter held a computer. Before greeting us, Josh referred to the recipe that was on the screen.

"Welcome to our home," he said in his lugubrious manner as he measured olive oil into a teaspoon. "We know you like to eat healthy, Charlie, so we're serving grilled chicken and pasta with organic red chard and toasted walnuts."

"Sounds great," I said truthfully.

I could have sworn I heard Zack murmur, "Where's the beef?" behind me, but when I looked around he was all innocent eyebrows as he set his cowboy hat carefully on a side table, crown side down so the brim wouldn't lose its shape. When he caught my eye, his mouth pulled into his bad boy grin and I felt relieved. The brief incident in the pickup had unnerved me.

"Can I help?" I asked, but Josh shook his head and gave me his popeyed, toothy smile.

"You'll want to freshen up," Taj suggested. "Zack, why don't you use the boys' bathroom up here, and I'll take Charlie down to the girls' bathroom."

I shot Zack a meaningful glance, hoping he'd get the message that he could look around while Josh was occupied and Taj was out of the way, then I followed Taj down the thickly carpeted steps.

The master bedroom was as simply but beautifully decorated as the upstairs. "Josh absolutely insisted on doing all the cooking tonight," she said as I exercised my powers of observation under the guise of admiration. Mainly I was checking for any place big enough to hide a briefcase in. "Isn't he an absolutely precious sweetie?" she added, with music in her voice.

I wasn't sure I could truthfully agree with this characterization, so I just inclined my head as though I were considering it. "How long have you . . . known him?" I asked.

Taj had caught the hesitation. She never did miss much. Her wonderful laugh rang out. "My stars, Charlie, why don't you just come right out and ask me how long we've been sleeping together?"

I put on what I hoped looked like an innocent expression, and she laughed some more. "We've been together three years now," she said. "We're still in the lovey-dovey stage."

"I've noticed," I murmured.

Her cheeks pinked up. "Josh is really handsome, don't you think?" she asked.

I could agree on that one, with one reservation which of course I didn't express.

She caught the reservation, too. "You're bothered by his nervous tic, aren't you?" she asked. "I forget about it; I'm so used to it. He can't help it, you know; he had Bell's Palsy years ago. Took a long drive with the car window down on a cold day. At least he thinks that's what might have triggered it. It left him with partial paralysis on one side of his face. So when he smiles, that part doesn't quite move right. His speech is affected, too. He can't talk as quickly as he used to."

I have had many occasions to feel guilty in my life—but that had to be the worst. Here I'd been calling Josh weird to myself, and all the time he was suffering from a physical disability.

Taj came over and gave me a hug. "Now don't you fret so, Charlie. I declare, you are sweet to be so distressed for another human being. All heart, that's you, Charlie Plato."

I felt even worse. Luckily, Josh called "Ho-o-oneeepot," down the stairs at that moment, and Taj let me go and hared off in response.

So now, you'd think I'd feel so guilty I'd forget about snooping, wouldn't you?

Ha!

I found a key on a chain. A tarnished chain. I got all excited, then upset, seeing that it was hanging on a hook on Josh's side of the walk-in clothes closet. If it was Walter's, and Josh had it, then he had to be the murderer, and Taj was going to have a coronary if her sweetie went to jail for the rest of his natural life.

Then something familiar about the key registered, and I recalled that I had a similar key on a chain hanging in my clothes closet. It was the key to the computer in CHAPS's office. I remembered the computer in Taj and Josh's kitchen.

This was ridiculous. Even if I found a key, I wouldn't know what it was to.

Dutifully going into the bathroom, I washed and rinsed my hands and ran them wet over my hair to calm it down. The vanity was loaded with enough cosmetics to make up the entire cast of *Grease*. I toyed with the idea of trying one or two things, but restrained myself.

When I came out, I headed straight for the closet again and this time noticed a briefcase propped against some other stuff. It didn't look anything like the black doctor's bag Bristow had talked about. It was a smart burgundy leather attaché that had been very well cared for during its obviously short life. It occurred to me that the librarian might have been mistaken about what Walter's looked like.

The briefcase wasn't locked. Inside it was a gold case filled with Josh's automobile showroom business cards, a newspaper with the crossword puzzle half completed, in ink, which always impresses me, several ballpoints and one Mont Blanc fountain pen, which I happened to know cost a lot of bucks. There was also a week-at-a-glance diary with the sort of cryptic notations most people use to indicate appointments. Tucked away behind the briefcase was a box containing several toys—belonging to Mikey no doubt: a model truck, a box of blocks, a bright purple, yellow and turquoise ray gun with a lightning flash on the barrel.

Really incriminating stuff.

I was rapidly running out of suspects. Prinny was pretty well crossed off. Josh wasn't as weird as I'd thought. I hadn't ruled out Bernie, though. And there was still Teddy. Maybe Teddy had left something incriminating around the house, and Savanna had transferred it to her apartment when she downsized. Maybe I could offer to babysit Jacqueline one evening and . . .

The thought of rooting around Savanna's home made me feel squirmy.

I carefully returned the briefcase to its proper place. As I was backing out of the closet, I heard a sound behind me and whirled to see Josh standing there. "My goodness, you almost gave me a heart attack," I said and laughed nervously, hoping he wouldn't ask me what I was doing.

He didn't, but he did glance at the closet, then at me. "Dinner's ready, Charlie," he said in a subdued voice.

To my relief, he didn't say anything to Taj about me snooping in their closet. I tried to think of some excuse, so I could bring it up myself and make it seem unimportant, but nothing came to me.

The meal was delicious.

"How are you getting along with Mikey?" I asked at one point.

Taj smiled in her serene way. "He's a great little kid. Mischievous, though. Takes all our energy to keep up with him."

"You like kids, too?" I asked Josh.

He nodded, his face doing its peculiar thing. Now that I'd been alerted, I could see the physical problem for what it was. It gave me pause. I'd been thinking that I was meeting more and more weird people lately. Then I'd found out about Mr. Perry's mental condition and Josh's palsy. Not to mention Taj's unhappy childhood. Probably there was an explanation for all apparent weirdness. Maybe in the future I ought to keep a civil tongue in my subconscious until I learned what the problem was.

There I went again, promising to be a better person.

"Didn't I tell you?" Taj said. "Josh is Mikey's father. He and his wife divorced soon after Mikey was born. Unfortunately, Josh hasn't managed to get complete custody of him yet."

So there was another lesson in humility for Charlie Plato. If Josh was Mikey's father, then he had been married to the woman who was working hard at drug counseling. Being a good-hearted angel, Taj was helping out. And I'd suspected Josh of loving her for her settlement from the bank.

"This is a great wine," I said lamely.

I helped Taj clear the dishes while Zack and Josh talked about cars. Evidently, Zack was thinking of trading in his pickup for an automobile. And I'd thought the pickup was part of Sheriff Lazarro's Western image.

"Josh is going to think I'm a terrible snoop," I told Taj as she washed and I stacked things in the dishwasher. "I looked in your bathroom for sanitary napkins—I forgot to bring any with me. I didn't see any there, so I looked in your closet. I should have yelled up to you, I guess, but I was a little embarrassed to say anything in front of the guys. So then Josh caught me coming out of your closet. I'm embarrassed after all."

"Don't be silly, Charlie," Taj said easily. "Josh and I both believe in the old saying that our home is your home." She smiled. "Follow me."

We went down to her bedroom. She kept Kotex in her nightstand. I remembered seeing the package. That must have been what had triggered my excuse.

"Did you look?" I asked Zack when we were back in the pickup.

"Yup," he said. "I wasn't goin' to, but there's somethin' about Josh seems mighty peculiar to me."

"Because he wears an apron when he cooks?"

That crack got me a look.

I explained Josh's medical problem. Zack nodded a couple of times, but didn't get a guilty expression. It seems to me men don't automatically feel guilty the way most women do. I think guilt is programmed into our genes before birth.

After a few minutes of silence, Zack glanced at me sideways. "Guess you don't want to know what I found, huh?"

I almost rose out of my seat in my excitement. "You found something?"

He nodded. "Tucked in the circuit-breaker box in the utility room. Next to the boys' bathroom."

"In the circuit-breaker box?"

"Used to stash *Playboy* in there myself when I was roarin' through puberty."

"That's all you found? A magazine?" My bubble of excitement popped.

"This one was randier than *Playboy* ever dreamed of bein', darlin'. The pictures were 'bout as explicit as any I'd ever hope to see."

"Naked ladies?"

"Not that innocent. This was S & M stuff, darlin'. Pretty near singed my eyelashes."

"Josh likes pornography?" Was this a clue?

"It would appear so." Zack shook his head as he pulled up in CHAPS's parking lot. "Havin' a taste for pornography doesn't make a man a murderer, Charlie."

I didn't reply. I was disgusted. I'm totally against censorship, but in spite of what anybody says about such stuff being harmless, I think it pollutes the mind of the beholder, and I wouldn't want anything to do with someone who indulged their prurient natures that way. If I'd known about this going in to Taj and Josh's house, I probably wouldn't even have eaten the food Josh had prepared.

"You goin' to invite me in for a nightcap or somethin'?"

Zack asked, with his wicked grin fully evident, eyebrows sexily puckish.

Twinges of interest gathered at the ready in a certain area of my lower parts. "I am not," I said firmly.

CHAPTER 15

Nursing homes everywhere seem to smell of antiseptic, urine and despair. In spite of its name, the Care and Comfort Residential Facility Zack and I visited shortly after noon on October third was no exception.

Wheelchairs half-filled a large multi-purpose room to the left of the entrance. A television set was blaring so loudly it was impossible to tell what the show was. Not that anybody seemed to be watching either the set or us.

A young woman in a white polyester pantsuit gave us friendly but voluble directions flavored with a Mexican accent, and we set off down a long, long corridor that also featured several wheelchairs, their occupants mostly somnolent. Either the residents were all on tranquilizers, or lunch was overdue and their blood sugar was running on empty.

Halfway along the hall a wiry-haired little woman in a cotton print dress, white cardigan and black lace-up shoes was determinedly sawing a table knife back and forth across the rolled piece of sheeting that held her in her wheelchair. As we walked by she looked up at Zack, gave him a sudden toothless grin and exclaimed, "Hey! It's Sheriff Lazarro!"

Ever willing to visit with a fan, Zack squatted to talk to her while I continued down the hall. A small room near the other end, the aide had said. One bed, one occupant. Olivia Emmett on the door's nameplate.

I'd wanted to go talk to the homeless people under the Condor railroad bridge, but Zack had reminded me of the volunteer librarian Bristow had mentioned, whom he considered a more salubrious lead. "You won't have to rappel down to the library," he'd added. Arriving at the library shortly after it opened, we'd discovered that Olivia Emmett had suffered a mild stroke six weeks earlier and had been taken to St. Joseph's Hospital. An impressionable hospital clerk had swooned over Zack and sent us here.

Just as I found the right nameplate and looked into the room to see a grey-haired woman asleep in the bed next to the window, I heard Zack yell "Whoa!" and turned to see him gazing back the way we had come. The little wiry-haired woman was scooting toward the front door at a surprisingly fast clip. Reaching it, she pushed it open and darted out into the sunlight. In Zack's right hand was the piece of sheet she'd been sawing away on.

Before I could react, Zack dropped the cloth in the abandoned wheelchair and hurried toward me. "You turned her loose?" I asked incredulously.

"Old lady begged me to," he said, sounding agitated. "Should I go after her? I can't believe she lied to me. Sweetest old lady. Said her name was Rina, and she never missed an episode of *Prescott's Landin'*. Said she had to go to the john real fast, and nobody would come see to her."

The sound of a raised male voice echoed along the corridor, followed by a female shriek. A second later two attendants barreled out of the multi-purpose room, glanced our way, then headed outside, presumably in hot pursuit of the runaway.

"Dang!" Zack exclaimed. "Who'd believe a little old lady could move so *fast*."

Catching a slight movement out of the corner of my eye, I touched his arm and shushed him. "Those two attendants will catch up with your friend Rina," I said quietly, then indicated the woman in the room. She had raised herself up on her elbows. "Miss Emmett?" I asked.

"I'm Olivia Emmett." Her voice was weak, but it had a refined sound. "Would you mind putting that extra pillow behind me?" she asked as I walked toward her.

"I'm Charlie Plato," I told her as I obliged. "This is Zack Hunter."

No hint of recognition as she settled herself comfortably. Not a television watcher, evidently.

"I heard somebody shouting," she said, looking at me with fearful grey eyes. She had a soft-skinned, pleasantly wrinkled face. I judged her to be seventy-five or so. She was almost as pale as the white pillows she was resting against, and she was obviously thin—her body scarcely raised the covers.

"One of the residents opened the front door and took off," I explained.

"We're not supposed to do that," she said. "People sometimes wander off and get lost."

Zack nervously resettled his cowboy hat, then hunched his shoulders.

"Do I know you, dear?" Miss Emmett asked apologetically. "I don't always remember . . . but it's nice of you to come and see me. I don't have family. I never did marry, and I was an only child. One or two of the people from the library have popped in, and my minister, but . . ." She chewed on her lips as though they were dry, and I poured some water from a jug on her night table into a glass and held it for her.

"So kind," she murmured.

"We haven't met," I told her. "Zack and I are co-owners of CHAPS in Bellamy Park."

A puzzled frown appeared between her wispy eyebrows.

"CHAPS is the country-and-western tavern where Walter's body was found," I explained.

"Oh dear." It hardly seemed possible for her to get any paler, but she did.

Zack brought a couple of chairs over from the other side of the room, positioned one for me then turned the other one around and straddled it. I've never understood why men so often sit like that—it looks very uncomfortable.

I sat down in the normal way and took hold of Olivia's thin, waxy-looking hand. "I understand you were very kind to Walter. A nice man at the library—Arthur Pelsner—told us you always talked to Walter and made sure he wasn't hungry and that he had a place to sleep."

"He said he had a shack, but it evidently offered little protection from the elements," she said. "When the weather turned cold or it rained a lot, he would go to a shelter. He seemed to take fairly good care of himself, except that he *would* drink." Her mouth pursed ever so slightly. "He also smelled really bad," she added with emphasis.

"Art told us that," Zack said.

"Excuse me," a male voice said from the doorway. "I'd like a word with you, sir, if you don't mind."

"The manager," Miss Emmett whispered. The man was wearing a suit. He was short, middle-aged, prosperous-looking, healthily pink-faced, but not, at the moment, completely content with his lot. Arms folded across his barrel chest, he gazed sternly at Zack.

Zack made sure his cowboy hat was at its proper angle and squinted back. For a moment the two men squared off like a couple of rams getting ready to clash horns, then Zack sighed and stood up. He was much, much taller than the suit.

"We don't appreciate people coming in and causing problems for our staff," the suit said, craning his neck.

"I don't appreciate people tyin' nice old ladies into wheelchairs," Zack said.

"It's not for you to dictate policy . . ."

"When my grandmother's a patient here, I've a right to fret about how you treat people," Zack said.

"*Miss* Emmett is your grandmother?" the suit asked, all eyebrows and pursed lips.

"He was adopted," Miss Emmett said with a lilt in her voice.

The suit sniffed.

"I may have to report your *policy* to the media," Zack said.

It was at that precise moment that the suit recognized Zack. His eyes became as round as his mouth, and he backpedaled rapidly into the hall. "Just see it doesn't happen again," he said lamely and bustled away.

"Mr. Parmentier's not really a bad person," Miss Emmett said with a twinkle in her eye. "He's just inclined to be a pompous ass."

"Thanks for adoptin' me," Zack said. Sitting down again, he smiled at her with that same fond look he'd formerly bestowed on Michiko Watanabe and me.

Miss Emmett twinkled at him. I thought she'd probably recognized him belatedly, too. "It was that or lose my reputation," she pointed out.

While Zack was puzzling that out, I brought her back to the subject at hand. "Do you know Walter's last name?" I asked.

She closed her eyes as if to think, but I had already caught the shuttered look that had come into them. When she opened them again, the guarded expression was still in place. "I have such a time remembering things lately," she said. "I think the stroke must have destroyed some of the little grey cells Hercule Poirot used to talk about."

"Charlie knows that Poirot dude," Zack said.

Miss Emmett looked somewhat puzzled. I sympathized with her.

"Zack and I are trying to find out who killed Walter, and why," I said. "The police have inquiries going, but it seems to be taking too long to get any answers. If you know anything at all, I wish you'd tell me. You can trust both of us."

She studied my face for a long moment, and I concentrated on appearing trustworthy and honest. "Did you know Walter?" she asked.

I shook my head. "I had never seen him before I found his body in our flower-bed after the earthquake."

Her eyebrows raised. "That was you on the news? Why did they cut the sound out as soon as you started talking?"

"I was cussing Zack for not letting me know the police had come to dig up the skel—the body," I explained. "I didn't notice the camera and mike until it was too late."

"But if you didn't know Walter, why are you trying to solve his murder?"

"Good question," Zack murmured.

I decided on the spot not to mention Igor and his threats to my health. Miss Emmett was already nervous. I didn't want to make matters worse. "It just seems to me that someone ought to care," I said. "Just because Walter was old and poor and homeless doesn't give someone the right to strike him dead and bury him. If it hadn't been for the earthquake, his body might never have been discovered. Whoever killed him should have to stand trial. That's the way justice works in this country."

Her face had softened as I spoke. "I know just what you mean, Charlie," she said softly. "May I call you Charlie?"

I nodded.

"I thought I was the only person in the world who cared about what happened to Walter," she went on. "I don't think anyone else even knew . . ." She broke off.

I waited.

Zack started to say something, and I made a quick backwards gesture with my free hand while continuing to hold on to Miss Emmett's.

"Nobody else knew who he really was," she whispered.

"But you did," I said, trying not to show my elation.

She nodded.

"Please tell me," I said. "Until we know who he is, we don't have much hope of finding out why he might have been at CHAPS or who might have had some reason to kill him."

She closed her eyes.

"We won't tell anyone," Zack said, leaning forward.

I scowled at him. "We can't make a promise like that," I said indignantly. "Whatever we find out, we're duty bound to pass on to Sergeant Bristow."

I looked back at Miss Emmett to find her gazing at me

quite kindly. "I think you are a very honest person, Charlie Plato," she said.

"Well . . ." I hesitated. "I try to be."

She let out a breath on a long sigh. "It's weighed on me that I should have told that nice police sergeant more about Walter when he came to see me," she said. "I haven't been able to sleep properly since. I worried so much I was afraid I'd have another stroke. I guessed, you see, when I saw on television about the body that had been dug up, I guessed it was Walter. I knew he was familiar with that area; he'd told me he had sung there once or twice. So when I heard all that about him being buried and that he wasn't much more than a skeleton, it upset me and I had the stroke."

"Walter couldn't have sung at CHAPS," Zack protested. "We haven't been open long—just since March—and he was probably already . . . well, already dead before we ever opened."

"Oh, I didn't mean he sang at *CHAPS*, dear," Miss Emmett said apologetically. "It was way back in the fifties when Walter sang there, in the same building, when it was called Banbury's. It was a dance hall. Some of the big bands used to play there. It was very popular, Walter said."

I gave her another drink of water, and she nodded her thanks. "I think the sergeant knew I was keeping information back," she continued. "I thought I was justified because when I reported Walter missing to the Condor Police Department—about a month after I first noticed he wasn't coming around—nobody seemed all that interested. Homeless people often move about, they said. Homeless people don't have roots—they come and go when they feel like it, or when they think the panhandling might be better elsewhere. But Walter *always* came to the library at a certain time on certain days. Never missed in—oh, five years to my knowledge. Sat in the same chair, read the same newspapers, left at the same time. When I reported Walter missing, I didn't tell the police who Walter really was—that was his secret to tell or not as he deemed fit. I didn't know of course that someone was going to kill him, might even have killed him already. I did tell them that Walter was dependable and punctual, but they weren't impressed. I also told them he'd had a very bad cold when I last saw him, and they said they'd check the local doctors and hospitals. I don't think they did. I called around, and nobody could tell me anything about a homeless man named Walter, but when I asked, they did tell me nobody else had questioned them about such a man."

Her forehead knitted into a hundred fine lines. "You might say I got my dander up," she said. "Why should I make Sergeant Bristow's job easier when his colleagues hadn't bothered to follow up on my report?"

She paused, looking directly into my eyes. "His name was Walt Cochran," she said with the air of someone making a significant announcement.

The name sounded a faint chord in my memory, but I couldn't place it. It brought a long, low whistle from Zack, however. "The singer?" he asked. "The dude everyone said sounded like liquid moonlight? Sang in the fifties, you said?" He scooted his chair closer to Miss Emmett's bed. "I thought he was dead. There was a retrospective on TV couple years back. A & E, I think. Everybody *acted* like he was dead."

"He is dead," I pointed out.

"I mean years ago," Zack explained. He shook his head. "Walt Cochran. My great-aunt Sophie played his records all the time when I was growin' up. It wasn't my kinda music, but I could appreciate the way his voice sounded. She told me when he was in his prime, women used to weep, hearing him sing. Some of them would literally pass out. Like teenagers swooned over Frank Sinatra and yelled, 'Frankie, Frankie!' Grown women fainted in the aisles when Walt Cochran hit the low notes. They were crazy over him. And he was crazy over them."

He gave a knowing kind of nod, as if to say he certainly knew how that was. "Old Walt had four or five wives. They all divorced him. Some kind of legendary womanizer, old Walt. Had a cult following like Elvis. Someone built a museum somewhere with contributions by his fans—filled it with memorabilia."

Miss Emmett's eyes were glistening. "His voice used to make *me* cry," she said. "Not that his songs were all sad; it was just the sound itself—so perfectly beautiful—pure gold."

"Walt Cochran," Zack repeated with an air of disbelief. "On the retrospective they said he started slippin' in popularity when Elvis came along. He must have been—what?— around my age by then."

He looked thoughtful for a minute, as though contemplating the idea of slipping, then shook his head and went on. "Then there were the Stones and the Beatles—the whole face of music changed."

"I've read the bios," Miss Emmett said. "Walter started drinking heavily in the sixties. Gambled, too."

"Didn't he go missin' in Las Vegas?" Zack tipped his cowboy hat forward and rubbed the back of his head. "Seems to me there were rumors about mob connections. I think he disappeared in the late seventies. 'Bout the time I was gettin' started in TV—those idiot teenagers space operas. Old-timers were talkin' 'bout Walter Cochran disappearin' all of a sudden, like 'Watch out, sonny, this can happen to you if you drink and gamble and get on the outs with the Mafia.' Old-timers all reckoned he'd died with his boots on. Concrete boots."

He shook his head. "And all the time he was alive."

"There were sightings, just like with Elvis Presley," Miss Emmett said.

"Yeah, 'cept Elvis really was dead." Zack frowned. "Didn't some newspaper publish a photo of Walt lookin' all wrinkly, around four-five years ago? Said he really was alive, and here was the proof. Turned out it was a computer-enhanced picture."

I've already admitted to being a regular reader of the tabloids. Parts of this story were starting to sound familiar. Celebrities who disappear or die while they are still reasonably popular seem to live on in American folklore, as if we can't bear to let them go. I thought I might have seen that picture myself. And the retrospective. A male voice like honey had begun to croon in my subconscious.

"You recognized him?" I asked Miss Emmett. Somehow I couldn't think of her as Olivia. Even lying on her back in a hospital bed, she had an air of dignity.

She rolled her head from side to side. "There was very little resemblance left. His hair was usually uncombed and dirty, and he had a raggedy beard. But once in a while when we'd talk, I'd think there was something familiar about him. One day I told him so, and he fumbled around in the bag he always carried and gave me this old newspaper clipping that told who he was. I was astonished. He swore me to secrecy."

"Did he tell you why he'd disappeared?" I asked.

Miss Emmett's grey eyes filled with moisture again. "He said he couldn't remember. He thought it had something to do with a fight over gambling debts, but he wasn't sure. He said someday he was going to make a comeback." She smiled tearfully. "He said that often, and I always agreed it would be a good thing to do, but to tell you the truth, my dear, I don't see how it would have been possible, the shape he was in."

"Arthur Pelsner told Sergeant Bristow about an old style briefcase Walter always carried around with him," I said. "Is that the bag you mentioned? Supposedly, he also had a key on a chain around his neck."

Miss Emmett closed her eyes again. I tapped Zack on the knee to get his attention.

He nodded. "I heard." He leaned forward to speak to Miss Emmett. "It was the kind of bag doctors used to tote with them when they did house calls, Bristow said."

"Black," Miss Emmett responded without opening her eyes.

Zack and I exchanged a glance, then stared at her.

After a few tense moments, she looked back at us.

"Do you have any idea what happened to that old bag of Walt's?" I asked.

"He gave it to me."

So. Maybe I wouldn't have to clean any more houses. "Do you have the bag here?" I asked, trying to sound casual.

She sighed. "I don't know where it is, Charlie, and that's the truth." Her eyes met mine, looking strained, obviously begging me to believe her. "Walt left that valise with me for safekeeping," she said. "The key went to the bag—I saw him open it many times—it was an obsession of his, to keep looking at whatever was inside."

"Did he give you the key?" Zack asked.

She glanced at him in a wistful way. "No, he didn't. Just the valise. I know you'll say I should have handed it over to the Condor police when I reported Walt missing, but I wasn't sure what they'd do with it, and I thought Walt might come back and want it, so I kept it. Then when I saw the report on TV and decided it was probably Walt they'd dug up, I'm ashamed to say I thought there might be money in the bag, and I thought I had as much right as anyone else to the money, because Walt had told me he was going to put me in his will. I thought I might just break open that bag and see for myself what was in it before handing it over. There might even be a copy of his will in there, I thought. But then I had the stroke, and the next thing I knew I was in here."

"When did Walt give the bag to you?" I asked. "And why? Did he say why?"

She nodded. "As I said, he had a very bad cold. He said he was worried about the cough, that he might be coming down with pneumonia. If he had to go into the hospital, he might lose track of his bag. Authorities didn't always take good care of homeless people's meager possessions, he said. So he wanted me to hold on to it for a while, just in case."

She closed her eyes again. She was obviously quite weak. Her eyelids had a translucent appearance. "It was right after Thanksgiving," she said at last. She opened her eyes. "I remember the library janitor taking down the pilgrim and turkey cutouts while Walt and I were talking. That was the last time I saw him."

"Last Thanksgiving?" I asked, and she nodded again.

"Do you think Walt really did have money?" I asked.

"I think it's possible, dear. He was not a well man, and his mind had certainly been affected by the liquor he'd consumed, and his lack of hygiene was appalling. But he usually made sense when he talked. He said he had made some investments that had done real well, and when he was gone the library would benefit. So would Bellamy Park Hospital where he'd been treated a couple of times, and a shelter he often stayed at, as well as a few people who worked at those places."

Was Igor one of those people? I wondered. Had Igor expected Walt Cochran to have his bag with him when he met him at CHAPS? Had he struck him down in anger when he turned up empty-handed? Was Igor's five thousand dollars in that black bag?

"You still had the bag when you had the stroke?" I asked.

She nodded as well as she could.

"Could it be at your house?"

"Apartment," she corrected, then turned her head from one side to the other. "I asked one of the aides who works here, a lovely young Vietnamese woman, to fetch me some clothes and toiletries a few weeks ago. At that time I asked her specifically to look for the black bag. But she couldn't find it anywhere."

"Maybe you hid it," Zack said.

She sighed. "I don't remember. I really don't remember." She was getting agitated, and I took hold of her hand again. Her skin felt dry and overly warm.

She smiled wanly at me. "This stroke was a funny thing. I haven't sustained any physical damage, they tell me, no paralysis at all. But for several days after I couldn't remember who I was, or anything about my life, not even my name. Now I remember most of that, but I don't remember having the stroke, or the period immediately following it."

Her eyes closed again. "I'm sorry, my dears. I'm feeling quite tired. I'm not sure I can. . . ." Her voice trailed away.

"May we come back another time?" I asked.

She said something very softly that I couldn't make out, but I decided to take it as permission to return.

"You could call me at CHAPS if you remember anything," I murmured.

She didn't respond, but her eyelashes flickered, so I left my business card on her nightstand.

On the way down the corridor, Zack poked his head around the door where his friend Rina had formerly been parked in her wheelchair. I stopped to look in, too. She was in bed, eyes closed, mouth open, snoring loudly, obviously worn out by her escapade.

Zack let out a relieved sigh.

"You like old ladies, don't you?" I asked as we walked across the parking lot.

He shot me a sideways glance to check if I were making fun of him, but I wasn't. "It's one of your nicer traits," I told him.

"I had an elderly great-aunt who took care of me when . . ." He broke off. "Yeah, I like old ladies. Seems to me they're often tougher than old men. As if all the carin' they do for other people through their lives makes them able to handle anythin' comes along."

I felt a sudden wave of warmth toward him that had, for once, nothing to do with hormones.

"My aunt was the one got me started actin'," he went on

in a musing tone. "She thought it might help . . ." He broke off, his mouth clamping shut, eyes turning hard.

Secrets.

I didn't push.

CHAPTER 16

We called Bristow from a phone booth on San Pablo Avenue, Bellamy Park's main drag, a wide thoroughfare lined with trees and wooden planters and brick sidewalks. He said he'd been trying to get in touch with us for the last couple of hours, and we arranged to meet in the espresso bar on the top floor of Lenny's Market.

I looked around shifty-eyed as Zack and I rode the escalator, hoping Igor didn't happen to be replenishing his larder. I'd almost forgotten what it was like to go somewhere without worrying about Igor watching.

"What's up?" I demanded as soon as we were all settled with froth-topped mugs of cappuccino and a basket of the rolls Lenny's bakery was justifiably famous for.

Bristow took time to slather butter—real butter—on his roll. Zack was doing the same thing. I thought of telling them it would stack up inside their arteries until their blood couldn't get through, but I've found people don't necessarily appreciate lectures about food and its effect on their health. Muttering to myself, I chomped down on dry bread.

"I tracked down Teddy Seabrook," Bristow said.

Ever since we'd called Bristow, I'd been worried that he had also come up with Walt's identity and we weren't going to be able to crow. I was really looking forward to letting him know a couple of amateur snoops had beat him to the draw.

Relieved that he hadn't mentioned Walt, I let a couple of seconds zip by before I actually took in what he'd said. "Teddy!" I squeaked.

He looked smug. Just wait, I thought.

"Teddy's alive and well and living in Palm Springs," he announced.

"With whom?" Zack asked with a cynical grin.

"Funny you should ask that," Bristow said. "Seems our Teddy now owns his own restaurant and shares living quarters with his sous-chef, who is of the male persuasion."

"Teddy came out of the closet," I said.

"He did indeed."

"Did you tell Savanna?" I asked.

He nodded, with a slightly reminiscent smile. I would ask Savanna about the reason for that smile, I decided. "So is there any possibility Teddy killed Mr. X—Walter—before heading south . . . and east?" I asked.

"Says not. He's making a statement to Palm Springs P.D. even as we speak. I certainly don't have anything to tie him to the scene."

He reached for another roll, opened up a pat of butter, then showed me his lovely even teeth. "So what did you find out from Olivia?" he asked.

Zack and I both stared at him, me with an open mouth.

Zack recovered first. "Mr. Parmentier told you we went to see her?" he asked.

Bristow nodded.

I gazed at Zack, stunned by the speed and intelligence with which he'd reached this conclusion. "Why would he do that?" I asked.

"Did he report me for settin' one of his old ladies free?" Zack asked.

"He did indeed. But that wasn't the main reason he called." Bristow wiped his knife carefully on his roll, letting the suspense build. "I *asked* him to call me if anyone came to see Olivia," he said. "I had no idea at that time that you were Olivia's grandson."

Zack's bad-boy smile had a little rue around its edges. "I told Parmentier that to rile him."

"Seems you succeeded." Bristow glanced at me and grinned widely. Evidently my irritation was showing.

"You *knew* Miss Emmett was in the nursing home," I said accusingly.

He nodded.

For a minute or two, I practiced breathing evenly so I wouldn't kick the sergeant on the shins and get arrested for assaulting an officer. "Would you mind informing me why you didn't *tell* us Olivia was in a nursing home?" I asked with commendable patience.

Bristow grinned. "I thought you'd enjoy using your deductive powers to track the old lady down." He lifted an eyebrow. "Didn't see why I should make it too easy for you, Charlie."

"Likewise, I'm sure," I said sweetly, and pointedly.

"You aren't going to tell me what you found out?"

I smiled.

"Walter was Walt Cochran," Zack said. Either he hadn't been following the conversation, or he wasn't going to allow me to enjoy a few minutes of one-upmanship at the expense of his good buddy.

Bristow's eyebrows climbed.

"The singer," I said.

" 'Such Sweet Magic'?" Bristow asked. " 'Love Me To-morrow'? 'The Other Woman'? 'Lazy Days and Busy Nights'?"

Now that I'd heard them, the titles of Walt's songs seemed familiar to me, too. I used to listen to Seattle's "old-ies but goodies" station when I was driving to and from Rob's clinic; "easy listening" is soothing when you're stuck in traffic. Once again, I could hear that honey-mellow voice crooning. Overlaying that memory was an image of Walt as I'd last glimpsed him, his bones encrusted with soil. I shud-dered.

Zack and Bristow were discussing Walt's disappearance. It occurred to me that we were still no closer to discovering who had stilled that wonderful voice.

"Why did you want to know who visited Miss Em-mett?" I asked.

"The guy at the library told me about the briefcase and key Walter carried with him at all times," Bristow said. "I asked Miss Emmett about the items, and she denied ever seeing them. I was pretty sure she was lying. Stands to rea-son if Arthur Pelsner saw them, she did, too. So after she had the stroke and went into the home, I asked Mr. Par-mentier to let me know if anyone stopped in or showed inter-est. Just in case."

He smiled rather smugly again, then stood up and went to get another round of cappuccino.

I looked quickly at Zack. He was frowning, as if he hadn't quite kept up. "Let's not say anything about that briefcase," I murmured.

"Why not?" he asked. "Isn't that aidin' and abettin' or somethin'?"

"Maybe so, but do we want Bristow badgering poor

Miss Emmett? Don't you think she deserves a little rest and recuperation? I believed her when she said she didn't know where the briefcase got to."

Zack nodded. "Me too."

"Okay then, it won't do Bristow any good if we do tell him. Why don't we wait and see if Miss Emmett remembers? Then we can report in."

Zack mulled, then nodded slowly. "Okay," he said, just as Bristow returned.

"Okay what?" Bristow asked.

"I just agreed with Charlie that she can do anythin' she wants with me next time we're alone," Zack drawled.

This time I didn't hesitate. Surely I wouldn't get arrested for kicking *his* shins. He was still laughing and rubbing his leg when it occurred to me that Bristow hadn't seemed unduly excited by our news about the identity of Mr. X, aka Walt Cochran.

Narrow-eyed, I studied the sergeant's face for several minutes as he blew lightly into his cup. Bristow's expression had gone beyond smug, beyond complacent, beyond cat-who-swallowed-the-canary.

My stomach descended to its basement. "You already knew the body was Walt Cochran," I said flatly.

His smile was tight and unbearably self-satisfied. "Bellamy Park P.D. always gets its man," he said.

I scowled at him. "How did you know?"

His grin turned as sunny as a spring morning. "Good old reliable dental records. Seems Walt was treated by a dentist in Las Vegas after some individual pistol-whipped him in the mouth during a nightclub brawl."

My own teeth flinched.

"According to the doc, most of Walt's teeth had already

been capped. Before caps are put on, the teeth are filed down. The damage was so extensive, the dentist had to remove everything and order in some falsies."

"When did you find all this out?" I asked.

"Fax came in this a.m."

"You *were* going to tell us?"

His eyes met mine, shining brilliantly with truth, justice and wicked amusement. "Absolutely."

He stood up. "Gotta go." He began to turn away, then swung back. He was still smiling, but the nature of the smile had changed from smugly self-satisfied to pleasantly friendly. "You guys did good, getting Olivia to talk. She ever mentions that briefcase, give me a call."

I nodded, hoping the heat I was feeling wasn't showing on the outside.

"What happens now?" Zack asked.

Bristow shrugged. "We do some more canvassing, asking about Walt Cochran this time."

I groaned. "The media's going to go crazy with this."

He nodded. "When and if they find out. I'm not telling. I'd strongly advise you to do likewise."

"It'll get out," I said.

He leaned down to me. "Foul whisperings are abroad: unnatural deeds," he murmured with suitable accompanying drama.

"Shakespeare?" Zack queried as Bristow strode off.

"The bard himself," I said. "*Macbeth*, I think. Bristow seems to like *Macbeth*."

I spent the next twenty-four hours, at work and at home, wondering what more I could do to track down Walt Cochran's murderer.

"You okay, Charlie?" Savanna asked me Wednesday evening. I was in the office, trying to balance the accounts for September. I was only missing a couple of dollars, and Angel and Savanna had each told me to give the bank the benefit of the doubt, but when I keep books I want them perfect. Also, I'm stubborn.

I glanced up and smiled at the picture Savanna made in her fringed red shirt, her blue-black hair tumbling past her shoulders. "You look so tense, sitting all hunched up like that," she offered in explanation.

My legs were wound around each other like pretzels. I straightened them out, saved my files on the computer and leaned back. "I get involved," I said.

"So I hear."

Now there was an interesting remark.

She sat herself on the edge of my desk, looking quite pleased with herself. "Explain yourself," I ordered.

"I heard you went on detecting after our neighborhood get-together."

"And what little bird passed that news on?" I asked.

She fluttered her eyelashes exaggeratedly.

"Let me guess. Would he be hirsutely challenged?"

"You catch on quick, girlfriend."

I laughed. "Did you meet him for a date, or an interview?"

She looked thoughtful. "All of the above. It was sort of in-between. He stopped in at my place Monday night to tell me he'd traced Teddy. He thought I might want to go after him for child support. I told him no, and we got to talking, and I found out he hadn't eaten yet, so I made a veggie frittata and we talked some more. That's about it."

"Anyone who eats your veggie frittata has to fall madly in love," I said.

She laughed. "Don't rush it, Charlie." She looked down, then up. "He's a nice guy. Jacqueline liked him."

"*Did* she?" I waited expectantly.

"Okay, Charlie," she admitted. "I like him, too."

I didn't feel like doing any more calculating after she left, so I wandered out into the main corral even though it wasn't yet time to start line dancing lessons.

One of my favorite things to do at CHAPS is to watch the guys dance. Okay, so the women do a good job, but men are not always the epitome of grace on the dance floor, right? Except when they're dancing country-style. "Smooth" doesn't begin to describe the way they move.

Most of them don't drink much—line dancing gets intricate—so there's no stumbling around or acting silly. One problem this causes when you own a tavern is that you have to devise ways to make a profit. The four of us had discussed having a cover charge, but were afraid it would put people off, so instead we charged $5 for a beer and $1.50 for a glass of water. Dancers drink a lot of water.

When I turned away at the end of the dance, I paused to regard an unexpected sight—P.J. sharing a meal with Taj, heads down, talking intensely. Taj had given me the impression she barely knew P.J. This was something to be looked into, obviously.

While I was still devising a method of approach, Taj looked up and waved me over to their booth.

"What's this? No ever-faithful, always attentive Josh?" I asked as I slid in next to P.J.—there was a lot more room on her side. "Has the sky fallen?"

Taj smiled as serenely as ever, then took a bite from her hamburger and chewed it thoroughly, swallowing before she answered. The woman's food choices were dreadful. The only time she ate healthy was when I ate with her.

"We had a fight," she said.

I sighed. "Someday I will learn not to make wisecracks until I've checked the area for hidden mines."

"No you won't, Charlie. And you shouldn't. Your quick wit is part of your charm."

"Hmm." I gave her a sympathetic smile. "Was it a 'never darken my doorstep again' fight, or a tiff?"

"More of a tiff," she said. "I'm worried about something he might have . . ." She broke off and sighed. "I'm sure we'll make up real soon. We always do. And the fight isn't the main reason Josh isn't here. His automobile company is having an open house—it's a big push to sell Lincolns."

"I wish him luck," I said. "I don't expect to ever be in that market myself."

She smiled. "How was your day?" she asked.

"Except that I can't balance CHAPS's checkbook, it was pretty boring. Tell me the bank's always right, and I'll give it up."

"Of course the bank's always right," she said. Then she added, "I came over to invite you to lunch yesterday, but you weren't around."

I nodded. "I was . . ." I hesitated. "Out," I said finally.

"Doing more detecting?" P.J. asked, giggling when I shot her a startled glance. I guessed my jaw had dropped.

"We've been comparing notes," Taj said. "P.J. came over to tell me you'd been hanging around her father lately, and she wasn't sure what you were up to. I told her you'd asked me about him. And her. And then I remembered you getting all pink around the gills when Josh caught you in my closet and the lame excuse you gave about needing sanitary napkins. I also remembered that a couple of weeks ago, you snapped at what's-his-name, the deejay. Sundowner? Sundancer. And then you apologized and said it was PMS, and I thought that two weeks was a heck of a long time to have PMS."

Her dark eyes twinkled at me, and I guessed the heat in my cheeks was showing. "P.J. and I went on to talk about that neighborhood gathering you had here. And we came up with kind of a wild idea."

"That you were maybe trying to solve the murder of the guy in the flower garden," P.J. put in.

I sighed. "Guilty as charged," I admitted.

"So what have you found out?" Taj asked, leaning forward eagerly.

"You don't really think my dad had anything to do with it?" P.J. asked at the same time.

I answered P.J. first. "Your father keeps hanging around, staring at CHAPS," I reminded her. "The first time I thought anything about it was right after the earthquake. He asked me if I had a leak in my pipes, and I thought that was a bit odd. But once I realized he was . . ." I searched my mind for a tactful simile for 'out of his gourd' and finally recast the whole statement. "Once I realized Prinny had a problem, then I knew he couldn't possibly have been involved."

Actually, I still wasn't all that sure. I kept remembering Taj telling me the big old guy had shown a tendency toward violence on occasion.

"But that *was* the reason you visited him, wasn't it?" P.J. persisted. "You thought for a while at least that he'd done the man in."

"I thought he might have *seen* something or someone," I said lamely, and she looked somewhat mollified.

"Had he?" she asked.

"Not that he's remembering."

"So what were you looking for in my clothes cupboard?" Taj asked.

I almost told the truth, but then I remembered I didn't want Bristow thinking I was all that interested in the briefcase and key. "I really was looking for napkins," I assured Taj. "Sometimes I have breakthrough bleeding midmonth." This part was true. My gynecologist wants me to have a D & C, but I'm putting it off.

It must have *sounded* true. Taj started in on her second hamburger. But just as I was letting myself relax, she wiped her mouth daintily with a paper napkin and said, "Give, Charlie. What have you found out so far?"

"Yeah," P.J. said. "We aren't letting you go till you tell us something."

I sighed and tried to think what I could say that would satisfy the two of them. However, Bristow didn't want word to get out that Mr. X was Walt Cochran, which limited me.

Sundancer was dithering around in his booth, headphones covering his ears, presently playing Trisha Yearwood's "Lying to the Moon." I hummed along for a few moments, stalling for time.

"Love that song," I said absently.

They were both gazing at me, waiting.

"Well, one of the gardeners at Hoshizaki remembered flowers being missing from our flower bed in January," I offered at last. "That would seem to indicate Wa—Mr. X . . ." Hastily I tried to cover up my near-gaffe. "What Sergeant Bristow thinks is that the missing flowers prove Mr. X died between the gardener's visit in December and the one in January. Then there's an old lady named Olivia Emmett, who I think might know something. Zack and I went to see her—she's in the Care and Comfort Residential Facility. Trouble is, she's had a stroke and can't *remember* what she knows, although other than that she's quite coherent."

P.J. laughed shortly. "Tell me about it. My dad recalls every detail when it comes to the history of Prince George of England, but ask him where he put his undershorts when he took them off and he's one big blank." She glanced at Taj. "You've worked with old people, haven't you, in your various charities."

Taj had pinked up with embarrassment as she always did when anyone talked about her good deeds. Waving a beringed hand around in a vague way, she said. "I do more work with children, but, yes, I've had some experience with the elderly at the Condor Senior Center. Most old people have blanks in their memories, especially following a stroke. But your old lady might have a sudden breakthrough," she added to me. "Quite often a memory suddenly pops up after being buried for ages." She chuckled. "It happens to me sometimes. Just the other day . . ."

I was fated never to find out what had happened the other day. Josh suddenly loomed over the back of the booth, eyes popping, teeth showing, fair hair shining like sunlight, his hands reaching down to pat Taj's plump cheeks. She covered his hands with hers, and they exchanged cooing noises.

I stood up. Now that I understood Josh's problem, I wasn't quite as unnerved by his odd facial expressions, but there was still the turn-off of that S & M pornography hidden away in his circuit-breaker box.

Apparently, P.J. didn't want to stick around and witness the grand reunion either. She slid out of the booth after me and murmured something about needing a beer. Which no doubt meant that as long as Zack was off playing poker, she was going after Angel again.

I headed back to the office, added two dollars to CHAPS's account in the miscellaneous category, saved the files to the hard disk and went back to the main corral. Rounding up Angel, at the same time rescuing him from P.J.'s clutches, I waved at Sundancer to announce the evening's first line dancing lesson.

CHAPTER 17

When the phone rang at nine a.m. on Sunday, I almost
didn't answer it. Not just because I was clipping Benny's
toenails, but because I hadn't made any progress in tracking
down Igor's money, or Igor, and I was very much aware
that I had only one day left. Tomorrow, if he was a man of
his word, and I had no reason to think otherwise, Igor would
present himself, knife in hand.

But then I recognized the snooty voice that spoke into
my answering machine, so I figured it was safe to snatch up
the receiver. "Mr. Parmentier?" I asked, snuggling Benny
under my arm. He was so happy to be reprieved from the
dreaded clippers, he nuzzled right in and went to sleep.

"Miss Plato? Miss Charlie Plato?"

"Yes."

"The young woman who visited Miss Emmett on Tuesday?"

"Yes."

"I thought that must be your card. I found it among
Miss Emmett's effects. I'm hoping you may be able to put
me in touch with her grandson."

"How would I . . . oh!" I'd almost forgotten Zack had
pretended to be a relative to get himself out of trouble.

About to chew the man out for reporting Zack to the police, I stopped cold. "What do you mean, her *effects*?" I demanded, feeling a chill lift the hair at the back of my neck.

"It is my sad duty to inform you that Miss Emmett died yesterday afternoon at four o'clock," Mr. Parmentier said. "I wish to contact Mr. Hunter—that *was* Mr. Zack Hunter, was it not? The actor? I require his advice as to funeral arrangements. As far as I know, he's Miss Emmett's only relative."

About to confess that Zack was nothing of the sort, I held back, thinking about the "effects" Mr. Parmentier had mentioned. Would they include a briefcase and key, I wondered.

After promising to find Zack and bring him along to the nursing home, I hung up and dialed Zack's number. Not quite an hour later, we walked into the Care and Comfort Residential Facility.

Before we could properly get our bearings and figure out where Mr. Parmentier's office might be, a high-pitched female voice hailed Zack from outside the multi-purpose room.

Rina, the Houdini of the nursing home set, was waving a table knife at Zack, her other hand clutching the rolled piece of sheet that held her captive in her wheelchair.

"I'm not helpin' you over the wall this time," he called back as she started wheeling briskly toward us.

Indicating a short corridor to the right, he grabbed my arm and almost hauled me off my feet in his haste to escape the poor old lady. It turned out to be the right choice, and we were soon facing the elegantly suited Mr. Parmentier across an expensive mahogany desk. The manager's office was furnished much more luxuriously than the rest of the place, and I entertained some dark thoughts about profiteering managers.

"What did Miss Emmett die of?" I asked sharply, once we were settled.

"A heart attack, according to her doctor," Mr. Parmentier said, his voice unctuous. "I called him as soon as an aide brought the dear lady's lack of pulse to my attention. Dr. Waldrop came as soon as I called, but unfortunately she had already slipped away from us."

"You have her effects handy?" Zack asked. I'd coached him on the way over.

Mr. Parmentier indicated a couple of cardboard cartons on the floor, and Zack and I started pawing through them, trying to act casual about the search.

It was mostly clothing. More flannel robes and nightgowns than anything else. A pair of slippers, crocheted in pink and blue; a small, elderly, battery-operated radio; a few paperback novels; a couple of vases; a photo album. There were also a wallet that contained a few dollar bills, some coins and business cards, and a key that Zack palmed and pocketed so smoothly that I wondered again about the murky parts of his past.

"What happened to her briefcase?" Zack asked before I could stop him. I hadn't mentioned the briefcase to him on the way over, thinking he'd probably forgotten about it. I hadn't wanted it mentioned in front of Mr. Parmentier.

The manager looked puzzled. "As far as I know, she didn't own one," he said. His eyes narrowed as if he were suddenly remembering Sergeant Bristow's interest in Miss Emmett.

"About the funeral arrangements," Mr. Parmentier

said. "I thought of asking her priest, but I don't know his name."

Questions popped up in the ever-fertile soil of my brain. Hadn't Miss Emmett mentioned her *minister?* Did Catholics call a priest a minister? The questions gave birth to further issues: Weren't Catholics usually fairly recognizable—a cross on a neck chain, a crucifix on the wall, a rosary nearby?

Suspicion reared. "When did the priest last come to see her?" I asked.

"Yesterday. The poor dear lady must have died right after his visit. One of the aides looked in after he left, and Miss Emmett appeared to be sleeping. When Cora checked again later, she realized Miss Emmett was dead. I can only hope the priest gave her the benefit of the last rites."

"What did this priest look like?" I asked urgently.

Zack gave me a puzzled look.

"I just caught sight of him for a moment as I passed the room," Mr. Parmentier said. "He was sitting on the other side of Miss Emmett's bed, wearing a black suit, talking quietly to her. A big man, I would say. A little stooped, perhaps, or just bent over to talk to Miss Emmett. He wore a clerical collar. Black hat. Like diplomats wear. A homburg. He walked with a cane, one of the aides told me later. She also said he spoke with an accent, but couldn't place it. She thought it might be Irish."

The person who came to mind was Prinny, who was a big man and had a pseudo-English way of talking.

"You're quite sure he was a priest?"

"He told Cora on the way in that he was Miss Emmett's priest. He certainly *looked* like a priest." He thought for a moment. "He had a deep voice, Cora said."

So did Igor. "Had he visited Miss Emmett before?"

"As far as I could determine after questioning the staff, this was his first visit. No one knew his name. Miss Emmett had not been with us long, you understand." He frowned. "Cora did seem surprised that Miss Emmett was a Catholic. She'd thought for some reason that the dear lady was a Baptist."

"Could I talk to Cora?"

He frowned. "Really, Miss . . . Plato, I hardly think that would be necessary. I'm not sure what to make of all these questions. You seem to be insinuating . . ." He broke off. "I can assure you this was a perfectly normal death. I can show you the death certificate if you wish. Dr. Waldrop had no hesitation in signing it."

He looked at Zack. "I really think we ought to be discussing your grandmother's arrangements, Mr. Hunter. Did she leave any instructions in her will, do you know?"

Zack stood up and rubbed the back of his neck, then glanced at me with his eyebrows slanted in that puckish way that always made my stomach clench. It struck me as ironic that *now* he was asking permission to speak.

"I'm afraid I don't have the right to take care of Miss Emmett's . . . arrangements," Zack said when I nodded. "I'm not really her grandson."

"But even if you were adopted, you are still responsible . . ."

"We were funnin'," Zack said. "I said I was her grandson so you wouldn't throw us out. Miss Emmett went along with the gag." He looked a little shame-faced. "I'm sorry. Of course, I'd be proud to send flowers, and attend the funeral, with your permission, that is."

"I see." Mr. Parmentier got to his feet, drawing his short

frame to stiff attention, his mouth opening to protest such deception. But then he hesitated. I could almost see him debating with himself—should he order us hence, as he had every right to do? On the other hand, would he want to risk offending a known celebrity?

Fame won out over propriety, though he did glance at the boxes we'd searched through. His lips tightened. "We *were* Miss Emmett's friends," I said hastily. "We did care about her. If we can do anything to help with her . . . arrangements, we'd be more than pleased."

Zack gave me an approving glance, which brought a glow to my whole body. Mr. Parmentier also favored me with a smile, which had no noticeable effect on my hormones.

"Perhaps you would consider giving the eulogy, Mr. Hunter," Mr. Parmentier said, turning to Zack. I could only suppose he thought this would give the nursing home some kind of cachet. Maybe he'd put up a plaque: "Zack Hunter spoke here."

I glanced at Zack, who was squinting again. Mr. Parmentier probably thought he was considering the suggestion. *I* thought he might be trying to figure out what a eulogy was.

Luckily, we were both spared having to answer. A very pretty young aide showed up at the door in a state of agitation and insisted Mr. Parmentier had to come and settle a dispute in the laundry room.

"Excuse me for a moment," the manager said.

As soon as he was out of the room, Zack and I scarpered. Zack headed straight for the outer door, but I turned right at the end of the hall and hurried up the corridor to Miss Emmett's former room. Zack did an about-turn and followed me without asking a single question. I think his nerves were frazzled.

Miss Emmett's room was occupied by another elderly woman who was sitting up in bed and eating from a tray. Three younger women hovered around her. I could only think there must be a waiting list for that bed to have been filled so quickly. What a depressing thought. In any case, I could hardly root through the drawers and cupboard with that many witnesses present. "Did Miss Emmett leave a briefcase in here?" I asked.

The woman looked at me blankly. Her friends or relatives followed suit. One of them finally said, "There wasn't nothing here when we moved Ma's stuff in."

I thanked her and started back down the hall alongside Zack, who still seemed nervous. We had just passed the room where Rina had ambushed Zack on our previous visit when we heard her calling, "Yoo-hoo." Zack sped up without looking around. Mr. Parmentier really had him spooked.

Feeling sorry for the old woman, I turned back and explained that Mr. Parmentier had chastised Zack for turning her loose the previous time. She shook her wiry grey hair impatiently. "Is your name Charlie?" she asked, with a funny sort of conspiratorial look in her faded blue eyes.

I felt my heartbeat accelerate as I nodded. "Olivia described you to me," she said. "I didn't believe anyone really had orange hair, but she swore you did and she was right." She had a cackling sort of laugh, but if you're stuck in a place like that, you probably don't get too much to laugh at, so I didn't mind.

"Why did Olivia describe me to you?" I asked.

"I went up to see her day before yesterday. She didn't

get around much. She said if you showed up again, I was to give you the bag she gave me to keep for her when she first came. She said she hadn't been able to remember what she'd done with it when you asked her about it, but as soon as she saw me she remembered."

"Is it a briefcase?" I asked, almost beside myself with excitement.

She frowned. "Don't know as I'd describe it as a brief-case," she said. "Olivia called it a valise." She shrugged. "See for yourself. It's in my locker there."

It took a minute for me to find the bag. It was underneath a lot of nightgowns, wrapped in an old pillowcase.

"What's in it?" I asked. But Rina had wheeled herself over to the window and was gazing wistfully out at the sunny courtyard. She didn't answer.

The bag was locked. It did look like the kind doctors used to carry—Mr. Pelsner had been right about that.

"I'll just take it along with me then," I said, but Rina didn't seem to be paying attention.

"Maybe I can come back and see you sometime," I suggested, feeling guilty about just walking off with someone else's property, something the police were interested in obtaining. Though I was going to turn it over to Bristow, of course. Eventually.

"I'll see you later then," I said, and took off down the corridor at a fast trot, hoping Mr. Parmentier wouldn't suddenly pop up and yell, "Stop, thief!"

I wasn't a thief, I assured myself. Walt had given Olivia this bag, Olivia had passed it on to Rina and instructed her to give it to me.

"You ripped off Rina's bed linen?" Zack asked as I hoisted myself and my booty into his pickup.

"Let's get out of here," I said.

He started the engine and tooled out of the parking lot. "Are we on the lam?" he asked from the corner of his mouth.

"I've got the briefcase," I said.

His eyebrows shot up, and he whistled. "Way to go, Charlie! You get the key, too?"

Clutching the pillowcase and its contents, I shook my head. "I didn't even think to ask Rina if she'd seen a key."

"You stole the briefcase from Rina?"

"Olivia told her to give it to me if I came back. She'd left it with her for safekeeping when she first arrived at the nursing home, then she forgot where it was until Rina went up the hall to see her a couple of days ago."

"We taking it to Bristow?"

"After we look at it."

"Charlie . . ."

"I just want to see if Igor's money's in there, Zack. If he shows up tomorrow with his sharp knife, I can tell him the police found a bag with money in it and there's no way I can get it for him. Then maybe he'll leave me alone."

Okay, I know my thinking was flawed. I could tell Igor that without it being true. I had no business breaking into that bag. But I'd gone to a lot of trouble to find it, and I wasn't sure Bristow would tell me what was in it, even though he'd practically ordered me to look for it.

And like Savanna said, I'm a natural-born, one hundred per cent snoop.

CHAPTER 18

I tried the key Zack had palmed, plus every key Zack and I had on our key rings before I thought of the key that would lock up the office computer. It worked just fine. I shouldn't have been surprised. I'd discovered years ago that keys to Rob's luggage would work on mine, which was a different brand altogether.

We'd carried the briefcase—still wrapped in its pillowcase in case Igor was watching—up to my loft. I'd double-locked the door and had even considered putting a towel over Benny's cage so there'd be no witnesses.

As I opened the bag I heard the rustle of paper and got all excited. Walt *had* stolen money from Igor, and it was right here in my hot little hands.

Except it had somehow turned into folded sheets of newspaper, stationery with various letterheads, notebooks full of hieroglyphics. Walt's handwriting was even worse than mine.

The pages were from the business section of the newspaper, and featured those columns of incomprehensible abbreviations headed NYSE and NASDAQ. The letterheads were quarterly account statements from many different mutual investment funds.

Sitting next to me on the sofa, Zack began whistling over the information on the statements while I was still squinting at the newspaper pages. "Looky here," he exclaimed, shoving a page under my nose. "Nineteen dollars and sixty-seven cents per share and check out how many shares he owned. And that's just one fund. He had a dozen at least. Don't miss the dividends, all plowed back in. And the capital gains, likewise. D'you have a calculator?"

I fumbled in my purse and brought out the credit card-sized calculator I use when shopping. Zack's fingers had difficulty hitting one button at a time, so I provided him with a pencil to poke with. He made notes of the totals on cocktail napkins from the basket on my coffee table, then added them all together.

We both stared at the final figure for some time. "Close to four million dollars," Zack said after a while.

There was surprise but no awe in his voice. Of course, he'd probably made that or more while *Prescott's Landing* was *the* program to watch. I, on the other hand, though certainly not poverty stricken, could not imagine four million dollars laid end to end.

"Where is it, then?" I asked.

"Well, accordin' to these statements, it was all safely tucked away as of last September. And the market took an upturn since then, so the shares should be worth even more."

"Miss Emmett said Walt showed her a clipping about himself that he took from his bag," I remembered aloud.

Shuffling through the papers again, Zack pulled out a yellowed piece of newsprint and put it in my hand.

It was a picture of Walt Cochran at a microphone. He wasn't a particularly handsome man, though he had a sort of roughhewn appearance that could be considered macho, and therefore attractive. According to the writer of the accompanying article, it was his voice that had made women melt.

The story dealt with Walt's disappearance. After appearing at one of the major Las Vegas hotels, he was supposed to sing with the symphony in Carnegie Hall. But he hadn't shown up in New York, and no one knew where he'd got to. The police had no evidence of foul play, but they weren't ruling it out.

"Here's somethin'," Zack muttered.

He'd found a business card for a Kenneth Turcell & Co., certified public accountants. Mr. Turcell offered complete services for businesses and individuals—tax preparation, accounting and bookkeeping, financial and estate planning. The address was on California Street in downtown San Francisco.

"It's Sunday," I said. "We'll have to wait until tomorrow." I shivered. Tomorrow, Igor's month was up. For some strange reason, I seemed to be developing a sore throat.

"We gonna give this stuff to Bristow?" Zack asked. "I have his home address. I can call him right now and . . ."

"I want to know what happened to Igor's money," I said firmly. "Once I find that out, I'll be happy to turn everything over to the sergeant."

"So how are you goin' to . . ." Zack gave me his narrow-eyed look. "You're figurin' on goin' to see this dude?" He glanced at the card. "Kenneth Turcell? You're gonna drag me all the way into downtown San Francisco to find out what Kenneth Turcell knows about Walt's money? He's not goin' to tell you, Charlie. Money dudes don't talk about their clients' financial affairs."

"Maybe he's a Sheriff Lazarro fan," I suggested.

I was joking.

Honest.

But I wasn't the least bit surprised the next day when Kenneth Turcell—a clean-shaven gent with a three-piece suit, a flat-top haircut, and a bedazzled smile, allowed Zack and me to be shown in to his beautifully appointed office as soon as his receptionist mentioned Zack's name. I hadn't even bothered to give mine.

"And this is the little woman?" Turcell asked after he'd tried vainly to outgrip Zack and had enthused over having him for a client for a good two minutes.

Zack's bad-boy smile showed he was expecting me to explode over that description. I may be skinny, but I could measure myself against Kenneth Turcell and come out a full head higher. Besides which, 'the little woman' implies a certain quality of meekness that is not in my nature.

But Zack had reckoned without my desire for information. I wasn't going to do or say anything to put Kenneth Turcell's back up. Instead, I smiled sweetly and offered my hand to be mangled while Zack introduced me and said I was one of his partners in CHAPS. As far as Turcell was concerned, I promptly disappeared.

"We came to talk to you about Walt Cochran," Zack said as Turcell gestured us to a couple of chairs in front of a mile-wide desk.

When Turcell's face fell, Zack quickly added, "After that, I'll maybe want to discuss my own financial situation."

Zack was getting pretty good at this sleuthing stuff. Maybe he could get into a new series as a con man.

The sunshine had returned to Turcell's smooth face. "I'm not sure I know . . ."

"Walt Cochran, the singer," I said. "His body was found

after the earthquake in August. You may have read about it in the newspapers or seen it on TV. He was found in our flower-bed. CHAPS's flower-bed.''

The accountant's puzzled frown gave way to dawning light as he seated himself behind his desk. "The skeleton? That was Walt?''

"This is confidential information," Zack said, and Turcell nodded solemnly. "We found your business card along with a passel of mutual funds statements in a briefcase that belonged to old Walt," Zack informed him. "We reckoned maybe you advised him on investments.''

Turcell nodded again, but he wasn't quite with us. "Walt Cochran," he said, then sighed. "I can't say I was sorry to lose him as a client. He was a lot more bother than . . .'' He broke off and looked from Zack to me with a suspicious light in his pale eyes. "Are you a detective, Miss er . . . ?''

"Plato," I supplied. "I'm not with the police. I'm private.''

Zack shot me a squinty-eyed glance for that deceptive implication, but he didn't say anything.

"I'm afraid I can't give away confidential information," Turcell began, but he broke off when Zack stood up and apologized for wasting his time. "Well, now, I suppose it wouldn't do any harm to tell you what I know, considering it's so little," he amended.

Zack sat down again, smiling smugly, and Turcell booted up a computer on the right of his desk. After a little study and a fair amount of keyboarding, he nodded and said, "After first swearing him to secrecy, Walt Cochran invested a fair amount of money, on my father's advice, in certain mutual funds. That was in 1978.''

He looked at Zack. "According to my father, there had

been rumors that the Mafia had caught up with Walt for gambling debts and . . . disposed of him, but the stories weren't true. Walt didn't want people to find out he was alive, however. He said he was tired of the rat-race, wanted to get out while he was still half-way popular. My father always felt the threat from the Mafia was real and that was the reason Walt had chosen to fade from public view. Either that or he was drinking so much he couldn't get steady work. When my father died a few years ago, I inherited Walt's accounts."

He shook his head. "Walt was not at all a satisfactory client. I never met him, but he drove me crazy. He was forever moving his money from one place to another."

He thought for a moment. "Walt might have been peculiar, even eccentric, but he was mentally astute and it *was* his money. He'd had the acumen to invest some of the money he'd made during his glory days. He was stubborn though. Both my father and I advised him regularly that with mutual funds it's best to take the long-term view, but every time the market fluctuated, he'd be sending instructions to transfer monies from his old funds to whatever new funds he'd picked out. However, his transfer authorization forms always carried his guaranteed signature. Sometimes he'd decide there was going to be a crash, and he'd withdraw all his funds, either by letter or by phone."

His mouth drew down at the corners. "He had an instinct, I'll give him that. The time before last that he drew everything out was in September, 1987, just ahead of the October debacle. He put it all back as soon as the market recovered."

"You can draw out funds by telephone?" I asked, surprised.

The accountant nodded. "If you request no more than

ten thousand dollars in any one day, the money is on its way the next day. And you can keep requesting."

I had a sudden horrible suspicion. "You said you weren't sorry to lose him as a client?"

He nodded again. "Walt drew out all his funds again last December." He consulted the computer again. "Over a period of three weeks. His instincts were wrong this time—there wasn't a crash, but he didn't replace the monies as quickly as he had done in the past. Instead, he telephoned and said he wouldn't be using our services anymore. He said he had a safe place to put his money. I had no reason to doubt him, and I can't say I argued with him. As I said earlier . . ."

His voice trailed away, and he went into a thinking mode, chin resting on right hand, elbow on the desk, eyes faraway.

I was doing some thinking myself. If Walt drew out four million dollars in December and was murdered in January, it seemed fairly likely the murderer had his money.

Evidently Turcell reached the same conclusion at the same time. "Damn!" he exclaimed. Judging by the wistful expression on his face, he was wondering how he'd let all that money get away.

"I guess you'd better let the police know all this," I said.

Zack looked puzzled. He hadn't quite caught up yet. "I'll explain it later," I told him and stood up. "We'll be reporting to the Bellamy Park Police," I said to Turcell. "Sgt. Taylor Bristow is handling the case. I'll tell him to call you, shall I?"

The accountant nodded absently. He was still staring blankly after that lost fortune as Zack and I left. He didn't even realize his potential client was making a getaway.

"Where to now?" Zack asked as we climbed into the pickup. He sat forward, gamely prepared to sally forth.

"Bellamy Park," I said.

"Taylor Bristow?"

"After a slight detour to call on P.J.'s father."

"You don't suppose P.J. will be home?" he asked nervously.

I shook my head. "She'll be at work. We'll only have Dee-Dee to deal with."

As we headed toward Highway 101, I could almost hear the gears grinding in his head. Finally, he said, "I guess whoever killed Walt took off with his money?"

"I'm not sure the murderer *took off* with it. It's more likely he stashed it somewhere."

"You think he's still around? The murderer?"

"It's possible."

He glanced sideways at me. "You've figured out who he is?"

I shrugged. "Not for sure, but I'm leaning toward Prinny again."

"Why?"

"Mr. Parmentier said the priest was a big man."

"Prinny's a priest?"

Sometimes I despair of Zack.

"When we visited Miss Emmett, she said her *minister* had popped in," I reminded him with commendable patience. "Priests aren't usually referred to as ministers. And Olivia didn't have Catholic accoutrements on her walls or on her person. So maybe the murderer *dressed up* as a priest and came to see her. I already decided Igor had to be the murderer. So maybe Igor is Prinny, and vice versa."

"Why would Igor come to see Miss Emmett?"

"He wanted to find out what happened to his money. Maybe he murdered Walt accidentally before Walt could tell him where he'd put his money. Maybe Igor murdered Miss Emmett. It's a bit coincidental that she died so soon after we talked to her."

"So what makes you think Prinny is the priest?"

"Mr. Parmentier said the priest was a big man," I said again. "He said one of the aides told him the priest carried a cane. Prinny always carried a tightly furled umbrella. At a glance, it might look like a cane."

A suddenly returning memory caused me to shudder.

"What?" Zack asked.

"I told Taj and P.J. I'd talked to Miss Emmett," I said. "They'd figured out I was investigating Walt's murder and insisted I had to tell them something, so I told them that." Stark horror had invaded my mind. "What if P.J. told her crazy father I'd gone to see Miss Emmett, and that's why he dressed up as a priest and went to the nursing home and killed Miss Emmett so she couldn't give any more information to me or the police?"

"Mr. Parmentier said Miss Emmett died of a heart attack," Zack pointed out.

"Yes, but what *caused* the heart attack?"

"It's all a bit far-fetched, Charlie," Zack protested.

I took in a deep breath, trying to hold the horror at bay. "You're right," I said, hoping he really was. "But I still think I should talk to Prinny. If he did go to see Miss Emmett, and I can catch him by surprise, he might just confess. He's blurted out a couple of sensible things since I first met him—like stuff about meeting his wife, and then the water leak he was worried about. After we see Prinny we can go talk to Bristow. I'm looking forward to telling him Walt was a rich man. We can call him up from CHAPS and arrange to meet him somewhere."

"You're still worried about Igor seein' you?"

"I intend to worry about Igor until I find out who he is, and Bristow gets him safely locked up. You may not recall that four weeks ago today Igor gave me a month to find his money, or else."

"Did he mean a lunar month, darlin', or a calendar month?"

I could have kissed him. It hadn't occurred to me to wonder. Maybe I had a couple more days. Then again, maybe I didn't.

Zack shot me a betrayed glance when P.J. opened her apartment door. Her eyes were red-rimmed. My first thought was that she was sick and that was why she had stayed home from work. "Oh, how sweet of you to come," she exclaimed as we stood semi-paralyzed in the hall. She ushered us inside. "How did you hear about it? I'm so worried. I keep thinking I should have stayed at the hospital, but the doctor said there wasn't anything I could do for my dad. With a head injury, only time would tell if he'd come around or not, and I should come home and get some sleep."

CHAPTER 19

I hadn't lost my voice for some time, but I lost it then. Zack and I both stared at P.J. for the longest time without speaking, then I managed to squeak, "Your father's in the hospital? What happened?"

She sat down on a sofa as if her knees had suddenly given out. "He wandered off again," she said. "He was sound asleep in his chair, and Dee-Dee took a chance and ran out to borrow some mayonnaise from a neighbor. She wanted to make tartar sauce to go with the fish she planned for dinner. When she came back, Dad was gone. She and the neighbor combed the area and couldn't find him, so Dee-Dee called me. We all drove around his favorite places, but he was nowhere in sight."

She gulped and sobbed, and I sat down beside her and pulled out several tissues from a box on the coffee table. Zack leaned against the wall, looking sympathetic but wary.

"When we got back to the apartment, a police officer was waiting. He told me Dad had been hit by a car on one of the back streets near the artists' co-operative. They took him to St. Joseph's."

"Isn't that the Catholic hospital?" I asked.

She nodded absently. "I can't understand how it could happen. According to the officer there's never much traffic around there during a weekday—the co-operative isn't even open except on weekends. Anyway, the driver didn't stop. Some lady walking her dog found Dad lying in the gutter with blood coming out of this huge cut on his head."

"It was a hit-and-run!" I exclaimed.

She nodded.

Me and my big mouth again. I'd questioned P.J. at the neighborhood get-together three weeks ago, and she had blurted out that it was okay for her dad to hang around staring at CHAPS if he wanted to. Loud enough for anyone nearby to hear. Loud enough for Igor or whoever the murderer was to hear and to wonder, as I had wondered, if Prinny had seen anything suspicious going on.

"Tell you what," I said, handing P.J. another wad of tissues. "How about Zack and I go over to the hospital and see how your dad's doing? I'll call you as soon as we find out something."

Her eyes lit up. "You are so sweet, Charlie. I just can't get over how sweet you are."

Then she glanced shyly over at Zack. "Maybe I should come with you," she suggested.

Zack came to attention, looking nervous. "No," I said firmly. "Like the doctor said, you need your rest. I promise I'll tell you as soon as there's anything to report."

Her mouth pouted a little, but then she drew a shuddering little breath and crumpled back against the sofa cushions. "Okay," she said in a lackluster way.

We found out the number of Prinny's room easily enough, but the nurses on duty didn't want to let us in, their recognition of Zack notwithstanding. But then I caught sight of an exceptionally tall man in a dark blue shirt and blue jeans talking in the hall to a doctor. The man had a smooth brown head that could be mistaken for no other.

Sergeant Bristow saw Zack and me at the same moment and strode toward us, looking so grim I glanced around for an emergency exit.

"I was about to send out an APB on you two," he said as he reached us. With a gesture of that same smooth head, he indicated a nearby waiting room and led us into it. "You've got some explaining to do."

"Let me guess," I ventured. "Mr. Parmentier called you again."

"He did. This very morning. Said he'd called you about Miss Emmett's effects, and you'd gone over there and rifled through them like you were looking for something in particular, *then* told him Zack wasn't Miss Emmett's grandson after all."

"He was probably angry because we left while his back was turned," I said soothingly, wondering if Rina had kept her lips zipped. If not, I wouldn't put it past Mr. Parmentier to swear out a warrant for my arrest. He'd never do it to Zack, of course.

"He wanted Zack to give the eulogy at Miss Emmett's funeral," I told Bristow. "And that was after Zack owned up. He's nothing but a celebrity . . ."

I broke off. Bristow's eyes were narrowing impatiently. Time for me to own up, I guessed. "We found Walt's brief-case," I said abruptly.

For all of ten seconds it was satisfying to regard Bristow's dropped jaw. But then his whole face clouded up, and I braced myself for the coming thunder. "At what time did you find the briefcase?" he asked in a deceptively mild voice.

I glanced at Zack, who shrugged. "Ten yesterday morning, maybe," I said.

Bristow looked pointedly at the clock on the waiting room wall. It was three p.m., and this was a whole day later.

"We were going to bring it in," I said. "I just wanted to clarify a few points first."

"Such as?"

"Well, there were a lot of mutual fund statements in the bag—"

"It wasn't locked?"

"Well, yes, it was, actually, but I just happened to have a key that opened it. I guess the lock was weak—it was a pretty old bag." Bristow's amber eyes could glow like a cat's, I discovered. There was an almost greenish glint to them. "There was also a business card in there, for a CPA in the financial district of San Francisco. So this morning we went to talk to him about what happened to Walt's money."

Bristow's attention was finally distracted from my wrongful behavior to my story, which was where it belonged. "Walt's money?" he echoed on a rising note.

Zack spoke up for the first time. "Accordin' to the mutual funds statements, old Walt was a millionaire four times over. But then this Turcell dude, the accountant, said Walt withdrew all of it last December."

"Withdrew it? Four million bucks? What did he do with it?"

"Well, we don't know," I said shortly. "I imagine that sort of information is easier for you to find out than for us."

I know the kind of body language that precedes sarcasm,

so I wasn't surprised when Bristow, after curling up one corner of his mouth and folding his arms across his chest, said, "Let me get this straight, Miss Plato, you're actually admitting there is something a police officer with years of experience behind him could do better than you?"

"There might be a faint possibility," I responded with some sarcasm of my own.

One thing about Bristow—one great thing—was his sense of humor. He laughed immediately and relaxed his posture. We were home free, I thought, but then Zack decided it was time for some chivalry. "You shouldn't blame Charlie too much," he said to Bristow. "She's done a great job of sleuthin', especially considerin' she's been scared to death of Igor all the time."

"Igor?" Bristow queried.

I groaned.

Bristow stalked across the room, stuck his head out the door and told a young cop who'd been hovering around to keep everyone out, then closed the door and indicated we should both sit. "Talk," he said to me.

I talked.

It was an hour before Bristow got through with his third degree. By the time he was through, he had reached into my head and scoured out every thought I'd had, every word I'd spoken, almost every word I'd heard, every action I'd taken, since that first awful moment when the ground opened and Walt Cochran's skeletonized foot popped into view.

The only consolation I had was that he did allow us to go in and see Prinny after I argued that Prinny was used to me now and might feel more comfortable talking to me than to Bristow. The only condition was that Bristow would remain in the room with us, and I would be given a list of questions to ask the old guy. Prinny, it seemed, had regained consciousness a few minutes before Zack and I arrived at the hospital.

The poor old man looked too big for the narrow hospital bed. He was hooked up to monitors and intravenous drips and oxygen, his head bandaged like an Egyptian mummy's. A nurse settled herself on a chair on the other side of his bed and gave me a look intended to let me know who was in charge here.

Prinny's eyes were open. They looked vulnerable and defenseless, the way people's eyes do when they normally wear glasses. They were rather a nice shade of blue-green, I noticed for the first time.

"Hi, Prinny," I said. "It's me, Charlie Plato."

He showed no recognition.

"How are you feeling?"

"I knew the Frenchies would get me one day," he muttered.

"Well, the doctor says you'll live to fight them another day."

His face brightened.

"Did you see who was driving the car?" I asked.

He closed his eyes, and I thought he'd drifted off.

I persevered. "What kind of car was it?"

"Man wore a black hat," he said.

He was in his 'answer the previous question' mode. I waited.

"Shiny car. Came up from behind."

When I was seventeen I had my appendix removed. As I was coming around from the anesthetic, a nurse gave me a few blasts of oxygen, and my brain seemed suddenly clear

and bright and capable of all kinds of creative thought. I'd
requested notepaper and had scribbled lyrics to at least
three songs while I was in this euphoric state. The lyrics
hadn't been any good, but I could still remember how clear
things had seemed to me at the time. With any luck they
were shining just as brightly for Prinny.

"Did the man in the black hat look like a priest?" I
asked.

Behind me Bristow made a small sound of impatience.
He'd pointed out that ministers also wore clerical collars,
and dark clothing, and had dismissed the report that the
man had *said* he was a priest as hearsay. Bristow didn't see
what difference it made, considering he was quite sure Miss
Emmett had died from a heart attack as her doctor had certified.

Prinny wasn't any help with the priest theory. He just
looked blank again.

"Do you remember telling me about a leak in my water
pipes?" I asked.

Zack and Bristow both made snuffling noises, but I paid
no attention. Prinny's eyes looked interested. "Outside
CHAPS," I prompted.

"Dashed cold that night," Prinny said. "It seemed
odd."

"What seemed odd?" I asked, barely breathing.

"Man digging in the middle of the night. Took it for
granted—leak in the pipes."

"What did the man look like?"

"Dark night. Overcast. No moon."

"How could the man see to dig?"

"Flashlight, of course. You've forgotten the flashlight."

"So what did he look like?"

Prinny's eyelids were fluttering, almost closed. "Black hat," he said in a wondering tone. "Two black hats. Black clothes. Must be villains, don't you know? A priest, you say?"

"I think that's probably enough," the nurse said.

Bristow protested, but looking down at Prinny I could see he wasn't going to be responsive again for some time. His face had relaxed completely, and he was snoring lightly.

I asked the nurse to call his daughter, and she promised she would. "So what do you think of my priest theory now?" I asked Bristow after we'd exited Prinny's room.

He rolled his eyes, then narrowed them. "Let's go get that briefcase," he suggested.

An hour later we saw Bristow off CHAPS's premises. Besides picking up the briefcase, he'd come at me with more questions and had dredged Zack's brain for answers, too. It was obvious he wasn't going to leave until he was convinced we'd told him everything we knew, so we held nothing back. He was especially incensed that I hadn't told him right away about Igor calling me. "I could have tapped your phone," he pointed out as we escorted him to his car.

"I told her she should have punched the record button on her answerin' machine," Zack said.

"I was too paralyzed to think of anything so practical," I said.

Zack couldn't let it go at that, of course. "She was afraid you'd yell at her for breakin' the law."

Bristow's exasperated glance would have withered me if I hadn't seen the glint of amusement in it. He liked me. No doubt about it. "I'll send a patrol officer over to keep an eye on you," he promised.

I let out a breath I'd been holding for the last month.

"Thank you." I should have left it at that. A nice farewell. Instead, I asked one more question. "Are you going to talk to Kenneth Turcell?"

"I am. And to Mr. Parmentier, and Cora, and Rina, and whoever else has anything to offer. I don't want you rounding up men in black suits," he warned loudly in parting. "Any rounding up needs doing, I'll take care of it myself."

I was laughing as Zack and I went back into the lobby. The sound echoed, scaring me. It was Monday night. If Igor had meant a lunar month, he could be hiding in one of these shadowy rooms, waiting for Zack to leave. "I still don't think Miss Emmett's death was due to natural causes," I said. "It's too much of a coincidence for her to die right after the man in the black suit visited her."

Zack grunted. At that moment I caught sight of him reflected in the plate glass window of Buttons and Bows. "You know," I said teasingly, "some people might call a man as tall as you a big man. And you always wear black. Maybe the black homburg was actually a black cowboy hat."

He grabbed me by the shoulders and swung me around to face him. He was smiling his bad-boy smile. "You're not serious, darlin'," he said, his hands sliding down to my backside.

I grinned up at him. "No, I'm not."

He sent me one of those zinger glances of his from under his eyelashes. Once again it was rush hour on the hormone superhighway, and all the little devils were yelling, "Let me at him!"

Zack's smile disappeared, and his mouth grew stern. I felt his big hands press me closer to his lower body. He was looking at my mouth, I realized, and the realization was enough to make my mouth soften and open a little. The lobby seemed suddenly remarkably short of air.

"Well, I can't for the life of me see where you'd get such an idea, Charlie," Taj's voice said from the shadows by the door.

Zack and I sprang apart, and I put a hand to my heart. "For goodness sake, Taj," I exclaimed. "I thought you were Igor. You almost sent me into cardiac arrest."

"Igor?" she queried, looking blank.

"Of course I don't think Zack killed Miss Emmett," I said hurriedly as she came forward, thinking it was best to leave Igor unexplained. She was wearing one of her beautiful suits, the kind that were cut so well you forgot she was a very large woman and thought only how smart she looked. Her hair was drawn up as neatly as always in its old-fashioned Gibson Girl style.

She shook her head. "I don't mean *that* idea. I mean the statement you made before, just as you were coming in. I guess you didn't see me following. I saw the police car and got worried about you. I watched from the bank's street-side entrance until the officer drove off, then came over to make sure everything was all right. That's how I happened to hear you." She seemed quite perturbed, which puzzled me.

"I don't even remember what I said," I protested.

"You implied that Miss Emmett didn't die of a heart attack," she reminded me. "Now, you told me and P.J. about Miss Emmett, remember, and how you couldn't get her to remember something she knew. And I told you old people often have a breakthrough. It stands to reason she remembered whatever it was, and the knowledge worried her so much her poor weakened heart couldn't stand it. It wasn't that long since her stroke, was it?"

"No," I agreed. I was going to tell her about Prinny's hit-and-run accident when I remembered suddenly that Prinny had said the car was a *shiny* car, and I thought, well, maybe it was shiny because it was *new*. And then I thought *Josh.* Josh worked at a posh European car dealership. He had access to a lot of shiny new cars. Josh wasn't a big man, but he was muscular.

While I was trying to process this sudden burst of information, Taj moved a little closer and I saw that she was very pale. "There's no earthly reason for you to think the priest killed that woman," she went on.

The air grew still around my ears. I could suddenly hear the sound of my own heart beating. I glanced at Zack, pretty sure he wouldn't have caught the slip. But I'd misjudged him, not for the first time. He was staring at Taj, his eyes narrowed, his whole posture wary.

"Maybe you'd better come into the office and sit down," I suggested to Taj. "You don't look too well."

CHAPTER 20

We got Taj settled on the sofa, then I brought her some water from the main bar. I brought a bottle of brandy too, but she waved that aside.

Zack closed the door as she sipped the water, and she cast a nervous glance at him. "I can't stay," she said, smiling up at me. "I just came over to see if you'd like to have dinner with Josh and me at Casa Blanca tonight. Josh is picking me up in a half hour or so."

"Hmm," I said noncommittally. Then I glanced at Zack and rolled my computer chair close to Taj and sat down. "I'm curious about something," I said. "What made you think the man I mentioned—the man in black—was a priest?"

Her expression was puzzled, nothing more. "You said so, Charlie. I told you, I came in right behind you. I heard you mention the man in black, the priest, whom you thought had killed Miss Emmett."

"I never used the word 'priest,'" I said emphatically.

"That police officer must have mentioned him, then. The sergeant. I heard him say something as I came out of the bank."

Zack shifted his position slightly. He was still standing

guard at the door. "Sergeant Bristow said he didn't want Charlie roundin' up men in black suits," he said. "He didn't say nothin' about a priest."

"Well, then, I guess I must have dreamed it," Taj said lightly.

"The problem is," I said, "that there does seem to have been a priest involved. The manager of the nursing home where Miss Emmett died told us a priest visited her shortly before her death. We wondered if he might have had something to do with her death."

"That's wild, Charlie. Priests don't go around killing people."

"We think he was just dressed up to look like a priest."

Taj's usually serene face crumpled like a sheet of paper that had been crushed and released.

"You have to tell us how you knew there was a priest in the picture, Taj," I said, keeping my voice casual so perhaps she wouldn't break down. "Prinny—Mr. Perry—was in a hit-and-run accident on Magnolia Street this morning. The car that hit him was shiny, he said. So I thought it was probably a pretty new car, and that made me think of Josh, because of his work. According to Prinny, the man driving the shiny car wore a black hat. The priest who visited Miss Emmett wore a black hat. Prinny also saw a man in a black hat digging in the flower-bed at CHAPS sometime in the winter. On a night when there was no moon."

"Is he dead? Mr. Perry?" she whispered, her voice trembling.

"The doctor says he's going to be fine. They'd given him some oxygen, which seemed to have awakened a few dormant brain cells. He was coherent for once."

A shudder went through her, then she lowered her head

into her hands and began sobbing, her big shoulders heaving. "How did you know the man in black was a priest?" I asked.

"I've been so afraid," she moaned.

"Afraid of what?"

Making a stupendous effort, she stopped sobbing and lifted her head. I rolled my chair back a little and reached to my desk for a box of tissues. After she mopped up, I put the pressure on again. "How did you know . . ."

She held up a hand to stop me, and the light glittered on her rings. "I didn't know," she said shakily. "I just guessed when you mentioned a man in black."

"Where would you get a guess like that from?" I leaned forward. "You're my friend, Taj. I want to help you, but you have to tell me the truth."

She took in a long, shuddering breath and sat up straight, looking very queenly. "I guessed that Josh had borrowed my Uncle Harley's suit again—the one that hangs in my hall closet," she said. "Uncle Harley was a priest. He was my mother's favorite brother. He died a long time ago. My mother kept his suit and hat, and I brought them with me when I left home as a sort of talisman. Uncle Harley was the only one of the family who was famous. He used to go on television and answer questions about families and how to raise teenagers—he'd done a lot of work with young people. People wrote him letters." She paused. "I always wanted to be famous," she murmured.

"I remember." She looked so vulnerable I wanted to sit down beside her and give her a hug, but I steeled myself and went on. "Josh had borrowed your uncle's suit before?"

She nodded. "I found it caked with dirt, in the closet, after Josh had been gone all of one night. It was the night after New Year's Eve. I asked him what had happened to the suit, and he said he didn't know anything about it. But there wasn't anyone else who could have taken it and then brought it back."

She looked pleadingly at me and then at Zack. "I love Josh. You know I love Josh. I never had anyone to love before. I brushed all the dirt off the suit, took it to a cleaners in Palo Alto, then hung it back in the closet. I never mentioned it to him again."

She hung her head for a long moment, then said, "It was my fault that Walt died. Josh would never have thought about killing him if I hadn't brought him home."

"You brought Walt Cochran to your condo?" Zack asked, sounding very startled.

I wasn't startled; I was in shock. My traitorous voice had gone again, and I wasn't sure it would come back.

Evidently Zack realized I was paralyzed. He took a few steps forward and put a comforting hand on my shoulder. "You knew who Walt was?" he asked Taj.

She nodded. "He came into the Condor Senior Center for meals several times before I figured it out. I'd met him once. When I was sixteen, he gave a concert in San Diego. I thought he had the most beautiful voice in the world. After the concert my friend and I went backstage to see if we could get an autograph. Walt was drinking and feeling sociable, and he talked to us for quite a long time. He even asked us about ourselves. I told him I'd always wanted to sing, and he said I should practice a lot. I told him it wouldn't do any good because I couldn't carry a tune, and he laughed and said neither could most of the new so-called musicians, but they were doing him out of a good living. Then he gave us autographs and shook our hands. I thought it was the happiest day of my life. I was devastated when I heard he'd disappeared and was thought to be dead."

"So then twenty some years later, he came into the Senior Center where you volunteer, and you recognized him," I prompted. My voice sounded rusty, but at least it had returned.

"About the fourth time he came in. That was last October, toward the end of the month. It was really cold. The center was crowded. He was standing to one side of the fire trying to get warm, and the firelight shone on him like a spotlight. A while before that he'd mislaid his false teeth, but he'd evidently found them and he had them in. It made a world of difference in how he looked. So I recognized him. I was so *thrilled*."

I could almost see the picture she was painting. The homeless people crowding around the hearth. Walt with his matted hair and ragged beard standing head and shoulders above the rest.

Taj had gone to him and introduced herself and told him she was a fan. He'd been delighted. He was relatively sober that night, and the two of them had talked. He'd told her the same story he'd given Olivia Emmett—that he really couldn't remember what had happened to him back in the late seventies, but he thought it was connected with a fight.

I remembered Bristow saying a dentist had removed Walt's capped teeth after someone pistol-whipped him.

Walt had told Taj he wanted to make a comeback. Just as he'd told Olivia. But where Olivia hadn't thought it was likely, Taj had offered to help. Typical Taj, always ready to reach out a hand to anyone in need.

"I met with Walt all through November," she said. "I wasn't able to keep him off alcohol altogether, but I persuaded him to cut down. About the end of the month, he caught a cold and I brought him to the condo."

Olivia had reported Walt missing at the end of December, I remembered, about a month after he'd stopped coming to the library. So he hadn't really been *missing* at that time. Taj had been taking care of him.

"I gave him the downstairs rooms," Taj went on. "Josh and I moved our stuff upstairs. That's when Josh got upset."

She shook her head. "He's always so clean. Josh. You've seen how he is. He couldn't abide the idea of Walt sleeping in our home. I kept assuring him it wasn't for long, but then he got really jealous about Walt and me having these long talks every night about how Walt was going to get on his feet and go back to work. Walt made me his manager. I was so excited. I couldn't sing myself, but I could give back to the world a singer everyone had loved, a singer whose voice sounded like liquid moonlight. Whenever he had doubts, I told him if Tony Bennett could do it, so could Walt Cochran."

She had bought clothes for him and had dropped his old ones from the railway bridge in Condor, where they'd probably been seized by eager hands. She had made him bathe every day and had cut his hair and shaved off his beard and given him lotions to smooth and soften his skin. By Christmas, even Josh had to admit Walt was a new man.

"Or rather the man he had once been," Taj went on. "He looked remarkably good considering all he'd gone through. We were sure he would continue to improve. He'd even promised to join Alcoholics Anonymous. Josh was far more amenable to the whole plan by then. At least he seemed to be."

Her face was crumpling again.

"What happened?" Zack asked gently.

Taj looked at him helplessly. "I don't know. We went through the holidays, Christmas, New Year's Eve. We thought pretty soon we could get Walt in good enough shape so we could get in touch with an agent and see about announcing his return. Oh, I could just see it so clearly. The newspapers, the television cameras, the fanzines. For once in my life I would have done something useful, something glamorous, something real."

I wanted to ask about Walt's money, but didn't want to interrupt the flow, so I kept silent.

So did Taj.

"Something went wrong, I take it?" I asked when it became clear she was having trouble continuing.

"I ate something New Year's Eve that upset my stomach," Taj said. "I felt ill all New Year's Day, so I took some medication and went to bed early that night. I didn't even hear Josh come up. When I woke up in the morning, Josh was sleeping beside me. Walt was gone. His new clothes were gone. The shoes I'd bought him. Everything. Josh swore he'd heard nothing, seen nothing, knew nothing. So, naturally, I thought Walt had just changed his mind and gone back to the streets. I was devastated, but of course I got over it, you always have to, don't you? I never saw him again."

"And then the body turned up in our flower-bed," Zack said.

She nodded sadly. "I knew. Even before you told Josh and me, Charlie, that night at CHAPS, that the body was an elderly man suffering from malnutrition, I knew. Walt had eaten well for that whole month he was with Josh and me, but that wasn't enough to make up for years of neglect. As soon as I heard about that skeleton and remembered the dirt on my uncle's suit in the closet, I knew Josh had to have killed him and buried him. I faced him with it, and he denied it, but as more information came out, it was pretty clear to me."

She reached for the tissues again and wiped her eyes. "I knew it was wrong not to go to the police, but I'd already lost all my big dreams about helping Walt Cochran make a comeback. How could I lose Josh, too? I told myself the world wasn't that bad off to be short one homeless person, but it's been so hard, Charlie." She was sobbing silently again.

"What happened to Walt's money?" Zack asked from behind me.

"I don't think Walt had any money," she said when she'd pulled herself together again. "He used to carry around an old bag and tell people, including me, that he was wealthy and would remember them in his will, but I never saw any money. And the bag had disappeared by the time he came to stay with me. He said he'd lost it."

She thought for a minute, gradually becoming calmer. "He did have a key on a chain around his neck, which I suppose could have gone to a safe-deposit box or something, but I don't know what happened to that either."

I remembered seeing a key on a chain in Taj and Josh's clothes closet. It had looked like my computer key, and my computer key had opened Walt's bag. Later, I thought.

"So I suppose all this means that Josh is Igor," I said to Zack.

Taj gave me a funny look. "Some guy called me a couple of times," I told her. "He disguised his voice so it sounded like a robot. Scared me to death. He said the man in the flower-bed stole five thousand dollars from him and since I'd discovered his body, I must have it. If I didn't give it back in a month, he said I was dead meat. Or words to that effect."

She looked totally blank for a minute, then said, "Well, my stars, Charlie, all those reports on television would attract all kinds of kooks." Her forehead wrinkled. "He said his name was Igor?"

I decided it was too complicated to explain I'd named him after a Sound Blaster scheduler, so I just nodded.

"Where's Josh now?" I asked.

It's odd how some questions get answered. The words were no sooner out of my mouth than we heard footsteps in the hall, then the door burst open and Josh barreled in, as if this were the last act of a melodrama and he'd heard his cue. Enter villain, stage right.

"What's going on?" he yelled.

He had a pistol in his right hand.

He was heading straight for Taj, and I was sure he meant to shoot her. I'd like to say I froze in my chair, because that would at least partly excuse my cowardice. But though my father had owned a couple of rifles, I'd only seen handguns on television and the movies and occasionally in a cop's holster, and all I wanted to do was get as far away from this one as I could. So I ducked my head, pushed off with my feet and shot my chair backwards across the wooden floor to where Zack was standing.

Correction. To where Zack *had* been standing.

Zack was no longer in the room.

I couldn't believe he'd run off and deserted me. I'd thought he was made of sterner stuff. Obviously I'd confused him with Sheriff Lazarro the way everyone else did.

Not having heard a shot, I pulled my shattered nerves

together and looked over at the sofa. Josh hadn't shot Taj. He was on his knees in front of her, his head in her lap. But the gun was still in his hand.

"It's all right, honeybear," Taj was murmuring to him as she stroked his gleaming blond hair.

Then Zack came back in the room and bent down to do a little murmuring himself. "I went to check on Benny and Taylor," he said. I took that to mean he'd called Bristow.

I stood up, thinking the two of us might just sneak out together as long as Josh didn't seem to be harboring any murderous urges. But before I could communicate this sensible idea to Zack, Josh got up from his knees and sat down on the sofa. The pistol was in both hands now, and he looked down at it then up at us and said again, in a very calm voice this time, "Tell me what's going on."

His face looked as if it were hurting. As if he'd just come out of the dentist's chair, and the novocaine was wearing off.

"Everything's fine," I said in my most soothing voice, sitting down again to prove it.

But then Zack pulled a chair over and proceeded to tell Josh every single thing Taj had said.

"Lazarro always used to confront the perpetrator," he said when I suggested he shut up.

"Lazarro had better writers than you have," I told him. "They made the bad guys give up right away."

Josh had moved the gun to his left hand. I couldn't remember if he was right-handed or left-handed. He put his free arm around Taj's shoulders. "I can't take this one for you, honeypot," he said sadly. "You'll have to take responsibility yourself."

I blinked. Taj had started sobbing again. Josh still held the gun in his left hand. He wasn't being aggressive about it, but it was there, and it was pointed in our direction. I certainly didn't want to try grabbing for it, and I didn't think Zack was that foolhardy.

Josh's eyes weren't popping now. Nor were his teeth bared in that awful smile of his that was more like a grimace. He just looked unbearably weary. And now that I thought about it, he'd seemed tired for a long time. Like ever since Walt popped up in our lives.

"I've suspected Taj of killing Walt ever since the earthquake brought him to light," he said as if he'd read my mind. "The night he disappeared, Taj put something in my soup. I felt very logy the next day."

Zack added a bit of information he'd missed before. "Taj says after you killed Walt, you dressed up in her uncle's priest suit and buried Walt in our flower-bed."

"Priest suit?" Josh queried. "I don't know anything about a priest's suit." If he was pretending to be blank, he was sure good at it.

"I kept hoping I was wrong," he said. "I couldn't confront Taj, because if I *were* wrong, she'd be so upset that I should think such a thing. And there was no way I could turn her in to the police. I love her, you understand." The look he gave Taj was a good imitation of loving, that was for sure, though it was sad around the edges.

Josh was gazing at me now. "That's why I threatened you, Charlie. I thought if I could scare you so you'd investigate Walt's death, I could find out the truth without getting Taj or myself involved."

He *was* Igor. I remembered how sick he'd looked when I'd told him and Taj the body was that of an elderly man who was malnourished. He'd have recognized that description, of course.

Of the two of them, Taj had seemed more convincing. It was difficult to know who to believe . . .

"How did you get your voice to sound so strange?" I asked. Gun or no gun, my enquiring mind needed answers.

The movement of his mouth was almost a smile, but it was a crooked smile. "One of my little boy's toys," he said. "It's a voice changer. It can make you sound like a man, a woman or a robot. Mikey loved playing with it."

I was furious to think I'd been tricked into terror by a toy! And then I remembered the odd-shaped thing I'd seen in the closet along with a model truck and a box of blocks. "Was it brightly colored?" I asked. "Looked like a ray gun?"

He nodded absently. "I hated scaring you, Charlie; you've been a good friend to Taj, but I didn't know what else to do."

"Do you know what happened to Walt's money?" Zack asked him. He's a single-minded sort of guy.

Josh went blank again, then his face cleared. "Oh, you mean the five thousand dollars I said had been stolen from me? That didn't really exist. I just made it up to scare Charlie into doing what I wanted."

"Walt's money must be floatin' around somewhere," Zack muttered to me. Then he did a little twitch of his shoulders as if he were putting on a coat, and his voice came out sounding like Sheriff Lazarro's again. "What are you intendin' to do with that gun?" he asked Josh.

Josh looked at the gun as if he'd never seen it before. Then he shrugged. "I don't know yet," he said. Which didn't sound too encouraging. "I found it in the glove compartment of the BMW," Josh added to Taj. "That's what made me rush in here like a crazy person. When I got to the bank they told me you'd left, but the car was still in the parking lot, so I figured you'd probably come in to see Charlie."

Taj was still quietly sobbing against his shoulder. He was holding her close, the gun steady in his left hand. I didn't see how this whole scene could get any more bizarre.

I was wrong.

"I loaned the BMW to Taj because her car's in the shop," Josh said to me in a dead sort of voice. "While I was debating whether to come in to see if Taj were here, I noticed some of the glass was broken out of the right turn-signal light. I bent down to look at it and saw stains on the car's paint. I thought they looked like blood. I thought that if they were blood I wasn't going to be able to protect Taj anymore. I couldn't let her kill more people. As I was looking for a tissue to wipe the stains and see what they were, I opened the glove compartment. That's when I saw the gun. It scared me so much I didn't even stop to think how it would look for me to dash in here waving it."

Taj sat up, and he gently kissed her face, which was flushed and tear-stained and very pretty. "I'm sorry, sweetness. I'm going to have to tell the police all of it now, the way you fixed Walt up and took care of him when he was sick. The plans you had for him. All of that. But I have to know first why you killed him. I thought you were obsessed by him, maybe even starting to fall in love with him. You were so excited about getting him on stage again."

For a few minutes I had been aware of slight sounds in the hall outside the open door of the office. It hadn't taken much imagination to figure out that Bristow and maybe another officer or two were shifting around out there, listening, waiting for a good time to step in and take over. The faint sounds were slightly closer now.

Now that Josh had said he was going to talk to the police, I felt a lot safer, but there was still relief in knowing they were out there. As long as Josh had the pistol aimed at me, I was going to worry about just how much experience he'd had with one. I mean, had anyone ever taught him how to *handle* a gun? Was there a bullet in the chamber or whatever it was called?

I didn't want the police coming in and maybe startling Josh until that gun was pointing in some other direction. Also, it looked like a confession might be forthcoming any minute.

Taj was staring straight ahead now, and her eyes seemed glazed, as if she were looking at some scene that existed only in her mind. "He couldn't sing," she said flatly.

Nobody was breathing. The sounds in the hall had stopped.

"I took him over to CHAPS because he'd told me he'd sung there—at Banbury's—in the fifties. It was his idea, because I'd told him the building was empty right then and I had a key. Michiko Watanabe gave me one a couple of years back when she and Joe went on vacation in Arizona. She wanted me to water the plants. She had a lot of plants. I never gave the key back."

She was silent again. Still nobody spoke. "I didn't think it would be a good idea to take Josh along with Walt, because I had this idea in my mind and I thought Josh might get jealous again. So I put a couple of sleeping pills in his wine, and he went off like a baby, and I drove Walt over to the building that was going to be CHAPS."

She paused, looking wistful and still very pretty. "There was still a microphone on the stage. Watanabes used to have Japanese singers in as well as dancers. I found the outlet and plugged the mike in and asked Walt to sing to me. I'd always had this fantasy of getting up on a stage and someone famous singing to me."

Josh frowned. "Walt wouldn't do it?"

Taj laughed, but there was no mirth in that laughter, only a harsh sobbing sound. And something was happening to her face. It was like the morph graphics you can get on computer software, melting, shifting into a mask of anger.

"He *couldn't* do it. He tried, but all that came out was this kind of husky croak. I told him not to worry, it was probably just because he hadn't used his voice in so long. And maybe he wasn't completely over his cold. A little practice and his voice would come back. But then he started laughing. He said we'd have to give up the whole idea. He should have known it wouldn't work, but he hadn't remembered until just this minute why he'd given up singing."

Zack and I were still staring, waiting. "He said he'd got in a fight with some guys he owed money to, gambling buddies, he said. One of them had hit him in the mouth with a gun and busted all his teeth, then another one picked up some kind of club and hit him across the throat. The pain was so bad, he passed out, and when he came around he was in a hospital, and the doctors told him his vocal chords were damaged and he'd never sing again. They told him he was lucky to even be able to talk. And that's when he decided to disappear. He didn't want anyone feeling sorry for him; he felt sorry enough for himself. He'd always been a drinker, so then he just kept drinking more and more. It would be a good idea to go get a drink now, he said."

The mask was still in place. "He was very sorry, he said. Life did have its little ironies, he said." Her fists were clenched so tightly her knuckles shone white as bone. "Little ironies," she repeated, her voice harsh. "People would have spoken of me with respect, with awe, because I'd found Walt Cochran and brought him back into the limelight. He'd smashed all my hopes for him, for *me,* all my dreams of becoming somebody. And he thought it was funny. *Funny!*"

"So you hit him with somethin'," Zack said softly.

She looked at him blankly, as though she weren't really seeing him at all, so fixed was her inner gaze on the past. "There was a hibachi on the floor. One of those little iron stoves the Japanese cook on with charcoal. I didn't even realize I'd picked it up until Walt fell down. It was really heavy, I discovered when I cleaned it up later. But at the time it felt very light."

There was a silence. "So then you buried him," Zack said into it.

She looked at him more normally than before, her voice becoming quite conversational. "Not at first. I left and got all the way home before I realized that if I buried him, nobody would know he was dead, so nobody would look for who killed him. Who was going to miss a homeless person? So I brought a shovel from home—I'd bought one when I worked on the kids' playground project in Condor. I took all of Walt's new clothes off, so they couldn't be traced to me. I even took his false teeth out."

She made a face. "I was up most of the night. First I buried him. That part wasn't too difficult. It was the night after New Year's Eve. Who goes out that night? The plaza was deserted."

Her eyes darkened. "I *thought* it was deserted."

I realized she was thinking of Prinny, but didn't want to interrupt.

"I cleaned up the stage area," she went on. "Then I took Walt's clothes and teeth and dropped them off in various charity receptacles all over the peninsula." She squinted at me, her eyes narrowed almost to slits. "If it hadn't been for the earthquake, nobody would ever have known. Even then it would have been all right, if you hadn't kept sticking your nose where it didn't belong."

There was a new note of hostility in her voice. The air in the room was now charged with electricity. I could almost feel Bristow and whoever was with him getting ready to burst in. Evidently Josh noticed something also. Looking startled, he took his arm away from Taj's shoulders and raised the pistol slightly.

Zack, Taj and I pounced on the gun at the same moment. I missed it entirely. We never did find out who actually pulled the trigger, but the gun went off with a tremendous crack and Zack sat down abruptly on the floor, his face turning the color of cottage cheese.

CHAPTER 21

"So," Zack said, "is it a wrap?"

"Just about," Taylor Bristow said. "Maybe a few minor loose ends to tie up."

It was four days later. Taj was in jail. Josh was out on bail until somebody decided just how innocent he really was. As far as I could tell, Bristow had arrived at CHAPS too late to hear Josh confessing he was Igor. I hadn't yet decided what to do about that.

Zack was leaning back against a pillow on my sofa, looking rakishly handsome with his hair tousled attractively, his left arm in a black cotton sling. The bullet had carved a groove through a few outer layers of skin on his upper arm. "It's only a graze," Zack had bravely declared to the assembled cameras and microphones on leaving the hospital. "What's one more scar?"

Bristow was in sweats, which made him slightly less intimidating, especially when he was sitting in one of my armchairs with Benny taking a bath on his shoulder. Rabbits do it like cats, so no water was involved.

"Who starts?" I asked.

Bristow showed me a smile.

"What happened to Walt's money?" I asked.

"I only give information in exchange for information received," he said. "Josh Gibson said something about being sorry he threatened you. What was that all about?"

"You think he was involved in Walt's murder?"

Bristow's eyebrows climbed, making his forehead furrow like corrugated cardboard. "You're not getting the picture of what's supposed to happen here, Charlie. I ask questions. You answer."

I gave Bristow my most innocent smile. "Maybe my answer depends on yours. Why won't you tell me whether or not you suspect Josh? Is it a state secret?"

His eyes glinted. Then he nodded. "Okay, Charlie, we'll do it your way. The only thing I have on Joshua Gibson is that he failed to come to us with his suspicions. It's not up to me to decide what charges, if any, will be filed. Apparently Taj acted without his cooperation." His eyebrows challenged me again. "So how come Josh said he's sorry he threatened you? I took that to mean he was your friend Igor."

"He could have meant he didn't intend the gun to seem like a threat to me," I said, which wasn't bad for spur-of-the-moment thinking. "A couple of times I got the impression he'd forgotten he was holding the pistol. He was in shock, I think."

I gazed meaningfully at Zack, trying to convey the message that as long as Josh was otherwise innocent, I wasn't going to press any charges against him for pretending he was going to do me in. The only other thing I knew about him was his liking for pornography. Reading dirty magazines wasn't against the law, as far as I knew. It seemed to me the poor guy was suffering enough. He really had loved Taj, no doubt about that.

"Igor must have been some off-the-wall character looking for cheap thrills," I said blandly. "He did mention seeing me on TV. You must get lots of calls from weird people when there's a murder involved. Especially when the moon is full."

"There was a full moon when Igor called?" Bristow asked.

I met his gaze head on. "Well, there was a full moon the night of the earthquake, and it wasn't quite three weeks later when Igor called, so it would more likely be first quarter, wouldn't it? So maybe he was still affected by the earthquake moon, or even the earthquake? But there was a full moon the second time he called. I can check my calendar, if you like. It's got all the quarters of the moon on it."

Even as I threw all this stuff at Bristow to bamboozle him, I remembered telling Igor that the body in the flowerbed was named Walter and he was a homeless man. He had hung up right away. He hadn't called again. He hadn't needed to. Josh had known for sure then that Taj had disposed of Walt.

Bristow's amber gaze was still fixed on my face. I presented a smile, and he sighed, then shrugged, which almost unbalanced Benny. Moving the rabbit from his shoulder to his thigh, he petted him gently until Benny resumed his ablutions. Then he evidently decided to give out with some facts.

"Taj helped Walt withdraw his money, notarizing or guaranteeing his signature on the necessary documents. She'd told him she was expecting another severe downturn in the market, and as she worked at a bank, and he was already irrational on the subject, he believed her. She used some of the money to buy his new clothes, planned on using more to hire some musicians and get a demo tape put together and for advertising and living expenses until she could get Walt reestablished. She wouldn't have touched the rest, she said."

He sounded doubtful. "Maybe she wouldn't have," I suggested. "Just because she was a murderer doesn't mean she was a crook."

Bristow gave me the kind of look that remark probably deserved. "She was a crook, Charlie. Her so-called accident at the bank? She staged that, hoping to get a big settlement. Seems the claims guy was suspicious but couldn't prove anything. He did manage to get the claim reduced, which Taj always resented, according to Josh Gibson. Her resentment worried him, he said."

I recalled Josh's nose twitching every time Taj mentioned her settlement. And I had thought maybe he was after her money. I'd done the right thing not to turn him in. I owed him for all my bad thoughts about him.

"So where's Walt's money now?" Zack asked.

"In a safety deposit box at the Plaza Bank."

"That must be an awful big box," I marveled.

Bristow sighed. "It's in checks, Charlie, all endorsed by Walt Cochran." He frowned. "The box was registered in the name of Edith Jones, for some unknown reason."

I thought I might explain about Taj's original name later. Depending on whether Bristow was nice to me or not.

"We're checking for the existence of the will Walt talked about," Bristow continued. "Maybe the people he promised money to will get it after all."

"Except for Taj."

He didn't dignify that comment with an answer. "Seems Walt had told her Miss Emmett was kind to him," he continued. "Taj remembered her name, and she wanted to find out if the old lady had the briefcase. She wasn't sure if there was anything in that briefcase that would tie Walt to her."

"And I told her where Miss Emmett was."

"Miss Emmett got discombobulated by Taj's questions," Bristow said. "Heart started fibrillating. Taj didn't get help, just sat and watched her die."

I felt sick. "What about Mr. Perry?" Zack asked.

Bristow nodded. "Interesting part there was that Taj bought her gun after she killed Walt. Says she planned to kill herself if it looked like she was in danger of being arrested. After Miss Emmett died, and Taj heard Mr. Perry was muttering about leaks in water pipes, she figured it was time to go. She was driving to the creek in her priest get-up to kill herself. Says she put on the black suit and hat so when we found her we'd know what she'd done to Miss Emmett. But on the way, she saw Mr. Perry wandering the streets, and it seemed like deliverance was at hand. It was just an impulse, she said. She didn't even have to swerve the steering wheel all that much."

I wasn't sure if I felt saddest for Walt, whom I hadn't known, or Josh, whom I'd formerly disliked, or Perry, whom I had suspected, or Taj. Taj, I thought. All she'd wanted in the beginning was a little bit of fame. I guessed she'd at least have that now.

I wasn't sure I'd ever get over Taj being a murderer. How could I ever trust my feelings about people again? I kept thinking of her serene face, her musical laughter. Something I'd read somewhere kept coming back to me: The brighter the sunshine, the darker the shadow.

Bristow stood up and deposited Benny in my lap, then grinned down at me. "I expect you're waiting for some kind of commendation from me?"

I made a face at him.

"You deserve one," he said abruptly. "But I'll deny ever saying it. All I'll admit saying to you is that police work should be left to the police. So I'll thank you to remember that in future. I really do thank you. Do you copy?"

I got the message and smiled up at him. "Won't you stay to dinner, Taylor? I'm fixing ratatouille."

He grinned. "Tempt not a desperate man."

"*Macbeth* again?"

"*Romeo and Juliet.*"

"I'll come and see you act someday," I promised. Then I asked, because even recent experience hadn't robbed me of my curiosity, "Why are you desperate to leave?"

"I have a date, Charlie."

I rubbed Benny's head with my thumb, and looked up at Bristow from under my eyelashes. "With Savanna?"

He shook his head. "With Jacqueline. We're going to play with her Mighty Morphin Power Rangers. Then she's gonna teach me the Barney song."

I laughed. "Your bachelor days are numbered."

He rolled his eyes. "That's what I'm afraid of."

"The Barney song?" Zack queried when he returned from seeing Bristow out.

"I love you, you love me, we're a happy family."

"Goodbye, Bristow," he said as he settled himself on the sofa again. With endearing clumsiness, he placed on my coffee table a bottle of champagne and a couple of glasses he'd carried up from the bar. Good stuff, too. Not my favorite Dom Perignon, but a worthy substitute. I put Benny carefully back in his cage and gave him a sheet of newspaper to play with. He loves tearing the news apart.

"How come you didn't wanna tell Bristow that Josh was Igor?" Zack asked.

"I'm waiting to see how it goes with Josh. If he really didn't get involved, I don't see much sense in kicking him in the teeth. I can keep a secret as well as anyone."

As well as Zack Hunter, anyway. I still didn't know anything about that year and a half that was missing from my partner's recorded life history. I'd have to search out that *People* story I vaguely remembered reading. Someday soon.

Kneeling next to the sofa, I helped Zack get the foil off the bottle, with much intermingling of fingers. Between us we managed to pop the cork without spilling a drop of champagne. Zack poured. We both sipped, making lots of eye contact, as if we were in an old silent movie. Zack's green eyes seemed darker than usual. My inner parts were playing leapfrog.

"Charlie," he said, then hesitated. For Zack, hesitation was a major personality shift. "What is ratatouille?" he asked at last.

"A sort of stew made with eggplant."

His lips stretched in a mirthless smile. "Maybe we could raid the restaurant and find a hamburger instead."

We did the eye contact thing again. It always worked in those old movies, right? I had the idea neither of us really wanted to go anywhere.

Which meant what exactly?

I took another sip of champagne and settled sideways against the sofa, within easy reach of anyone who might want to make any sudden moves. "That was quite an adventure we had," I said.

"Not a bad team," he agreed in an absent-minded way.

"What would you have done with that gun if you'd got it away from Josh?" I asked.

He grinned. "Damned if I know. I just didn't want Taj to get hold of it. How about you?"

"I missed it altogether. I'm glad of that—I'd hate to think I might be responsible for you getting shot."

"You did go after the gun, though," he said.

I felt vaguely proud of myself. Maybe I wasn't a dedicated coward after all. "I guess my motivation was the same as yours," I said. "Do you suppose Taj would have shot herself? Or us?"

He shrugged, winced with pain and sat up straighter, re-settling the sling on his left arm. Then he ran his right hand through his hair, which he often did when he was about to make a pronouncement.

I sat up straighter myself, allowing my heart to pump a little faster.

"There's somethin' I need to talk to you about, Charlie," he said with unaccustomed solemnity. "I'm not sure how you'll feel about it, but I gotta tell you anyway. I just can't keep it to myself anymore."

So what if I'd made a vow to be celibate for a couple of years. So what if I were a substitute for the radiant flight attendant Melissa, who was apparently on an extended journey. I was young, healthy, I'd just escaped death by a fraction of an inch. Life had new meaning. Life was meant to be lived. You're only young once. Opportunity knocks but once. *Carpe diem*—seize the day.

There were probably another hundred or so clichés I could have used to excuse the irrational act I was anticipating, but I didn't have to dredge them up after all.

"We need to talk about your position," Zack went on, frowning.

"My position?" I was disoriented.

"Naturally, there'll be some money in it for you. We can work out any kinda agreement you want."

I finished the rest of my champagne in one gulp.

"It'll mean more responsibility for you, but not a whole lotta work, considerin' you regard my presence as purely decorative." He sent me one of those zinger looks from under his eyelashes.

"What on earth are you talking about, Zack?" I asked.

He smiled his bad-boy smile, but I already suspected I wasn't going to like his answer and I didn't respond with my usual hormonal rush.

"I'm not gonna be around for a while," he said. "Had a call from my agent followin' my appearance on television yesterday. Seems John Donatelli, the producer, caught the interview."

I'd caught it myself. I'd wondered if my ex-husband Rob would see it, remember my connection to Zack and maybe call me and tell me how much he missed me. Not that I wanted him back. I just wanted to see myself as irreplaceable and unforgettable. So far the dust on the telephone hadn't been disturbed.

Our man in black—Sheriff Lazarro made flesh—had told Miss Perky newscaster and the rest of the couch potatoes in the country, in his own modest, folksy drawl, how he'd managed to outwit the master criminal Taj Krivenko— killer of the helpless and homeless—and bring her to justice, without heeding the risk to his life and limb. I'd kept waiting to hear him mention my name, but it had somehow slipped his memory again.

"Donatelli remembered he liked my style in *Prescott's Landin'*," Zack went on. "He wants me to play the lead in a new pilot for a musical mini-series. Country-western theme. Set in a town like Branson, Missouri. Lotta singin' and line dancin' and guitar pickin', with a mystery for me to solve. Catches on, might turn into a weekly series. Could go on for a year or two. Great advertisin' for CHAPS, Charlie."

I shot to my feet.

"What?" he asked.

I couldn't even speak, I was so mad. In the aftermath of our shared adventure, I'd forgotten my own rule about not getting ditsy about Zack Hunter. Instead of taking advantage of that to seduce me, as any red-blooded American male should have done, he was taking advantage of the adventure itself in order to further his career.

"Out," I said.

"Charlie?"

"Out. I'll talk to you tomorrow. When I calm down. If I calm down. Right now, I just want you out of here."

He unfolded himself to his full height, reached for his cowboy hat and put it on, looking bewildered and slightly hurt and lean and unutterably sexy. "Women are the strangest critters," he said as he exited the room.

I sat and fumed for a full half-hour, furiously informing myself that somewhere along the line I had to develop more common sense when it came to men. But eventually I saw the funny side of me sitting there contemplating making a move on Zack, while he was contemplating making a move out of town and I started to laugh. With a smile on my face, I got up and went into my kitchen area and began collecting the ingredients for ratatouille.

As the pot was simmering, I thought, wait a minute—a *musical* country-western mystery series?

With singing and dancing and guitar picking?

Nah, it'd never catch on.

I felt better.

Please turn the page for an exciting sneak peek of

Margaret Chittenden's newest Charlie Plato mystery

DEAD MEN DON'T DANCE

now on sale wherever hardcover mysteries are sold!

I glanced at my watch. It was time for Zack to make his speech so everyone could go home and we could get the place cleaned up for tonight's opening time. Sunday evenings weren't as popular as Wednesdays, Fridays, and Saturdays, but we still drew a good-size crowd.

Catching Zack's eye, I tilted my head toward the mike. He nodded and climbed up on stage to stand directly below the blowup of himself. Very dramatic. "Y'all listen up now," he said in his nice folksy down-home drawl.

Everybody started applauding as if he'd said something immensely clever. The fan-club members stood up straighter, a few with hands to their hearts as if they were saluting the flag.

"It sure is nice of y'all to help me out here," he added before starting in on his prepared speech, which he'd memorized like a movie script. Angel was right, Zack was a quick study. He talked earnestly and well, with appropriate gestures, slipping easily into his old Sheriff Lazarro persona.

It was a good speech; thoughtful, intelligent, laying out his position on the future of Bellamy Park, covering the hot issues he and Winston stood for. Yes, of course I wrote the speech. What did you think?

When the applause finally died and people headed for the exits, all pumped up to begin campaigning, I took myself off to the office to add some names to our telephone tree. I hadn't even got the computer booted up before Zack and Macintosh and Winston wandered in.

"I wanna show the guys the dartboard," Zack explained.

I sighed. We'd hung the dartboard on the back of the office door so we could let off steam once in a while—there's something very satisfying about the thunk of a heavy brass dart embedding itself in a boar-bristle board. Once in a while the four of us held a minitournament while discussing business decisions or problems.

Recently Zack had transformed the dartboard by pinning one of Gerald Senerac's campaign flyers over it. Winston did his imitation of a neighing horse when he saw the darts sticking out of Senerac's patrician nose. Macintosh looked embarrassed—maybe over the darts, maybe over Winston's laugh.

Pulling the three darts out, Winston stepped back and plunked them one at a time into Senerac's high forehead, then removed them and handed them with a flourish to Macintosh, who accepted them reluctantly.

It took a couple of minutes for Macintosh to get the board in focus, then he flung the darts in a floppy overhand. Two bounced off the board and onto the floor, one stuck to Senerac's right cheek. Macintosh walked over and yanked it out right away.

Zack took it from him, gathered up the other two and fired each one into Senerac's throat. "Straight to the jugular," he declared, setting Winston off on another whinny.

"I never thought I'd wanna get me a picture of Opal Quince," Winston exclaimed.

Opal Quince was Winston's opponent—a seriously weird real-estate lady, with formidable teeth, who had made something of a career out of writing letters to the editor of the *Bellamy Park Gazette.*

"Opal hasn't said anything really bad about you so far," I pointed out to Winston.

"There isn't anything bad to say," he said with a smug smile. "Besides which, you're not up to date, Miss Plato—Opal has a letter in this week's *Gazette* accusing me of being in cahoots with Zack to take over the town and use it as a set for television movies, like *Northern Exposure* did to Roslyn in Washington state."

Zack smiled wryly. "Opal says *I'm* an agent of the devil, like all other actors who portray violence on TV."

This campaign was shaping up into a battleground for crazies, I thought as Zack escorted his buddies out.

I was sliding open the window to clear out the odor of Old Spice when Zack returned. Heat poured in, causing the air-conditioning to cut off. The sun glinted on the windows of the Adobe Plaza bank next door. For all of ten seconds I thought longingly of cavorting in the waves at Half-Moon Bay, then I closed the window.

"I've been wantin' to ask you somethin' all day, Charlie," Zack said as I turned around. He was leaning back against the doorjamb. He sure did know how to lean.

I did some leaning of my own, settling my elbows behind me on the windowsill. "Ask away."

"You happen to know a good deodorant?"

"Your social life falling off, Zack?" I was doing restraint well today.

He squinted at me. At least I *thought* he was squinting. It's hard to tell with Zack, because he's perfected this way of narrowing his eyes that makes him seem to be gazing off into a dust cloud created by stampeding cattle. "I'm talkin' about my new car," he said. "It has a funny smell. It must be fierce for me to even notice it, considerin' I got my nose busted on *Prescott's Landin'* and I don't have much sense of smell."

A month earlier one of the guys in our cleaning crew, leaving after a hard night's work, had absentmindedly put the group's van in reverse instead of drive, then stomped down on the accelerator. The resulting backward leap had flattened Zack's old pickup against CHAPS' very sturdy adobe wall. The new car was a Lexus Zack had purchased a week ago right out of a swank automobile showroom in Menlo Park.

"Why don't you get one of those little green paper trees you can hang on the rearview mirror," I suggested. "Probably it's just new-car smell. It'll fade in a few days. Unless there's something wet in there. Mildew makes for a pretty foul odor."

Zack frowned. "I was thinkin' maybe it's BO. You remember that episode of *Seinfeld*—the valet at a restaurant brought Jerry's car around front and there was this tremendous stench of BO after. They built the whole episode on tryin' to get rid of the smell, but it kept gettin' stronger even after Jerry had the car ionized at the car wash. Everyone who sat in it carried the smell away with them."

Sometimes Zack has difficulty drawing a line between real life and television. While I was trying to think up an answer that would be suitably insulting, his eyebrows slanted up in the puckish way they had, and a glint showed in his green eyes. Evidently he'd been teasing me.

Ambling across the office, he put a hand on the windowsill

on each side of me, and leaned in so that his face, and body, were barely an inch from mine. "What do you think, Charlie? How *do* I smell?" he asked softly.

He smelled *clean. Masculine.*

I read recently that a human's blood-vessel system is sixty thousand miles long and has more than an acre of surfaces. All of my sixty thousand miles had their surfaces pulsing.

"I wanna thank you for all your help gettin' today's shin-dig off the ground, darlin'," he said, looking at my mouth. "That poster is a real winner, Charlie. You are a woman of a thousand talents." His eyes glinted. "Maybe a thousand and one?"

Images of Scheherazade danced in my head. Like her I was constantly thinking up ways to stay out of the sultan's bed. Well, at least half of me was. My physical self kept saying go for it; my mental processes had a lot more self-respect.

"I have to get back to the computer," I said lamely. "I have to update the telephone tree. Several people volunteered this afternoon."

"Is it truly urgent?" he murmured.

Luckily, at that moment, I caught a slight movement in the vicinity of the doorway and glanced sideways to see Zack's friend, Marsh Pollock, looking in.

"Come on in, Marsh," I said hoarsely.

Zack looked over his shoulder, but didn't move away.

Marsh was thirty-nine, three years older and a couple of inches shorter than Zack, which put him right at six feet. His thick, prematurely grey hair was cropped short and curly, a look that was devastating with his tanned youthful face. Zack had good muscle tone. Marsh was buff. As the new owner of Dandy Carr's gym, he had to be.

Marsh had bought the gym from Dandy in February, after the old man suffered a minor heart attack and decided to retire to North Hollywood to be near his daughters. He'd kept Dandy Carr's name for the place—out of respect for the old guy, he'd told me. When Zack had met Marsh at the gym, he'd invited him to take Dandy's place in the Bellamy Park Irregulars, who used to play poker on Wednesday evenings but now got together on Sundays.

Marsh was wearing a white polo shirt with Dandy's logo on it, tan walking shorts, and boat shoes, a nice change from the western outfits I was usually surrounded by. He always looked as if he'd just walked off a yacht, and he had the kind of vivid blue eyes some sailors have when they've spent years looking at the vastness of the ocean. Though when I told him that, he laughed and said he'd never been to sea in his life.

Right now his eyebrows were climbing. "Should I come back later?" he asked.

"Much later," Zack murmured, looking at my mouth. "Two, three weeks. A month maybe."

I gave him a push and he shifted to one side, smirking. "He's harassing me," I told Marsh, making my voice brisk, aware I'd probably colored up. "I'd report him to my boss, but I don't have one. Did you come to volunteer for the campaign committee?"

"Sorry, Charlie. I've made it a practice never to get involved in politics." He switched his focus to Zack. "I was in the vicinity, dropped in to tell you I can't host tonight's poker game in the gym office even though it's my turn. I'm having the office painted tomorrow and the workmen cleared all the furniture out today."

Zack shrugged. "My house then? I can probably catch Macintosh and Sundancer if I hustle." He glanced at me sideways. "If Charlie can bear to let me go," he added.

"I'll try to soldier on," I said.

I fully expected Marsh to leave with Zack, but he remained in the doorway. I purposely moved over to my desk, sat down and booted up the computer, hoping he'd take the hint. But he didn't.

A couple of times Marsh had come close to coming on to me, but I'd bristled in time and he'd backed off. I hoped he wasn't going to try again today. I had enough to do fighting off Zack.

Besides which, I wasn't quite sure what I thought of Marsh Pollock. I pride myself on my ability to read people but I couldn't seem to get a handle on him. He always had a sort of knowing smile hovering around his mouth, which was attractive, but irritated me no end. Which probably meant I was also attracted to him, I admitted to myself with a sigh.

He perched himself on the edge of my desk. "Are you and Zack . . . ?" He let the question hang.

"No," I said, more explosively than was warranted.

He let the silence grow. "How come you don't work out in my gym, Charlie?" he asked. He had a gravelly sort of voice, which made everything he said sound as if it had hidden meanings.

I kept my gaze on the computer screen as I retrieved the telephone-tree file. "Your gym is always crowded with perky young things in spandex, and macho guys spattering sweat on the mirrors," I said. "I prefer the gym in Condor.

It has all this neat old equipment—separate bench presses with long handles, old-style leg-lift and leg-press machines. I especially like the rowing machine and the treadmill; they don't have any monitors that check your pulse rate or tell you how many calories you're burning. And the place is usually empty at the time I work out."

I always babble when I get nervous, and something about this man made me nervous. When I finally managed to stop, he leaned forward and said in a conspiratorial way, with that funny little smile in place, "You'd look great in spandex, Charlie."

A line of zzzzz's appeared on my screen. I hit Backspace several times to wipe them out. Once again I caught movement in the doorway. Busy as Union Square today. This time it was Lauren Deakins, Zack's fan. For once I was glad to see her. "Hi," I said. "Can I help you?"

She stammered something about Zack. Apparently she'd come looking for him. Darting glances from me to Marsh, who had twisted around to see who I was talking to, she gripped the doorjamb and looked as if she were about to burst into tears.

"I think Zack probably left," I lied. I was beginning to worry about this young woman.

"Oh well . . . okay, I guess . . . thank you." Flushing miserably, all the way up to her thick eyebrows, she finally managed to detach herself from the doorjamb and take herself off.

"One of Zack's fans," I explained to Marsh.

"An apparently proliferating breed," he said with a grin, then went on as if there'd been no interruption. "I could work with you on a program as your personal trainer, Charlie, no extra charge. You really need to bulk up a little."

"In other words I'm too skinny? Don't you worry yourself, Marsh, I'm very healthy. I eat right and I eat regular."

Stand by for a minihistory here. I'm actually almost obsessive about eating regularly. After my parents demolished themselves and their Cessna in a thunderstorm near Tahoe during my last year of high school, I'd gone into a tailspin and had apparently decided to starve myself by the time I graduated from the University of Washington. At that time, I fortunately took a job with a doctor in Seattle. Though he was a plastic surgeon, he recognized anorexia when he saw it and got me into therapy.

Unfortunately, he also married me, then periodically forgot that fact when his more glamorous patients came up from Hollywood (in disguise) to consult him. I decided that in this age of AIDS his little hobby was probably even more hazardous to my health than anorexia. So I divorced him and answered an ad Zack had spread around a few newspapers, which, of course, had led me to my current situation.

"What do you say, Charlie?" Marsh asked, leaning closer.

My patience, never my primary virtue, was wearing thin. There'd been enough testosterone floating around in this office for one day.

"Thanks, but no thanks," I said sharply, then added for good measure, "I really do have a lot to do, Marsh. If you don't mind, I'd really like to . . ."

He slid off the desk and raised his hands in surrender. "Okay, I'm leaving. But we'll talk again, Charlie Plato."

I stayed irritated for a good five minutes after Marsh was gone. Mostly with myself. I'd actually caught my breath when he leaned close. And he'd noticed.

Muttering to myself, I was nonetheless getting on with

my work when Zack came strolling in again. "What now?" I demanded when he just stood there frowning.

"All of a sudden, that smell in my car stinks worse than a road-killed skunk, Charlie," he said. "Car's been sittin' out there in the heat of the day since I got here this mornin'. Seems like maybe somethin's gone rotten."

I sat back and looked up at him. "Did you check the trunk? Maybe you left some food in it. Did you take one of your dollies on a picnic lately?"

He took a couple of minutes to think about that, then shook his head. "I can't get the trunk open, the catch is jammed."

"It's a new car, why would the catch be jammed?"

He took off his cowboy hat and looked in it, as if it would provide some answers. After replacing it, he said slowly, "The catch wasn't jammed when I brought the car home. Leastways I don't think it was. First time I noticed it was when I went fishin' yesterday with Winston and Angel and Ted Ennis, over to Pillar Point. I had to put my fishin' gear in the backseat. I meant to run the car over to the dealer, but then I remembered him sayin' he was takin' his son to visit his grandparents in Ashland, Oregon, so I thought I'd wait until he came back."

His forehead was furrowed and he seemed a little pale. "I wish you'd come take a sniff, Charlie. I'm sorta worried."

Angel was our worrier. Not Zack. "Worried about what?" I asked.

"I just want you to come see what it smells like to you."

"What it smells like? How am I supposed to know what it smells like?"

Zack was no longer among those present. I had no choice

but to save my file, shut down the computer, and follow him out.

There were still a few cars in the parking lot. When I went back in, I'd need to start clearing out the lingerers. The sun was really baking down, in spite of the shade of the ancient oak trees. I could feel heat bouncing back up from the plaza paving stones, making my jeans wilt.

Zack's gleaming new luxury car—a beautiful forest green—was parked well away from the other cars and the buildings. He wasn't taking any chances on another befuddled janitor.

A little breeze had come up, which seemed to promise a cooler evening. First breeze since the heat wave started a few days ago. It felt good wafting around my face. At least it felt good until we came close to the Lexus and I caught a whiff of the odor Zack had talked about. That wasn't new car smell. Nor was it mildew. Or BO.

My stomach did a double somersault. I stopped walking as suddenly as if I'd crashed into a brick wall. All the blood left my head.

Zack scanned my face. "That's what I thought," he said.

Once you've smelled death you don't ever forget it; you can't mistake it. We had both smelled death when I found that skeleton in our flowerbed.

Something or somebody dead was in the trunk of Zack's car.

AMANDA HAZARD MYSTERIES
BY CONNIE FEDDERSEN

DEAD IN THE CELLAR   (0-8217-5245-6, $4.99)

DEAD IN THE DIRT   (1-57566-046-6, $4.99)

DEAD IN THE MELON PATCH   (0-8217-4872-6, $4.99)

DEAD IN THE WATER   (0-8217-5244-8, $4.99)